GREYHUFFINGTON

THE **EISENBERG EFFECT** BOOK TWO

TRIGGER WARNING

PLEASE READ THIS SECTION!

Seeing this note means the book you are about to read could contain triggering situations or actions. This book is subject to one or more of the triggers listed below.

Please note that this a universal trigger warning page that is included in Grey Huffington books and is not specified for any particular set of characters, book, couple, etc.
This book does not contain all the warnings listed. It is simply a way to warn you that this particular book contains things/a thing that may be triggering for some.

This is my way of recognizing the reality and life experiences of my Romance friends and making sure I properly prepare you for what is to unfold within the pages of this book.

violence
sexual assault
drug addiction
suicide
homicide
miscarriage/child loss
child abuse
emotional abuse
mental illness
infidelity
infertility
cancer
criminal activity

CONTENTS

GREYHUFFINGTON

lyric

THE **EISENBERG EFFECT** BOOK TWO

lyric

THE *CREED'S* *Wind Flowers* and *Baccarat* combination was unmatched on my skin. With one in my left hand and the other in my right, I sprayed even, strategically positioned pumps onto my freshly showered and moisturized skin. The moment they were applied was as critical as the combination. It was paramount that the particles were able to embed themselves underneath the first layer of skin for longevity in addition to my personal scent being one of the key notes of the final fragrance.

The glass bottles sounded on the marble countertop of my bathroom as I sat them both down. There was something about putting my perfume on in the mirror that made it feel and smell even better. Spraying blindly was never an option, even when crunched for time. Racing against the clock wasn't the case at the moment, but my actions wouldn't change if it was.

"Alright, Lyric, twenty minutes." I sighed, inhaling the uncompromising combination.

My reflection stared back at me, prompting a smile. The flawlessness of my skin was tempting. Every day, I concealed it with my obsession with a perfect beat, but tonight I was experiencing a change of heart. The twenty minutes it would usually take me to polish my face could easily be spent with the three little people that I missed more than I could verbally express.

Forget it. The decision was made as quickly as possible. A quick peek through my bedroom and at my vanity, I tilted my head and considered what I was getting myself into by stepping out for the evening bare-faced. With a shrug, I used my fingertips and began making gentle tapping motions along my jaws, chin, and forehead.

The smoothness of my skin was so satisfying. No matter how much makeup I piled onto it, I took good care of it. Bi-weekly facials from my esthetician were part of my self-care routine that I wasn't willing to sacrifice for anything or anyone. They were mandatory, much like my next breath, for survival.

Palming my cheeks, I tore my eyes from the mirror and stepped into my bedroom. The black button-down and fitted pants to match laid across my bed as if it was my first day of school or the first day of my new job. With the excitement of family dinners brewing in my bones, I could relate to both sentiments.

The once monthly event left my cheeks red, blotchy, and burning from the constant laughter, smiles, and conversations that went on for hours. Combined with my favorite season of the year and I was in heaven. Autumn was the time of year that reminded me of just how blessed I was. The amount of time I spent alone and at home sipping honeyed tea and cocoa while reading my favorite romance novels always left me in a state of bliss and thanking God for such a rewarding life.

One by one, I slid the threads onto my skin. The silkiness of the shirt caused small, fine bumps to line my arms, shoulders, and back. A chill ran down my spine, followed by an exaggerated shiver that made me feel tingly inside. My eyes watered slightly but cleared with a simple blink.

I pulled the black, thigh-high Manolo Blahniks up after I'd gotten my pants over my roundness. The tail of my shirt covered far too much of my bottom half for my liking. I quickly fixed the issue by tucking it loosely into my waistband, but not enough to see the empty belt loops that I had no intentions of filling. I pulled on the black blazer and stepped closer to the wide, floor-length mirror that I was already staring into.

Perfect. I admired my reflection, noticing only a few things that were missing from the equation. In a few seconds, I was inside my closet and standing over my jewelry case. I tapped the combination of buttons that I knew would grant me access to some of my most prized possessions.

Clack.

The disarming of my safe sounded. I lifted the top and removed the Audemars that had been gifted to me for Christmas. My oldest brother, Luca, had upgraded me, again. I wasn't complaining. Between him and Laike, I wasn't sure whose gifts were better. Next was the roped diamond necklace that I loved more than I cared to admit. It was quickly followed by two bracelets that Luca had been generous enough to purchase as well. The diamond earrings were already in my ears.

There. I smiled, stepping back and taking a look in the mirror inside my closet. It was the same as the one in my bedroom. I slid the head wrap from my forehead and watched my loose, barrel curls fall from under-neath. With a little fingering, they lie perfectly on my shoulders and hung slightly down my back.

I tidied up as I walked through my bedroom and bathroom to disable the lights. On my way out of the garage door, I grabbed the large, black Chanel bag that was waiting on my kitchen counter. The lights of my truck flickered as I unlocked the doors before stepping onto the custom epoxy flooring, a gift of Laike's in addition to the garage and G-Wagon that was parked inside of it.

When he felt inclined, he utilized his God-given talent and architectural degree. Six months ago, I'd been blessed with his latest project, a fully customized two-car garage that he somehow attached to my home. His ministry wasn't mine, so I'd never understand.

Numbers were my thing and I knew them well. It was the reason I was the most sought-after accountant for those who didn't exactly punch a clock to earn their money. The people that couldn't walk into a bank with the kind of cash they were seeing called me to clean their money and store it safely so that the biggest criminals — the government — of them all didn't get suspicious.

But, just like Laike, sometimes I put my real estate license to use when my clients were searching for homes. Selling homes weren't my passion but the career allowed me to store extra cash in the bank to cover the expenses of my lifestyle. The bill was hefty but selling two to three multi-million dollar homes a year covered it for the most part. My brothers covered the rest.

With the fob strapped to my visor, I lifted the garage and backed out slowly. Once my front end was in the clear, I lowered it. Remembering both Laike and

Luca's warnings, I stayed put until it touched the pavement. Coming home to an unwanted guest inside of my home was their worst nightmare and when my garage was installed, the chances increased substantially.

With it came a gate that Luca had installed along with a new security system. When it came to my safety they spared no expense or detail. I was thankful for it, too. Between the two of them, my dad could hardly do his fatherly duty. They were too busy thinking that I was solely their responsibility.

On my way. I texted my best friend and brother's wife, Ever.

See you in a few. She responded, immediately.

It would, indeed, only be a few minutes. She and Luca lived only ten minutes away, higher in The Hills. Their home was a dream. Laike had designed it beautifully, but the final product was more than either of us had imagined.

I exited our thread after seeing her response and slid my finger down my screen. Teyana Taylor's *Let's Build* was next on my playlist. Without a second thought, I pressed play. Then, after taking a quick glance at my surroundings, I began to reverse out of my driveway.

The gate opened as I pressed the button to separate it into two parts. When I was out of it completely, I pressed another button to seal it, again. With Teyana's voice booming through my speakers, I watched until it the metal met at the center.

The route to Luca's place was as scenic as they came. Everything along it was beautiful. The same could be said for my home but the higher in The Hills, the more dreamy the entire environment became.

The narrow roads led to astonishing views and breathtaking homes that were owned by people whose skin resembled mine and those with a bit more melanin infused. It was always a joy seeing Black faces watering grass, taking walks, and washing their cars in the driveway. Channing was the epitome of Black culture, every inch of the city. And, we loved it for that.

It wasn't long before I was pulling up to Luca's gate. I pressed the numbers required for entry, and the gate opened for me without hesitation. The long, spiraling driveway was one of my favorite features. It was much like mine but on a larger scale. During our monthly Sunday dinners, it was iconic to walk outside and find our fleet of vehicles lining it.

I pulled to the very beginning of the gate without an issue. There wasn't a doubt in my mind that I'd be the last to leave. I helped Ever put my babies to bed after each of our Sunday dinners to take a bit of the stress off her and Luca's hands. Though they worked well as a team, it felt so good helping out. I preferred the task alone, but she couldn't help herself. She never could when it came to her girls.

The little one that she was carrying would be

making his debut soon, and I could only hope that she'd release the shackles she had clutching her ankles when it came to parenting. It was her life. She had all the help in the world, but she still managed to care for the girls on her own. With Luca's help, of course, the tasks mostly stayed between the two of them.

There wasn't a need to sound the bell when I stepped onto the porch. Luca knew that I had arrived. His state-of-the-art security system and his insanely accurate intuition kept him on his toes. When the door of his home swung open and he stood on the other side of it with Elle in his arms, I wasn't surprised.

"Just weird." I scoffed, shaking my head.

"Just ready," he returned, pulling me inside and into his chest. "Hello to you as well."

"Hello, Luca," I responded, inhaling his familiar scent.

He was home for me. Laike was home for me. But, Luca, he and I had a connection that was so much deeper. He'd rescued me. As I was dragged across the parking lot of my apartments, my skin getting second and third-degree burns from contact with the concrete, and my eyes swollen shut he pulled into my complex. At the sight of me being beat to a near pulp, he lost all control, firing a single shot into my ex's head and killing him. Kill shot. His had landed him in jail for eight years, and for the entire eight years, my heart broke a little more each day.

I didn't think I could ever repay. But then he met

Ever, and somehow I felt like she was my consolation prize. Not that she was an item or could replace the years of his life that he'd lost but her being in his world made it so much better and helped me sleep a little better at night knowing that I was the one who connected them.

Together, they'd built the cutest family that didn't seem to stop growing. I could only hope that Ever wasn't tired of giving Luca the children he desperately desired by the time I finally found someone to call my own and give him babies, too.

He'd saved my life. I'd sent him a love that he could grow old with. Our connection was just different. Besides, he was the oldest and he treated me as such. Without verbally doing so, he reminded me of it every day of his existence. Even his tall, thick frame brushing against my shorter, thinner one revealed our dynamic. *Big me, little you*, it read and not in a negative light either. *Big brother, little sister* was more accurate.

"TT Lyric!" Emorey's little voice burst through the air.

I lowered my gaze in search of the body that matched but didn't see her. It wasn't until I witnessed Luca's legs part that she appeared. She had him wrapped around her pinky finger, and he wasn't going anywhere any time soon. Ever giving him so many girls was right up his alley although he played like he was desperate for a son. He'd told me time and time again how much the girls reminded him of me and how much more he loved them just for the simple fact.

Luca was only four when I was born, but there was no way you couldn't tell him that he wasn't my father from the moment he laid eyes on me. He was my protector. He was my peace. He was my heart. So, seeing him with girls of his own was always tear-jerking.

"Where's Emorey?" I pretended not to see her, turning in every direction but the one she was in.

"I'm here, silly, between Daddy's legs."

"Oh, there she is." I gasped, laying eyes on her again but acting as if it was my very first time.

"Yes. Here I am. You want to go to my room with me, TT?"

"Of course, Em. I came early to spend a little time with you girls. Where's Essence?"

"She's in our room."

"Okay. Get a head start. I'm on my way."

I stretched my hands, demanding Luca hand over Elle. When she wasn't on her mother's boobs, she was attached to his hip. The little girl was spoiled rotten between her siblings and her parents. There was so much love in their household that you could feel it from the moment you entered their gates. I admired them and was slightly jealous that they'd all found their person. Ever and the girls had Luca and Luca had Ever. It was an emotional rollercoaster seeing the family thrive whenever I encountered them.

"Come on, baby girl."

Elle climbed down and into my arms with her chubby arms and legs. She was gnawing on her fingers as if she hadn't been fed but I knew that couldn't be true. Every few minutes, she was begging for something to fill her chubby cheeks.

"Go spend time with your wife until the rest of the clan gets here. I'll be hanging with the girls."

"Appreciate that." He rushed off, obviously excited to go spend some alone time with Ever. Their healthy obsession with one another was everything that I craved in a partnership.

"Try not to make her go into labor, Luca. We still have a few more months before my nephew touches down."

"I can't make no promises, but I'll try to keep that little nigga cooking as long as I can."

"As long as you can?" I chuckled.

"You know what I mean."

Ugh. So stinking cute. I loved seeing my brother in love. It looked so damn good on him and it was so good for his skin. It looked better than mine, and I spent thousands to make sure it stayed flawless. His was effortless.

I marched up the other set of steps to get to the girls' room. Elle's nursery was combined with her parents' bedroom, but she would be chilling with us for the time being while they did what they seemed to love most. *Ok, I'm definitely hating,* I admitted as I hit the top of the enormous staircase. *Did Laike really have to make them that wide and have to add that many? They* seemed to never end.

"It's Laike. Of course he did."

Only two years my senior, Laike was the other part of my heart. I loved him much more than he gave me credit for. He swore I saved all my love for Luca and though he was somewhat accurate, the love I had for him was unwavering. He would ride and he would die for me. I'd do the same for him.

Because we were so much closer in age, we were the typical sister and brother duo. He made it apparent that he was the boss of the relationship, but he also gave me space to be whoever it was that I wanted to be. It probably had a lot to do with his busy schedule and fleet of women that he had to keep track of. As I thought more about it, it definitely had a lot to do with his busy schedule and fleet of women that he had to keep track of.

Nevertheless, he'd put it all on hold to make sure that I was cared for, not wanting for anything, and out of harm's way. While Luca was the grumpiest of the pack, Laike was the most nonchalant. He cared for nearly nothing and no one. Anyone outside of our circle meant nothing to him – *except Baisleigh.*

Since they were teens, he'd had a soft spot for her. Though he didn't care to admit it now because he'd fucked up with her so much, we all knew the truth behind his lies. He was still scarred from the decision she made to stop accepting his bullshit and move on with her life.

"You want to hang with TT Lyric?" I bounced Elle in my arms as I made my way down the hallway. Her drooly smile made the worst of my days better. She was pure light just like her sisters. I could only imagine my nephew would be hell because the girls were just too perfect.

"Look, Essence. It's TT Lyric," Emorey announced when I entered the room with Elle in my arms.

"Hi, Essence."

"I missed you, TT!" Essence jumped up, leaving her dolls behind to hug my leg.

Truly the sweetest girl I'd ever met, there was a special place in my heart for Es. The oldest of the three, she was the gentlest with the patience of an elder. She was the least talkative of the tribe as well, preferring to blend than stand out. Essence loved the shadows while Emorey thrived in the spotlight.

Elle was still under examination. Her age hadn't allowed us to determine exactly who she was shaping up to be but we were seeing more of Luca in her spirit by the day. She had acquired Ever's softness, however, but she could be as grumpy as her old man when she wasn't having her way.

"I missed you more, Es," I admitted.

It had been a full week since I'd seen either of their faces, and I was beating myself up about it, too. I tried my hardest to go by the bakery or come by their home at least twice weekly to give Ever a hand and catch up, but I'd been wrapped up in client work. It had consumed me all week, leaving me exhausted and with little energy to do much of anything.

"What are we playing here?"

Even in my thigh highs, I lowered my body to the floor where Essence had the enormous dollhouse split down the middle and opened wide enough to see and play on both sides. I was immediately taken back to my childhood when dollhouses and stuffies were my favorites.

"Ariel, the one right there, is starting her first day of school and is trying to find out what she wants to wear. Daddy took me to the store and got me these clothes for her today," Essence explained, holding a small pail full of doll clothes.

He is ridiculous, I thought as I nodded and watched Essence sit it between us. I could only imagine he'd chosen every piece of clothing that could fit the doll and even some for the other dolls in their collection for future play.

"Okay. We have a lot to work with. Let's get Ariel together for her first day."

I sat Elle between my legs and within seconds, she was off to do her own thing. She, too, loved dolls at her tiny age. Hers were much bigger and age-appropriate so that she wasn't swallowing shoes and accessories while no one was watching.

"I want to get her together, TT Lyric," Emorey chimed in.

"You're more than welcome to help, baby."

As we fell into play, my heart lightened. Around Essence, Emorey, and Elle was one of my happiest places. Their innocence was admirable. The world hadn't tainted them yet and to be around such an abundance of purity made my soul smile.

lyric + keanu

THE SMELL of seafood penetrated the air. Surprisingly, it was the same air that I'd been inhaling for the past forty-five minutes without as much as a whiff of it. I was certain Ahmad, Luca's personal chef, was preparing food prior to my entry but with the girls at the forefront of my thoughts, I didn't notice the prominent stench in the air.

We were keeping it simple this Sunday. Drinks of choice, lobster, shrimp, scallops, pre-cut crab legs, corn, sausage, steak, whole potatoes, and mini potatoes were on the menu. Ahmad's special seafood sauce was in large bowls around the long table and strategically placed so that everyone could reach one.

"He's not a good option in my opinion, but we will see what they have to say about it next week. The boy needs a bit more experience. Throwing a ball isn't always enough," my father told his boys while shaking his head from one side to the other.

"But it's what we're missing. We need somebody who can throw because Dotty can't throw to save his life since that hand injury. He should remain benched or give his spot up on the team so that someone else can have it. He's done for," Laike responded.

Luca's silent nod was followed by, "All he needs is a good arm. We can handle the rest. We just need someone to throw. We can get the touchdown, but we've got to get the ball in Crawford's hands to make that happen. Dotty ain't the answer anymore."

Although they hardly mentioned anything other than sports at the dinner table, it was always great having my three men in the same space. With every-one's schedule, it wasn't often that we could make it happen.

"Alright. Alright. Enough about tossing a ball," my mother interrupted.

"I second that," I chimed in.

"Oh hell, what do y'all want us to talk about? The latest bullshit bags y'all want from the store or your last trip to the spa?" My father chuckled, relaxing his shoulders and slightly reclining in his seat.

"Not exactly," as a matter of fact, I replied.

"Babe, maybe now is a great time to tell them."

Ever, with all her gentleness, changed the subject without making temporary enemies amongst the men. It was her specialty. She possessed a softness that commanded everyone's attention when she entered a room, spoke even a few words, or shared her light.

"Tell us what?" my mother asked, stuffing Elle's mouth with a chunk of crab meat from the Dungeness stack she had in front of her.

"That we've decided on a name for our son," with a smile, Luca answered.

"Oh, have you?" I could feel the ridges of my cheek harden as my lips curved upward.

"Yes. We have." Ever looked up and toward Luca.

The love that rested in them as she waited for his response was so obvious that even a blind man could see it. To love someone as much as Luca and Ever loved each other had to be painful. Not in a negative way, either, but in the most beautiful one. I knew it had to because watching from a mere two feet away caused a sharp pain in my chest.

"Lucas Elijah Eisenberg," my brother proudly stated.

"A very strong name," my father added, nodding in the process.

"Y'all must didn't consider Laike as an option?" Laike followed up.

"Please, Laike," annoyed, my mother chastised him.

"Put that on the list for your seeds," Luca calmly stated.

A verbal response wasn't in Laike's best interest, so he settled for a middle finger in Luca's direction.

"I love it." I put my two cents in the pot.

"So do I. A little of you both in there," Mom agreed with me.

"Just like Elle," Ever reminded us.

"Right, like Elle." I caught on instantly, always loving how well her name conveyed their unity.

Bzzzz.

Bzzzz.

Eyes wandered around the room trying to find the source of the betrayal. Cells weren't allowed at the dinner table on Sunday. It was the only two to three hours we were able to spend with each other monthly and wanted it to be uninterrupted.

"Babe," Ever tried whispering after she realized he was the culprit.

"Tonight is an exception, love," Luca assured her as he slid a finger down her cheek.

"Tonight's an exception," she repeated with a smile after Luca lifted the phone for her to see who was calling.

He slid his hand across the screen and then placed the call on speaker. When the operator's voice sounded on the line, my heart's beating halted. It was far too loud to hear anything beyond it. I needed silence to comprehend and digest every word that was spoken from this point moving forward. She continued speaking as I listened intently, hanging on to every syllable.

"You have a prepaid call from," there was a slight pause.

"Keanu," his voice, like molasses, slowly graced the line.

"To accept, press three. To decl—"

Before she was able to get anything else out, Luca pressed the number that would connect us to the awaiting caller. There was static on the line before it cleared. I waited with hiked breaths and curious eyes until he finally spoke, bringing peace to the chaos that had quickly swarmed me.

"What's up, nigga?" Ken greeted Luca.

"Shit," he responded, "I got to send messages through niggas to get you on the line. What part of the game is that?"

"The same part you played when you were down."

"Fair enough," Luca chuckled, "but it's been three weeks since I sent the message."

"I'm still waiting for your point, big dog."

"Why you calling now, nigga? I needed to holler at you three weeks ago."

Luca smiled, knowing that he was going to get under Ken's skin if he kept at it. He knew exactly why Ken was calling. We all knew. It was the only reason he'd brought his phone to the table and it was the only exception.

"I'm calling so you niggas can tell me happy birthday," Ken admitted. "Call Laike ass. I need him on the line, too."

"He already here."

"Happy birthday, black ass nigga!"

"LAIKE!" my mother yelled.

Because everyone was an adult, she and my father didn't trip much about the profanity that they used. As long as they kept it to a minimum. Words like damn, ass, and shit were among the few they were allowed to say. Otherwise, my mother and father found it disrespectful. Any hardcore profanity was not permitted. They didn't care whose home they were at, they'd cut into the guys swiftly. I hardly exercised the privilege they'd given us. In so many ways, I still felt like I was the baby of the bunch and wasn't allowed to do everything my older brothers were.

"What happened?" my father turned to ask her.

"Happy birthday, Keanu," my mother said, ignoring both my father and Laike.

"Happy birthday, nigga," Luca followed up.

"Happy birthday, Ken. We love and miss you."

"Happy birthday, son," my father told him.

"Appreciate that," he replied, his smile obvious on the other line.

Before I could gather my thoughts and wish him a happy birthday as well, he began again.

"Where's Lyric?" His concern was as genuine as he was.

I felt Ever's fingers clasp my knee and squeeze. A golf ball-sized lump of air formed in my throat, trapping my words behind it. But even if they weren't stuck back there, I could hardly form a complete thought to even begin to speak coherently.

"Right here stuffing her face," Luca informed him.

With a second nudge from Ever, my heart pumped again and my brain began to function properly. A sip of water helped me remove the lump from my throat and speaking came easy.

"Happy birthday, Ken!" I shouted loud enough for him to hear me.

"Appreciate that so much, baby girl."

He didn't mean anything by them, but those last two words stuck with me. They clung to me, blurring my vision and drowning everything out around me. I couldn't hear anything and neither could I see.

Minutes passed before I was coherent again. The fuzziness of my ears subsided, and the smiling faces around me became clear again. Ever's gentle rubs against my leg slowly brought me back to life, back to reality.

"Aight. I'm going to holler at you. Three months down."

"Three to go."

"Love you, bro," Ken said before the line died.

The energy of the room immediately shifted. Everyone knew and understood Ken's situation, and we all hated it for him. His loyalty was never to be questioned. Just like Luca had, he was spending his time behind bars due to the unwavering love of a sibling. Kale, his younger brother, got himself into some trouble that would've ended his future in the NBA before it even started. Instead of allowing one mistake to determine his brother's future, Ken took it upon himself to take the charge that was meant for Kale.

For it, he'd been sentenced as a first offender and given a year in prison. He would only have to serve six months of it if he kept on the straight and narrow. So far, he'd done well. But with each day that passed that he was still behind bars, I felt the pain of losing a loved one to the system a little more. Tonight wasn't much different. It felt like forever since I'd seen his handsome face or heard his voice. As relieved as I was to hear from him, the moment was bittersweet. He deserved freedom, not confinement.

"Well, we're going to head out, Luca. Tonight was such a pleasure, per usual." My father broke the uncomfortable silence that coated the air.

"I enjoyed seeing you all so much," Ever responded, recovering while Luca was still attempting to.

"Luca!" Laike yelled from the other end of the table before nodding his head toward the gazebo. Everyone amongst us knew what he was hinting at except the three small faces that were seated between the adults.

"I'll be back in a few," Luca explained to Ever as he stood.

"It's fine, baby. I'm going to get the kids ready for bed. I understand. Take your time."

"Do you need help getting this cleaned up?"

"No ma'am," Ever expressed to my mother, "that's why we wrapped the table with plastic. Everything is going straight to the trash bins except the glasses we drank from."

"Good. That was smart."

"Trying to work smarter and not harder." She chuckled.

"Well, I'm going to kiss my babies and then get out of y'all's way. Those two will be a minute back there. They're missing their third musketeer and it's eating them up... just like when Luca was away."

I simply listened, choosing to remain quiet because I was unsure of what to say. The brain fog had reappeared. So, in silence, I sat.

lyric + kenn

"ARE YOU OKAY?" Ever asked, pulling Elle's pants from her chunky legs.

"Yeah. Why'd you ask?"

"Because you haven't said anything since we ended the call with Ken."

"Yeah. I'm fine," I lied.

"You're not, Lyric. I saw the sadness in your eyes from the moment Luca answered the call."

Turning toward my friend, I swallowed the pile of

saliva at the back of my throat and tilted my head. I was trying to find the perfect words to express my sentiments but couldn't quite put together the right combination. As I gnawed on the inside of my lip, Ever waited for whatever was to come.

"What is it, love?" she questioned, patiently waiting for me to spill but also knowing that I needed the encouragement. "It's okay, Lyric. It's me you're talking to."

"You ever felt like you were in love with someone, but you've never had the pleasure of actually loving them? Like, you don't remember the month, day, hour, or year it happened. You just looked up and this person was a piece of you, though they have no idea how you actually feel?"

"I loved Luca the moment I laid eyes on him. I loved him more than I'd ever loved any man in my entire life in a matter of seconds. Before he got out of your truck the day we picked him up, he owned my heart. He didn't know it or know how I felt, but I knew he was my person. I knew that he was for me. So, I understand, Lyric. I promise I do."

"That's how I feel about Ken. I feel like he's for me but it's not as easy as I'd like it to be. There's history. He's family. And what's crazy is that's the very reason I trust him and I trust that he'll never put my brothers in a compromising position. I feel like he'll handle me and my heart with care, but I'm like his little sister."

"Did you hear the same man on the line as me,

Lyric?" Ever asked as she placed Elle into the water with Emorey. Essence was feet away in the shower having the time of her life.

"It meant nothing, Ever."

"Who are you trying to convince? Yourself or me? Because I heard him and have been hearing him loud and clear since the moment I met him. You're beating yourself up about nothing. He wants you just as bad as you want him, no matter what risks are involved."

"I don't think that's true," I admitted.

"You won't know until you ask him. Will you? Now is a better time than any. He's sitting still. His ears and his heart are both open."

"I'm not going to see that man and embarrass myself pouring my heart out to him in a visitation room. He'll just call my brothers, and then I'll be too shamed to even come out of my house for the next five years."

"That won't happen. You and I both know it. He wouldn't humiliate you like that."

"Then why suggest it? Because there's always a small possibility that he will."

"Write him."

"What?"

I could feel the scrunching of my features as I looked at Ever like she'd grown two heads. Just like Luca, she wasn't fazed. The two definitely belonged together. They were the epitome of unbothered.

I grabbed Emorey's sponge and soaped it up. Her

little arms shot in the air, already knowing what time it was. She loved baths and so did Elle. If Ever would allow her to, she'd take three or four each day. However. Bath time wasn't the easiest for Ever with her belly growing more and more daily. She'd just reached the six-month mark and was glowing.

"Arms up!" I told her anyway, but only because she loved hearing it.

"Arms up!" Emorey repeated.

I looked over to find Elle's arms in the air, too.

"Awww. Pumpkin, you're getting the hang of this thing, too?"

The few teeth that she had in her mouth were on full display as she smiled, drooling in the process. She fell right in line with the other girls, resembling Ever. However, my brother hadn't gone down without a fight. She had his nose and the structure of his large, round eyes. She had ears just like him, too. We all had those Eisenberg ears. There was no denying them. Lucas would have them, too.

"Write him," Ever clarified as she picked back up where we'd left off, "tonight. For his birthday. He has that email thing. That's how Luca had me send him a message to call weeks ago before sending a message through someone else. It's simple and only costs a few cents. He can see the message and respond fairly quickly. He just didn't respond to us because there wasn't a need. We didn't give him anything to respond to. We just told him to call us."

"And he still didn't do that."

"Well, because it's hard in there, Lyric. You guys said Luca never called either. They're just trying to get their time over and done. I can understand the lack of communication. Who wants to constantly be reminded of what they're missing on the outside?"

"You're right."

"So write him."

Sighing, I slumped on the floor of the bathroom with shoulders hunched and posture slouched. My thigh-high boots were long gone and replaced with the pair of slippers I kept at Luca's for nights like this one. Nights when I wanted to do more than keep the girls company. Nights when I was ready to make my brother and best friend's lives easier. Nights when I was in full auntie mode.

"I'm not going to write him, Ever."

"I mean this in the most loving way, Lyric, but seriously babe. You have to grow the hell up. You've avoided any type of relationship for the last ten years, depriving yourself of happiness and while I know that it had a lot to do with Luca, I know for a fact that it has had something to do with Ken as well. You've been waiting for him. You're still waiting for him, and he's waiting for you. I can see it in his eyes when he looks at you. I can hear it in his voice when he speaks to or speaks of you. He wants everything to do with you, but he doesn't want to overstep any boundaries you might have set unknowingly."

"You think so?"

"I know this, Lyric. Stop waiting or you'll be waiting until you're old and gray. You've told me more times than ever in the last two years that you're ready to find a love like mine and Luca's. Well, being a pussy won't get you there. If I'd let Dewayne's mistakes stop me from opening my heart to Luca, I wouldn't be where I am today. I'm so happy that it makes me cry most nights.

"When I'm making love to Luca, I sob like a baby because that man makes me feel like I'm the only girl in the entire world that he has ever and will ever love. His love for me is overwhelming and sometimes flares my anxiety because I'm always wondering how the hell I got so lucky. Luca is a very selective man, and he doesn't hang around just anybody. If Ken is his only best friend then I know he's worth the shot. Give him a chance to love you to tears. Trust me, it's the scariest, most rewarding feeling ever. Write him."

"Write him," I repeated with a nod, "I should just write him."

"Yes. Please. Tonight."

"And say what?"

"Whatever your heart tells you to."

Whatever my heart tells me to? The question rang loud in my head.

"Come on. It's time for you girls to get out and get your pajamas on," Ever announced as she tossed me a towel for Emorey.

With her arms stretched out, again, she stepped up and into my arms. I wrapped them around her little body and lifted her into the air. Carefully, I made my way to her bedroom and laid her on the bed. Ever sat next to Emorey with Elle bouncing in her arms. She'd laid out pajamas for all three girls.

"How have you been feeling lately?"

"Tired as usual. I feel like I'm on a never-ending, extremely rewarding spinning wheel. I just feel so blessed and so tired at once."

"You have three little ones, a husband, a business, and a child on the way. You've pretty much been pregnant two years straight. Your body is probably in overdrive."

"Yeah. After Lucas comes, I'm putting a gap between our next set of little ones. Maybe we'll try again when he's two and out of diapers," Ever explained.

"Luca will wait as long as you need him to."

"I know, but I don't think I can. I honestly love being pregnant. I feel so purposeful. It's the highlight of my days, Lyric. I be so damn happy for no reason at all, and I don't like the idea of birth control or pulling out. I'd rather he leave it there."

"Ever, I really don't want to hear that shit. You do remember I'm his sister, right?"

"Yes, but you're also my best and only friend besides Baisleigh. I'm not going into vivid details. I save those conversations for her."

"Good, because I'd hate for our friendship to end over it."

"Shut up."

"I'm serious," I warned, "but I don't know how you're going to get around that. Maybe just try the birth control for a year."

"It's not even an option for Luca and me."

"Then, I hope he learns to pull the hell out or you two can be expecting another one by your six-week checkup. I can bet my last dollar on it."

"We're going to figure something out. What's going on in your world?"

"Numbers. Numbers. And more numbers," I shared. "But you already knew that."

"Any new flames?"

"No. No one makes it past the phone stage and everyone else is friends with those two downstairs. I can't catch a break, honestly."

"You will. In about three months' time. Just wait and see. I have a good feeling about this one."

"TT Lyric, you sleep in my bed with me?" Emorey asked.

"Not tonight, Emorey. Maybe we can all have a sleepover soon. Gets some manis and pedis and facials. What do you think?"

"Yes. But, when?"

"Soon. Probably when Mommy has your brother. She and daddy will need the house to themselves."

"Okay. Mommy, can you have my brother tomorrow?"

Ever and I shared a hearty laugh. Emorey's impatience was comical. She wanted her way and anything else was an insult.

"You all ready for bed, kid?" I asked, pushing her pretty, blonde curls out of her face.

"Yes."

"Good, because it's bedtime. Which story would you like me to read tonight?"

"You pick."

"Okay. Lay down, and I'm going to grab a special book to read to you. We have to wait on Essence to get her jammies on and get in her bed first."

Essence was a little woman. Her level of independence was scary. Just as I mentioned her, she walked into the bedroom with her bathrobe wrapped around her body.

"I'm all done."

"Look at you big girl, all squeaky and clean," Ever cheered.

"I brushed my teeth, too!" she shouted, excitedly.

"Good job, Es." I clapped my hands as I told her. "Go ahead and put on your pajamas. I'm picking a bedtime story, now."

"Okay, TT Lyric."

She was her mother's child. The calmness of her spirit was enchanting. I gazed at her bouncy curls as she made her way to her bed where Ever had laid her pajamas as well. She didn't take any shortcuts when it came to her children, and I loved that about her. San helped out many days to alleviate her from her duties, but even then she was always on point.

lyric + kenzi

BOTH GIRLS WERE sound asleep when I crept out of their bedroom. It was going on ten o'clock. Aside from a few light sconces in the hallway, the Eisenberg residence was dark and quiet. I didn't have to peep in on Elle to know that she was asleep with her mother's boob dangling from her mouth. It was the same routine nightly until Ever woke in the wee hours and went to bed or Luca got lonely enough to retrieve her.

"Let me walk you out," I heard Luca's voice but couldn't pinpoint his location.

When he appeared from the shadows beneath the steps, I knew that he'd been tending to his other best friend, Glock. The tri-colored, short, and stubby dog was the most well-behaved I'd ever encountered. He was much like his owners, unbothered by anything and everyone. Not even the children could work him up.

"Putting Glock down for the night?" taking in Luca's appearance, I asked. It was still uncanny how much he and Laike resembled each other. They were identical twins. Laike had just been born two years later. It was as if our parents had birthed the same boy twice.

"Yeah. And wanted to catch you before you snuck out," he admitted.

"Is everything okay?"

"Yeah. Everything is good on my end. I'm just trying to figure out if that is the case for you. Lately, you've seemed... I don't know... sad."

"Me? Sad?"

My questions were in vain, especially knowing how intuitive Luca was. He could sniff out any sign of trouble on my end. I still think it was how he ended up in my parking lot the night Chauncey put his hands on me. He was due there anyway, but he'd come so much sooner than he was expected. He was at least twenty minutes early and that never happened. He was usually a few minutes late for dinner.

"Don't insult me," he chastised. "What's going on in that pretty head of yours, baby girl? Is there something wrong? Something you need to talk to me about? Something I can help with?"

"I'm fine, Luca. Just going through the motions."

"Don't lie to me, Lyric. You've never done it, so don't start now."

"I don't know what you want me to tell you, Luca." I sighed, pressing my back against the wall. He'd stopped so I followed suit.

"The truth," he declared.

"Well," I cleared my throat and spoke, "seeing you

so happy and so loved just feels me with as much joy as it does... I don't know the word I'm getting at but it reminds me of what I don't have."

"Who's fault is that, Lyric?"

"I can't say it's all mine because I tried. That didn't turn out well for me or anyone that I love."

"That was a decade ago, Lyric. I've been so afraid that it's the true reason behind you not accepting love from another man since but hearing you confirm it makes that shit so much worse. Listen, I did my time and I'd do that shit again. I have no regrets so why do you?"

"You left us for eight years, Luca. That hurt worse than any heartbreak. That hurt worse than the pain of not having someone. You guys have spent your whole lives protecting me. The least I can do is keep you two out of jail. I can control my actions, but I can't control what someone else will or won't do. I never imagined Chauncey would do what he did but look where that got us. It's easier to just steer clear instead of trusting that someone will have your best interest at heart."

"I get that, Lyric, but hear me out. You could walk into a store and be minding your own business and someone violates you. Who do you think is coming to check that motherfucker? Me or Laike, whoever is closest. You could be driving and someone hits your shit. When they jump stupid with you, who do you think is coming to check them? Me and Laike. You could be enjoying your night at the club and a nigga starts tripping. Who do you think is coming? Me and Laike. Ain't no saving us, baby girl. We're here to do our jobs and because you're trying to keep us out of trouble won't stop us from doing it.

"We don't send hitters, Lyric. We are the hitters and the heaviest of them all when it comes down to the people we love. So, don't worry about us. Whatever will happen, will happen. Take care of yourself and we will handle the rest. Let some nigga love you down, Lyric. You deserve it. My kids need some cousins and shit to play with. How else will they know how to fight? Your first ass whooping always be from your cousin. Laike ain't giving me shit, so I need you to come through."

Nodding, I agreed. "Seriously, we'd be lucky to get a steady face out of Laike."

"Exactly. You're our only hope. So, promise me you got me."

"I got you."

"Aight. Now, let me walk you out so that you can get home. Text me to let me know you made it."

"I will."

We started for the door, again. When I reached my truck, I felt Luca's arms around me. I rested my head on his chest and inhaled his familiar scent. It was one of my favorites. After a few seconds, we disengaged and he opened the door of my truck for me.

"Goodnight, Lyric."

"Goodnight, Luca."

FROM THE SECOND I stepped through my door, I began removing articles of clothing. By the time I reached my bathroom, I was fully undressed and ready for my shower. But as I started the water, I came to the conclusion that I preferred soaking over a long shower. My garden-style tub was a dream and ideal for extensive bath times.

I stood from the ledge of the tub and slowly dragged my body across the bathroom until I reached my sink. Underneath it was an entire cabinet full of the most divine fragrances paired with soap to create a rich, lathery bubble bath. The large bottles had been gifts from Ever whenever she felt like forcing her favorite relaxation tactics into my routine.

It wasn't often that I did or even wanted to sit in the tub. I preferred showers, the longer the better. But for once, I wanted to rest with my thoughts and figure a few things out. Luca's words were at the top of my list. Then, there were Ever's words. And, lastly the words I'd compile in a potential email to Ken.

Still, I wasn't too fond of the idea, but as I poured the thick liquid at the bottom of my tub and adjusted the temperature of the water, the urgency of it hit me like a sack of bricks. The thudding of the water against the bottom of the oval-shaped pit reminded me of my rapidly beating heart. *What will I say?* I wondered.

Before the running water ceased, I was stepping inside and lowering my frame. It disappeared underneath the fluffy bubbles, instantly protesting for my tranquility. I closed my eyes as I listened to the ferociousness of the running water.

Keanu. His chocolate skin was so smooth and so perfect. Though it had been months and months since I'd encountered him, I could still smell the peppery fragrance that he wore so well. The amber and citrus made my nose tingle and my nostrils flare.

Vividly, I could recall the day that I realized my adoration for him was deeper than that of a family friend. It had been over a year since I'd seen him and the night of my prom. In my sparkling dress with my prom date on my arm, I watched as Ken slid from the driver seat of the Lexus he was driving.

Luca exited the passenger side. High out of their minds, the two of them made their way to the curb where I was posing for pictures. Though I was so happy that my brother had kept his promise and made it in time to see me off, it was Ken that I couldn't keep my eyes off. The heartbeat that formed between my legs as his gold teeth shined beneath his smile was a clear indication of my true feelings for him.

I'd known him all my life or at least for as long as I could remember. But at that moment, he felt like a stranger, one that I wanted to get to know. *Keanu.*

That's who I was interested in. I knew Ken like the back of my hand.

The bubbles surrounded me, finally reaching my back and alerting me of the water's dangerous height. My eyes popped open as I slowly slid toward the faucet and turned it off completely. When I shifted backward again I was careful not to move too fast or with too much emphasis. The water was near the top of the deep dwelling and would spill over with too much movement.

Dear Keanu, I began inwardly.

"This isn't middle school, Lyric." I chuckled.

Happy birthday, Keanu. I replaced it with, already liking the sound. *Yeah. That's better.*

I closed my eyes again and allowed my thoughts to roam. If I was going to take the leap that I was contemplating, I wanted to do it with accuracy and purpose. Ken wasn't just anybody and this wasn't a situation I could walk into with that frame of mind, either. It was imperative that I understood what it would mean for the both of us if the email I was planning to send served its purpose. Therefore, penning a cute little love letter wouldn't suffice. He'd read right through me, just like Luca and Laike did all the time.

With my body submerged under water, the words began to flow in the back of my mind. Slowly, the idea was vivid and so was the email's context. I knew my angle and I knew just how I'd work it. There was nothing I wanted to leave him to question or ponder on. Each point that I made, I would expound upon and any question I could think of that would arise I'd answer before the words ran out.

With my water still at a near-scorching temperature, I belted from the tub and snatched the bathrobe from the hook on the wall beside it. The words were at the tips of my fingers and before I forgot a single one, I wanted to put them onto paper. Well, in an email in this case. Skipping my nightly facial routine for the first time in months, I rushed through the bathroom and into my bedroom. I made a mental note to return before bed for a shower and to complete my religious facial regime. For now, none of that mattered.

I plopped down onto the cushion of my office chair, simultaneously tapping the keypad of my iMac to start it up. After punching in my passcode, the screen altered a bit to display my desktop and the photo of Essence, Emorey, Elle, and I that I loved so much. Just as I opened the Chrome application, a notification bell sounded and a new email popped up on the right side of my screen.

Ever Eisenberg.

Here's the link that you'll need to set up the email service. It only takes a few seconds.

Attached was a link that I clicked immediately. I chuckled at the fact that my friend knew me so well. She had definitely awakened and remembered the conversation we'd had. Before she passed out for the night, in the comfort of her own bedroom, she wanted to make sure that I was reminded as well. Fortunately, I was on the same page as her. The email would save me a bit of time and research.

eNMATE was the website that launched from the link I'd clicked from Ever's email. Just like she'd stated, it only took a few seconds to create my account and find Ken. He was the only Black, male Keanu in the system which made locating him that much easier.

I added money to the account for us both to participate in the two-way emailing service. It was only a dollar and seventy-five cents per send and the same amount to receive. Though I made it through the set up rather swiftly, when I clicked the tab to compose a new message, my heart swelled in my chest and my thoughts ran to the furthest corner of my brain.

Grow up. Ever's words caused me to smile as I shook off the nerves that I was feeling inside. She was right. I needed to get my shit together and put my fears behind me. If she could see the admiration that Keanu supposedly had for me, then I didn't understand why I couldn't. Ever would never steer me wrong, intentionally, so I knew there was truth to her revelation. I'd only seen the poor girl lie once and that was to keep my brother out of trouble. She hated to do that even.

Keanu,

I'm wishing you the happiest of birthdays today. I know that your situation isn't ideal for any of us but let's just count this year as a blessing in disguise. I don't have to go into grave detail about who I am because I'm certain you've already gathered that from my information that's probably displayed on your screen right now. My list of reasons for being here is so extensive that I'm hoping there's room in your inbox and in your heart to receive it.

Though these words are long overdue, it's quite difficult to sit here and write them. But I felt it was time to share these feelings I've acquired for you over the years with someone other than Ever for once. If I'm overstepping boundaries or you simply don't feel the same as I do, then you have my permission to disregard this message altogether. Hell, maybe I shouldn't be writing it at all, but I'm too invested now to stop.

Since the night of my prom when you stepped out of your Lexus wearing a red Ralph Lauren cap, tight eyes from the buds you'd consumed, dark denim, and a white shirt to match, my heart has belonged to you. It was that very moment when I realized I was more interested in Keanu Brinks than I was Ken. I'd known Ken all my life and though he was already part of my family, it was Keanu that I truly desired companionship with.

As I grew, so did my feelings for you. Even when I didn't see you at all during the time Luca was away, my heart was still attached to you. Every man I've ever encountered or was involved with was always compared to you. He's not dark enough. He's not tall enough. He's not tough enough. He's not wild enough. He's not clean enough. He's not him. He's not Keanu.

It's been my plight since that night, no matter how different it might've seemed. I only advanced in prior relations with others to keep my mind off you. But like a boomerang, I always end up right back here, feeling exactly how I felt when I heard your voice on the phone tonight. Feeling like it's you for me and me for you.

Your presence takes me under. I feel like I'm floating most times, but since you've been gone it's felt like I'm underneath the water, drowning. I wept the night that you went away, and I find myself on my knees praying for your safe return every day.

I miss you like I miss Sunday mornings at my parents' before church. I miss you like the melodies and love-driven lyrics of old R&B. I miss you like a long, lost love that I'll never get back again. I miss you like I miss you – like only I could miss you.

My calendar is marked each day that you're away. I'm counting down until you come home like you're coming home to me. Maybe one day, huh? Maybe soon?

When I'm alone at night and I begin to touch myself, it's you that appears behind my lids. I've wondered for far too long how well we'd mesh together, how my body must contour to your frame, and how we probably fit together like two puzzle pieces.

I often imagine the faces of our children and what being loved by you must feel like. A cozy autumn night with cocoa in-hand and a sappy flick playing on the television. Does it feel like that? Or a stroll on the beach as the sun sets in the background with sand between my toes. Is that what it would feel like? Maybe roaring thunder and rain after a drought. Could that be what it feels like?

I've wanted to love you for so long but as each year passes the idea seems more and more like a figment of my imagination – like it could never be my reality. Could it be? Could you and I be more than a blissful moment in my head each night before bed and at the top of the morning when my eyelids part?

Sometimes when your gaze lingers on me, I wonder if I'm imagining it or if you might actually feel the same way that I feel. Or anything even remotely close. How do you feel, Keanu? I'm desperate to know.

Tonight I asked Ever if she thought it was possible to be utterly in love with someone that you haven't had the pleasure of loving on. She told me she loved Luca from the moment she saw his face. I was relieved knowing that I'm not bat shit crazy and the things I feel for you are possible.

Because I'm in love with every inch of you. The darkness of your skin. The perfection of your smile. The gold teeth that you love hiding your pearly whites behind. Your dimples, both of them. The curves of your wide nose and the fullness of your lips. Your eyes, as curious and big as they are. Your fearlessness. Your loyalty. Your pride. I'm in love with every part of you, even the darkest ones.

I'm just hoping I'm not in this alone. Stepping out on a limb and sending this message shows me just how *smitten I am with you. Just how deep my feelings run for you. I'm just wondering if you're feeling the same way, too.*

Lyric.

Without reading over my words and without hesitation, I pressed the send button. If I read through it, I knew that I'd be changing things or deleting the message altogether. I wanted my raw, honest, and unfiltered thoughts to reach Ken as I intended versus the polished ones proofreading my words would result in.

"Did I really just send that?" I squealed, already feeling the embarrassment that was to follow.

Immediate regret swarmed me. I was an Eisenberg and our pride was everything, but as I sat considering what I'd just done, mine was displaced. My chest burned, aching as I stared at the computer screen. *Your message has been sent* stared back at me. I wanted to puke as I read it for the fifth time in a row.

I really just sent that. In silence, I pushed myself away from my desk and thought.

"I really just sent that," I said aloud as I stood to my feet and treaded across the floor.

When I reached the hallway, my mouth was still hanging and my heart was still on the ledge. Absentmindedly, I drifted to my bedroom and into my bed. Once I was underneath the covers, I pulled the bathrobe from my body and draped it across the other side of the bed.

I wasn't sure how, but I was hoping sleep found me

sooner than later because the thought of the act I'd just committed was too overwhelming to survive the night. It had only been about two minutes since I'd pressed send, and I was already wishing I could unsend the email.

I melted between the sheets, a deep, stressful sigh leaving me as I rolled onto my right side. It was the most comfortable side to sleep on. As I closed my eyes, I cringed at the thought of going to bed without administering my facial products, tying my hair up, or sliding into some night threads.

Tonight is the exception, I determined, knowing that I wouldn't be able to conjure the strength to do either now that I was under the sheets. I closed my eyes and released the breath I'd been holding. The long, exaggerated air left my lungs and was quickly replaced with new oxygen as he appeared behind my lids.

lyric + kevin

THE MORNING SUN WAS BRUTAL. It shined through my big bay windows, interrupting my sleep. I'd gotten up at my usual 5 a.m. meditation and yoga, but my tired eyes wouldn't let me stay awake after the shower I had at 6 a.m. When my exhausted gaze reached the clock on my nightstand, I noticed it was after eight.

"Hhhhhhhhhhhhhhhhhhhuuuuuuu," I yawned, tossing both feet over the side of the bed and stretching my arms in the morning air.

The silkiness of my pajamas caressed my skin as I stood to my feet. I turned around and checked the satin pillowcase for my headwrap but luckily, it wasn't there. My hands went to my head instantly and I found it there, sitting nicely. Satisfied with the success of my morning nap, I trekked toward my bathroom.

The moment I stepped into the space, the motion detector sensed me, flooding the space with light. Though I'd already completed my hygiene tasks, brushing my teeth again was a requirement. As I stared back at my fresh, heavily moisturized face I was consumed with plaguing, cumbersome thoughts.

My actions could ruin a perfectly good friendship, I reasoned, remembering what I'd done the night before. The words of my message played loud in my head, each one more cringy than the last.

I often imagine the faces of our children? I questioned. *Ugh.* Disgusted, I shoved the toothbrush into my mouth and shoved it back and forth. Though the deed was already done, I was praying that somehow Ken didn't get through the entire message that I had sent. There was a part of me that knew he would read every word, every syllable, but one could only hope that he stopped after realizing the message's context.

For three minutes, I stared back at the mirror, brushing my teeth with furrowed brows and eyes that kept rolling upward in my head. Needing control over every situation and having none over this one was grueling. Anxiety clenched my lungs, giving the illusion that I couldn't breathe although it was apparent that I could. The tightness in my chest was evidence of my anxiousness, which made a second morning shower seem more ideal than just one.

As I contemplated it, I came to the realization that another shower wouldn't solve my issue. The best I could do was forget it even existed. After I cleaned the toothpaste from my mouth with my water pick, I dried my mouth and exited the bathroom. My next stop was the kitchen so that I could prepare my favorite breakfast meal.

Two boiled eggs, light seasoning, and a tall glass of water always gave me a good head start. And just before I left the kitchen, I'd squeeze fresh orange juice to get my workday started. It was all routine, which I happened to thrive off. Knowing exactly what my day consisted of helped keep me on the straight and narrow daily.

It wasn't until I made it to the kitchen that I realized it was time to reorder my groceries. The last of my eggs had been used the morning before. Shit. I combed the shelves of my massive fridge with my eyes, wondering what I could put together for a decent meal. I settled on a bagel and cream cheese.

The plain bagel was cold to the touch when I grabbed it from the bag. That quickly changed when I stuffed it in the toaster and placed the rest of them back in the fridge. I grabbed a glass from the cupboard and filled it with filtered water from my fridge.

"Ahhhhhh." The first sip eliminated the dryness of my throat and slightly washed away the taste of my toothpaste. I wanted it at a minimum by the time my bagel was ready for consumption.

The buzzer on the toaster sounded as I rounded up the oranges that I'd be using for my juice. I rushed over to grab the warm, thick bread and placed it on a glass dish. Another sip from my cup, and my water was half gone. I stood in the same spot until I'd finished it off. It wasn't until then that I began coating my bagel with cream cheese.

With such a small meal, I didn't bother having a seat. I stood where I was, shoving the bagel down my throat piece by piece as I created a mental checklist of my day's tasks. The first was reordering my last cart of groceries for delivery. In a few short minutes, breakfast was complete, my orange juice had been made, and my to-do list was still forming. Certain that I'd forget to put something from my list on paper once I sat down, I expedited my exit from the kitchen, deciding to tidy up when I returned for a lunch break.

I strolled through my home with a glass of freshly squeezed orange juice in a glass, humming the lyrics of *Protect Her* by Sabrina Claudio as I made my way to my home office. My chair was still pulled from under my desk, partially. I slid onto it in my jammies and tapped the keyboard of my iMac to get it started. I wasn't settling down for the morning. Not yet. I still needed to get dressed and apply my makeup. For now, it was imperative that I created the list that would guide me through the day.

Ill-prepared, my heart sank into my furry slippers when the screen changed after typing in my password. I was quickly reminded of what I'd tried so hard to forget – and had succeeded for the last few minutes.

The green check mark was big and bold on the screen, confirming my message had been sent. With a heavy sigh, I hovered over the red X that would remove the page from my view completely, but curiosity just wouldn't allow me to click it. Instead, I moved the cursor down and over a bit, clicked the full URL and hit enter on my keyboard.

The page refreshed, but the green check mark had disappeared. It was replaced with a record of sent and received messages. The only one in the column of messages was mine. Not only had it been sent but there was record of it being received. My palms perspired instantaneously.

He read it.

"He read it!"

Nausea hit me like a sack of bricks. I could feel the bagel I'd eaten minutes prior rise to the top of my stomach, threatening to surface. I stared at the screen, my eyes wide and refusing to close even for a millisecond. *He read it.*

I felt sick to my stomach knowing that my feelings had been exposed in such a desperate manner, but I was even sicker realizing that Ken had gotten my message and didn't bother responding. My secret wasn't between Ever and I anymore. The source knew, too, and from the looks of it, the feelings weren't mutual.

NOTE.

Between the covers of this book is **my** art piece — beautifully paired words structured for **my** creative satisfaction and later consumed by others for enjoyment.

It's **leisure for you**, it's **life for me**.
This is just a book to most. **It's art for me**.
My art. I've had *my* time. Have **yours**.

happy reading

GREYHUFFINGTON

lyric

THE **EISENBERG EFFECT** BOOK TWO

ONE

keanu

"YO, WHO THE FUCK IS THIS?"

A call came through for the third time, and it was the same number on the line. Wanting details on the urgency of the call and who was behind it, I waited for them to respond. My dick was still wet and still lodged in Malika's tightness. The last thing I was interested in was talking to whoever was on my line, demanding my attention with the constant redial.

"Ken. What's up?"

Keeping my stride and not missing a single stroke, I continued to give her exactly what she'd been begging for the last two nights. My free time was limited and though I preferred spending it alone, tonight was one of those nights that I preferred spending it inside something wet and gushy. Malika was the perfect candidate. I'd been sliding into her for a full year and her pussy didn't disappoint.

Her low moans lulled me as I tried to fill her stomach and chest with my eight inches of hard, Magnum-wrapped dick. Like a champ, she acquired every inch I had to offer, but not without attempting to run first. But with my legs pinning hers down with her calf, she was unable to scoot her way up the bed. She had no other choice but to bury my lumber deep within her walls.

"This pussy I'm in so speak your peace or get off my line. Who is this?"

My patience was as short as the weekend and lolly-gagging on the phone while I was trying to put both Malika and me to bed for the night wasn't ideal.

"This Ward from over on 4th."

"Yeah. What's the emergency?"

"Shit, man. I thought you'd probably want to know that I've been seeing your brother doing his thing down here or whatever. I've been to the kid's games. He's got something. He's a star man. The last thing I want him to do is fuck off his chance at getting up out of here on a sack of dope."

"My brother?"

My beating heart sped in pace, blurring my vision as I tried to comprehend what was being revealed to me. Finally, my dick deflated and movements halted. I could feel the tightness of my face and flaring of my nostrils as I tilted my head, anticipating a response.

"Yeah. Kale Brinks. I've seen him play. I don't forget faces like that."

"And you saw this shit with your own eyes?"

Slowly, I removed my dick from Malika's wetness and slid backward in her bed until my feet touched the floor. I headed into the bathroom that was connected to her bedroom and started the water in the sink.

"Just did, but I've been seeing it for a few weeks now. Maybe three."

While the water warmed, I removed the condom from my skin and rolled it up in a wad of toilet tissue before flushing it down the toilet.

"And you just calling me?" I probed, holding the phone steady between my shoulder and ear. If I even glanced at the mirror in front of me, I was certain I could see the steam coming from my ears. My blood boiled as I continued to listen to Ward.

"I'm just getting ahold of your number."

"He still out there?"

It didn't matter where he was, I would find him before the night was out. Some things couldn't wait to be addressed and Kale calling himself slanging was one of them. A scholar by day and basketball star player by night, he had no business jeopardizing his future for the hell of it. Kale wasn't hurting for money and neither was he trying to survive. He was simply trying to get his head knocked off by me, a jack boy, or police. Luckily, I'd be the first to give the private school, straight-A student the wake-up call he desperately needed.

Kale, slanging? Slanging what? I pondered.

"Yeah."

"4th and what?"

I grabbed one of Malika's fancy towels that matched the others strategically placed around her bathroom. I'd listen to her fuss later. For now, I needed to clean my balls and thighs of her remnants before hitting the door.

"Audelia."

"Appreciate that."

"No problem," Ward said as I ended the call.

"Leaving so soon?" Malika appeared, leaning against the doorframe with her arms folded and sad eyes.

Refusing to get caught up in her beauty, I focused on the task at hand. I cleaned every inch of my center, removing any evidence she'd been bouncing on my dick or that I'd been swimming in her ocean seconds prior.

"Yeah. Got shit to do."

"Can you at least come back?"

"I can't give you an answer to that."

"Why not?" She insisted on more information.

"Because lying isn't my thing, and I'd rather say

nothing than something I know could end up being a lie."

"So basically you're not coming back?"

"If I do, I do. If I don't then I don't. Tripping now won't help in your protest to get me back here later."

"I'm not tripping. I just miss you and you just got here."

"And gave you what you really wanted, Malika. Let's not act like we don't know what this is."

"I want it to be more," she declared.

"Oh yeah?" I sniggered, "Have you told that to Antwan and Dex? The other two niggas that be climbing up in your shit, probably leaving their seeds behind for the next nigga to find?"

Silence was her only response.

"I didn't think so. Let's just keep this a buck. We have good sex and a good time when we're together, but neither of us is ready for whatever you're thinking in your pretty little head."

In the full year that I'd been in Malika's bed, I hadn't once considered removing the magnum, no matter how good she felt. That should've been the sign she needed to understand my train of thought when it came to whatever it was we had going on. Together, we were a good time. It ended there.

"So, you're saying that all I am to you is a piece of pussy?"

"If that's the hill you want to cry on, I'm going to let you. But arguing ain't it for me. Debate a nigga *that gives a fuck. I don't. I've got to roll. Don't wait up."*

I'd already made it up in my mind that I wouldn't be returning. There wasn't a woman in the world that could tell anyone that I wasted my breath or energy going back and forth with her. I didn't have the capacity – not for a nigga or a female.

I located my jeans near the foot of her bed and slid them back on. My Forces were next to my pants, making the transition simple and easy to get them on my feet. When I was redressed, I scurried through her front room and was out of the door seconds later with one thing on my mind – Kale.

Underneath the Channing City lights, I mashed the gas of my matte, black Camaro, weaving through traffic that the nightlife brought about. It was Friday. Everyone was happy to be taking a break from their work week and getting some drinks in their system.

The twenty-minute drive to a forbidden part of town where Kale had no business being was cut by eight minutes; the motor of my new toy being just what I needed to get me across the city in haste. When I reached the intersection of 4th and Omen, I slowed my engine to a creep so that he wouldn't be alerted of my arrival. It wasn't easy to conceal the horsepower underneath the hood but it was worth the try.

I reached the corner of 4th and Audelia undetected. Kale was too wrapped up in his heated phone conversation to even notice me when I stepped out of the car and on his turf. Had I been a hitter or had come to shake him down for his paper, it would have been such a sweet lick. Kale wasn't on his toes. He was lacking.

So easily, I entered his personal space. From the few words that I heard him utter, I quickly came to the conclusion that he was talking to our aunt, Brandi, the woman who'd raised us both. Me from the age of four when my granny took sick and Kale from the day he left the hospital. I was already out of high school and had found my own lane by then. We were twenty years apart, making me more of a father figure than an older brother.

To say I took my job seriously would be an understatement. Kale made that thing in my chest beat. And seeing him risking everything I'd worked so hard to give him and everything my aunt and uncle had instilled in him broke it. Split it into tiny pieces that would take time and effort to put back together.

"Get in the fucking car before I beat your ass out here in front of all these niggas you fronting for," calmly, I stated, close enough for only Kale to hear me.

Causing a scene wasn't in my plans, but I would if it came down to it. When Kale ended the call with our aunt, lying to her about his whereabouts, he turned in my direction with his head lowered and eyes on the ground. He raised a finger and began scratching the back of his neck, a sign of discomfort that I'd learned a long time ago. I led the way to my car, which was only a few feet away, daring him with my eyes to make a questionable move.

I made it to the car first, Kale shortly after. As I watched him lower himself into my passenger seat, it was taking everything in my not to stomp a hole in him. Not only was he jeopardizing his future, but he was making a fool of the people who loved him the most. My aunt and uncle worshiped the ground Kale walked on. He had the best of everything, and they busted their asses each day to make sure that he got it, in addition to everything that I was already giving him.

"What the fuck are you thinking?" I boasted the second my door closed and I restarted my engine. "Huh?"

Kale said nothing, only stared straight ahead out the front windshield.

"I asked you a question, nigga. What the fuck are you thinking?"

"Nothing man. Just trying to make some extra paper before I'm off to college."

"Then, get a fucking job!" With emphasis, I pushed out the words. "A nine-to-five! Because otherwise, you won't make it to college. What the fuck are you selling out here, Kale?"

"A nine-to-five won't help me stack the money I'm trying to stack, Keanu. I'm not a boy anymore and I'm tired of sticking my hand out to Brandi and Jeff or you each time I need something. Do you know how that shit feels? Reminding Brandi that I need briefs for my ass?" He huffed, obviously frustrated.

"You're seventeen, bro. You're far from a man. You're a kid and you should stay a kid for as long as you can. That shit runs out quickly. Them niggas you call yourself hugging the block with, they are surviving and will do anything it takes to get that dollar – including you if they see you stacking that bread you keep talking about and they're not. You have no idea what comes with this lifestyle or what it takes to maintain it."

"It's simple enough. I haven't heard you complain once about it."

I bit a hole in the side of my tongue, drawing blood as my thoughts raced. Kale didn't have a clue about shit, but swore he knew everything. He didn't know anything about the streets. His head belonged in the books or between one of them cheerleaders legs but not on the swivel after running across the wrong nigga or the right cop.

Seething, I responded, "What I do is not your fucking business. I bleed so that you're untouched. I get my hands dirty so that yours can stay clean. I deal so that you can dunk the fucking ball and stay the fuck out of dodge. I'm in the streets so that you can stay in the gym! My head is in the game so that yours can stay in the books. You feel me, young nigga?"

My chest ached as my eye began to sting from the fire I felt inside. My engine roared as I pressed the pedal, rushing Kale back to his side of the tracks where he belonged. I had every intention of revealing his where-abouts to my aunt and uncle in addition to sharing with them his actions and the reason behind them.

"If you want to stack some money," I gripped the steering wheel as I barked, "then you tell me you want to stack some fucking money and I see to it that you stack as much as you want. My money is falling out of the fucking safe because I can't get rid of the shit fast enough and you're out here taking chances for what I can hand you in the blink of an eye!"

Whoop! The blue and red lights followed by the familiar sound made my aching heart sink into the bottom of my shoes. Kale's eye bulged from his head as he whipped his neck around to confirm what we both already knew. I contemplated trying my luck and flee-ing, but the last thing I wanted to do was get Kale involved in what could end up a deadly pursuit.

Cops didn't always play fair, but I had a better chance of talking them out of a ticket or search than fleeing on the busy Channing streets. Had we been on the expressway, I would've ghosted him the second he hit his lights but running through the streets filled with pedestrians at this hour would only end in tragedy.

"Fuck," I groaned, "what do you have on you?" The wheels in my head began churning.

Spooked, Kale snapped his neck in two directions without saying a single word. From the front windshield to the back windshield, he continued going back and forth with his eyes.

"Kale. What do you have on you?"

I continued to travel down the street as if the lights weren't on and the siren wasn't blaring. Until I made sure Kale was straight, I didn't intend on pulling over.

"Fuck, man. I can't go to jail, Keanu."

The strife and grit that he'd displayed a few seconds earlier had dissolved and the little seventeen-year-old boy that I knew reappeared. This Kale was the one I recognized. This Kale was the one that I refused to let get himself into trouble. This Kale was the one I'd never allow to fall short on my watch.

"You won't. What do you have on you?"

Whoop! Whoop. Whooooooop! Blue lights shined in front of me, causing me to swerve, nearly hitting the curb as I tried to avoid hitting the police car that had pulled in front of me. There were now two laws on us. One behind us and another in front of us. I had no choice but to decelerate.

"What do you have on you?"

Kale reached into his pocket, hands shaking as he struggled to remove whatever was inside. Before he was able to show me what the plastic I'd heard rattling contained, his door was being pulled open as he was being pulled out.

"Get on the fucking ground!"

Simultaneously, I was pulled from my side of the car and forced to the ground as well. Before I could react or comprehend what was going on, cuffs were being slapped on my wrists and I was being led to the hood of the police car that had been following behind us.

"Don't fucking move," I heard behind me.

"Do it look like I'm moving, nigga?" I asked.

"Don't fucking move."

"I see this motherfucker likes to hear himself talk," I concluded, tuning him out completely.

It was obvious that he was one of the ones you hated crossing paths within uniform. On the street, they'd have an entirely different demeanor. The badge and gun made them feel superior. With or without my tool I was the same nigga.

I watched as they forced a shivering Kale onto the hood beside me. Seeing his wrists cuffed behind his back broke something deep within me that I don't think could ever be repaired. The tears that stained his face, and the sound of his low whimpers were daggers to the chest.

"Chin up," I demanded, "Whatever it is, it's mine."

"I'm sorry," he apologized.

"It's cool. Big bro got you. Just keep your mouth shut."

"Okay."

I watched intently as the flashlights darted across the car. Within a few seconds, a clear baggie was lifted into the air. Dangling it, a chuckle surfaced.

"Well, look at what we have here, Staples," the cop on the passenger side called out to his fellow officer.

Squeezing my lids together, I groaned inwardly.

Even from my position, I knew what the bag consisted of. I didn't have to be any closer and neither did I need it in my possession to determine its contents.

"Pure cocaine," one of the police from the other vehicle sang as he slid out. "Pure cocaine."

I drew blood, gnawing at the inside of my lip. When I reopened my eyes, Kale's orbs were on mine. Refusing to reveal my apprehension, I smiled in return.

"It's aight, lil' bro."

"Which one of you does this belong to?"

"If you would've run the tags before you pulled us out and cuffed us without reading us our rights then you'd know whose it is. Do your job. We're not going to do that shit for you," I spoke to the one asking the question.

"You're going to do well in jail," he returned, giggling uncontrollably.

"I'm well wherever I plant my feet," I assured him.

lyric + kevur

"BRINKS."

My name being called snatched me from my thoughts. Since the night they'd happened a year and a half ago, the events replayed in my head like a broken record. That night was one I could never forget. Not only was it my first offense, but it was the push that

Kale needed to keep himself on the straight and narrow and his head in the books.

It had changed the trajectory of both of our lives and as much time and money it had cost me, hearing Kale's excitement for college and his future in basketball on the line made it all worth it. The gun and ounce of coke that were found in the car had gotten me sentenced to a year, but with good behavior, a hell of a lawyer, and drug programs, my time was sliced in half.

"Yeah?"

"It's your time," the CO informed me.

I stood to my feet while simultaneously scrubbing the memories of the small holding cell and the one I'd stayed in the entire six months from my head. When I walked out of the doors, I wanted the six months of wasted time to be a blur that was so complex, my mind couldn't fathom what it must represent. This was my very first and my very last prison stint.

Every inch of my six-four frame stretched until I heard my bones crackling and popping. Without haste, I proceeded out of the cell door that was slowly opening to accommodate my new status. I was officially a free man but until I was on the outside it wouldn't register. Through one door after another and then three gates too many, I hit the pavement. It was identical to the concrete that I'd just walked across to get through the gates, but the shit just felt different. It was the one that commemorated my emancipation.

"That's what the fuck I'm talking about."

Kale's words hit me dead in the chest. The smile on his face as he beat his chest a few feet away from me caused my cheeks to rise as I shared the same sentiments. Reunited and that shit felt so fucking good.

"Lil' bro," I dragged.

"You out that bitch," he cheered, clapping his hands as he circled the spot he'd just stood in. He'd entered his first year of college but flew home for the day to make this moment happen. I could've had either Laike, Luca, my aunt, or uncle to scoop me, but Kale wanted this moment. He deserved it, so it was his to have.

After three full circles, his balled fist went up to his mouth as he blew a heavy, unsettling breath into the small space between his palm and fingers. The tears that slid down his face were evidence of the relief he felt seeing me again. Because not everybody made it out.

"I'm out that bitch," I agreed, "and my stomach touching my fucking back."

"Then let's fill it. You ain't got nothing? A bag? A piece of mail? A letter? Nothing?"

My calendar is marked each day that you're away. I'm counting down until you come home like you're coming home to me. Maybe one day, huh? Maybe soon?

The words that I'd remembered like my favorite line of a Jay track surfaced.

"Nah. They can burn all that shit."

The gray sweats were the only thing I was bringing

with me and that was only because I needed clothes on my back when I left. If leaving without a thread on my skin was possible, then I would've. I wasn't bringing anything with me from my time in jail, *except her words*.

"Just baggage I don't need or care for."

"Bet," Kale responded, hopping into the passenger seat of the matte black Grand Cherokee.

Laike. I knew who was behind the set of wheels that was in front of me. I'd mentioned purchasing the Trackhawk once on one of the rare calls I made home and this nigga had it delivered straight to the parking lot.

Phweoooooooeeeet. I whistled, rounding the truck to get a good look at my new muscle.

"This nigga don't miss," I whispered.

Ready to get the hell out of dodge, I kept my admiration to a minimum. There would be plenty of time to learn more about my ride and its capabilities. For now, I wanted to put my current view in my rearview. Home was heavy on my heart.

I'm counting down until you come home like you're coming home to me.

"Buckle up," with a grunt, I advised Kale while I slid into the driver's seat.

"Say less."

Though I wasn't sure who Kale had pumping through the speakers, the bass on the track sounded superior coming from the speakers. I hiked it up a notch, bobbing my head as I accepted the iPhone that Kale handed me. The plastic was still on the screen. With a nod, I placed it in the cup holder and put the truck into gear.

lyric + keann

HUFFINGTON MILLS WAS where I rested my head, but Dooley was home. When I pulled into the gated community, making a pit stop at the security booth to give my name, contentment devoured me. It had been six months too long since I'd crossed the barriers. I vividly remembered the day that I surrendered my freedom. The morning was as somber as it came as I pulled out of my subdivision. To be home again meant everything.

I wept the night that you went away, and I find myself on my knees praying for your safe return every day.

As I pulled into the driveway, the words that I'd read a hundred times and remembered so well replayed in my head. I silenced the engine and hopped out of the car with Kale on my tail. He'd occupied my space for four months before entering his first semester of freshman year.

I paused briefly before stepping up to my door, allowing the security system that Laike had installed to identify me and have a chance to read my vitals. If they didn't check out, then utilizing a key was necessary. When I heard the locks turn, I rejoiced inwardly.

"I uh," Kale started, scratching the back of his neck, "I kind of…"

"Got some shit to get into?"

"If you don't mind. If so, I can just cancel and hang with you."

"It's cool, kid. I'm not sweating it. Just be safe."

"I will," he promised, scurrying off toward the garage.

Before I went in, I'd given him my Camaro to have. I wouldn't need it, and I was certain I'd be in search of a new set of wheels by the time I touched down. Laike had already made that happen, so it wasn't even on my agenda anymore.

I heard the roaring engine of Kale's whip as I entered my home. The freshness was welcoming. Just as I'd requested, Luca had refurnished every inch of my pad. I walked into the newness that I'd craved the last three months of my bid. The earth tones blended well with the dominantly black pieces and revealed that there was a woman's touch involved.

Hers? I wondered but as quickly as the thought surfaced another did.

This nigga, I chuckled as soon as my eyes landed on the large box of magnums. It was next to the Welcome Home sign. It had Luca's bullshit written all over it.

Bypassing the madness happening on the console table, I headed upstairs to the master suite. There was one particular place I had in mind. When I breached its surface, I peeled every piece of clothing from my body.

Shit. It felt good to be out of the gray sweats. I replaced them with a pair of basketball shorts and a tank. Finally, I could breathe again because for the last six months, I felt like I was barely staying afloat.

Your presence takes me under. I feel like I'm floating most times, but since you've been gone it's felt like I'm underneath the water, drowning.

Like lightening, the words from the computer screen flashed before my eyes. I'd been drowning, too, and until this very moment, I couldn't catch my breath. Being told when to shower, piss, shit, eat, hoop, and socialize was not ideal for a nigga who'd lived a limitless life. Though I'd adapted, the entire ordeal felt like an outer body experience. It was my first and my last time in that motherfucker.

I picked up the fresh grays from my closet floor and dumped them down the trash shoot in the hallways next to my bedroom. Upon my return, I entered the bathroom where I stared back at my reflection with a half-smile.

"Boy, you look rough," I admitted, pulling at the bulkiness of my hair.

For six months, it had been growing like wildfire. I refused to let the niggas in the barbershop cut it. That task was one that only I could accomplish. I was too specific and too particular about how I wanted my shit, and I hadn't found a barber that could achieve the same results as me. That's why I'd been cutting my own hair since I was nine. The first and last time a barber fucked my line over was my eight birthday. For a year straight, I practiced and perfected my technique. By November 28th of the following year, I was nice with it.

I pulled out the deep drawer and removed the cape, clippers, brushes, scissors, alcohol, and the rest of the things I'd need to get myself together because whoever the nigga in the mirror in front of me was, I didn't recognize. He was buried beneath six months of knotty, black hair – facial included.

"Alexa, play something I'd like to hear," I called out to one of the white gadgets I had all around my home that made my life a lot easier.

When Meek Mill's *I Got the Juice* blasted through the speakers, my smile widened as my head began nodding to the beat. All wasn't lost upon. At least Alexa still recognized me. For now, I'd settle for that.

As I listened to the lyrics, matching them word for word in my head, I prepared my utensils. And though I promised to leave every and anything that went on within the six months, I was locked away in the past, there was something – or someone rather – that I simply couldn't.

As I grew, so did my feelings for you, she'd written.

I gazed at my reflection in the mirror as I began to reveal the man behind the wool one stroke of my clippers at a time. Lost in the thought, I didn't realize just how long I'd been standing and chopping away until I was patting my face and neck with alcohol that stung, drawing me from the daze I was in.

My bare feet tapped the marbled floors of my bathroom, sending a chill down my spine. When I reached the glass shower, I turned the digital dial to six and a half. It was the perfect temperature. Not too hot or too cold.

Without hesitation, I stripped down a second time and stepped behind the glass barrier that kept water from exiting and cold air from entering. The warm water hit my dark skin, forming a stream that slid down my body upon contact. For the first time in six months, I closed my eyes while allowing the steam to rise up my nose and clear my airways.

I'd come to the realization long ago that I'd taken long, hot showers for granted all my life. Not anymore. I was more than thankful for the peace of mind they brought me and the safety net having one in my home afforded me with. There wasn't a nigga in the whole joint that had tried me after I put the first one on his eyes in under five seconds.

I had barely slept on my bunk a full week before the bullshit started. But as quickly as it had risen, it settled. Niggas did not want the work that I had to offer them — *inside or out*.

As the beads of water tap danced on my skin, I considered the rest of my day's events. Before I did anything else, I needed some decent, uninterrupted sleep in the comfort of my own bed. It was new along with the bedding on top of it, but I was certain I'd sleep like a newborn once my head hit the pillow.

My shower ended twenty minutes later and after four rounds of scrubbing. It was imperative that I removed all traces of the past six months, even from my skin. With a towel around my waist, I strolled into my bedroom and sat on the edge of the bed.

Home. There was nothing else like it and I missed it so much that I was contemplating not leaving. Spending the day clearing the fuzziness surrounding my release sounded so much better than anything else I could think of wanting to do in Channing – *almost*.

So instead of trying to convince myself otherwise, I slid the pair of briefs I'd tossed on the bed before cutting my hair and showering up my ass. Five seconds later, my bedroom light was out and I was underneath the covers. Sleep came easy much like everything else when comfort wasn't an issue.

lyric + kenna

DARKNESS DEVOURED every inch of my home. With the back of my hand, I rubbed my right eye and then my left to clear them of the debris that hindered my vision. My view of The Hills would never get old. I stared out of the floor-to-ceiling windows that every home deep within the community had been built with so that everyone could indulge in the beauty of the scenery.

"Haaaaaaaaaaaaaa," I yawned, eyes and mouth watering simultaneously.

My stomach sounded immediately after. I hadn't eaten shit all day and knew that it was time to. But first, I needed to take a piss and brush the exhaustion from my breath. Before I could do either, I checked the time on the cell that Kale had given me earlier. It was after nine.

"Shit, I was tired."

There were two missed calls on the line, one from Luca and one from Laike. I remembered both of their numbers by heart. I'd bet my bottom dollar that when I didn't answer for one, the other called and betted they'd get me to pick up. That could only mean that the niggas were together. It hadn't been a full hour since they'd hit my line. Before I called either of them, I needed to make a more urgent call first.

"What's up?" Kale answered, projecting his voice over the music in the car.

"Shit. You good?"

"Yeah, bro. You don't have to worry about me. I promise. I'm staying out of trouble."

He already knew exactly what I was calling about.

"Where you at?"

"Edgewood."

He was in familiar territory. That's where we were raised with our aunt and uncle. That's where I met the Eisenbergs. We lived across the street from one another our whole lives. They were family. With a shake of my head, I recalled not being surprised to see Liam Eisenberg waiting for me outside the jailhouse after I'd been bonded out the morning after everything went down. It was him who'd shared their family lawyer with me and made sure that I didn't pay a dime out of pocket. Luca and Laike were no more of his sons than I was. We just didn't share the same blood.

"Bet. When are you heading back this way?"

"You miss me?"

"Nah. Not really. Enjoying my own company, actually. Just trying to keep up with you."

"Around midnight."

"Aight."

"Okay."

I ended the call and dialed Luca's line. He was the first to call, so I figured he deserved the return. I wouldn't hear the end of the shit when I saw Laike, but I'd deal with his shit later.

"My nigga," Luca answered on the second ring.

"What's good?"

"Shit. You're sounding very fucking free right now. I prefer that," he shared.

His lack of enthusiasm as he was clearly excited

was classic Luca behavior. He was by far the least bothered nigga I'd ever met in life – aside from his father. According to the streets, I was next in line. Laike was right after. There was a fine line between unbothered and not giving a fuck when it came to us both. I doubt that either of us gave a fuck about much if it didn't involve the ones that we shared blood with or loved unconditionally.

"Tell that nigga I see how he's moving," Laike's voice erupted in the background.

Chuckling, I requested, "Tell him I miss him, too."

"That's probably what his soft ass wants to hear. I think he wants a kiss or some shit," Luca teased.

"Fuck you," Laike boasted.

"Ever does it and does it well, my nigga. She needs no help. But he said he misses you, too."

Tonight I asked Ever if she thought it was possible to be utterly in love with someone that you haven't had the pleasure of loving on. She told me she loved Luca from the moment she saw his face. Her words resurfaced. Closing my eyes, I shoved the message from my thoughts as I tried regaining control of them.

"Y'all definitely on the level I'm trying to be on. Where you niggas at and where are y'all headed?"

"We're at Laike's crib about to head to Oat + Olive in the next thirty minutes."

"Sounds like a bet. I'll see you niggas in about an hour."

"Say less."

No more words were exchanged. We both ended the call just as I stood from my bed and stretched my limbs to the limit. Oat + Olive was a vibe. I'd only been about three times but every time, I'd enjoyed the few minutes I stayed. Tonight would be different, though. I had nowhere to be and not a single piece of pussy lined up that would chop away at my time in the spot. I was free in every sense of the word. Tonight, it was whatever.

TWO

lyric

THIS HOOP OR THE TRIANGLE? I gazed in the full-length mirror in my bedroom, trying to decide which earring suited the black, long- sleeved romper that was painted onto my skin. My face was flawless, covered in mostly Fenty along with the rest of my favorite beauty lines. Aside from the earring situation, I was pretty much ready to walk out of the door.

Triangle, I decided. There was just something about it that gave me uber sexiness and that's exactly what I was aiming for. It had been almost four weeks since Collin and I had been dating and tonight was feeling like the night I'd finally give him a piece of the cake he'd been waiting to devour.

Luca was adamant about me entering the dating scene, so much so that he'd taken it upon himself to find me a therapist to work out whatever issues I'd had with dating seriously. The eight-week, twenty-four session program did wonders for me. The guilt that I carried for Luca's imprisonment was still intact, but it was no longer hindering me from finding the love of my life.

My date for the night would be arriving at any minute, and I wanted to be ready. In my Valentino platform booties that were the perfect match for the chilly February winds in Channing, I trekked across the room and back into my closet. I needed to grab my other earring and return the LV hoops. They simply didn't match the vibe I was aiming for tonight.

Just as I slid the second earring into my ear, my phone pinged. That could only mean that Collin had arrived. His timing was impeccable, always was. I respected his time just as he respected mine which is why I hated to keep him waiting. He was always prompt.

Perfect timing. I grabbed my clutch and headed

straight for the door, but not before pumping a few more puffs of my perfume on my chest and arms. When I exited my home, Collin was outside of the gate waiting for me. Outside of his pearly white ride, he stood awaiting my arrival.

"Good evening," he greeted as I approached, extending his arms for me to snuggle between.

"Good evening," I replied, admiring his handsome features in the dark as I wrapped my arms around his neck.

"You ready to roll?"

"Yes."

"I've already punched the location into the GPS. It says we should be there in about ten to twelve minutes."

Collin drove like an old man, slow and without haste. It was the only reason I didn't like riding with him. I preferred taking my own car, but there was just something about riding in the passenger seat with a man that was as fine as Collin with a bank account as fat as his, too. He was a numbers guy, too, but more into stocks and investing.

His portfolio was astounding and his worldly possessions were evidence to prove it. There wasn't anything Collin wanted and couldn't have at the moment. He was at the top of his game – according to him and his account statements that I viewed when he first signed on as a client of mine.

"Sounds accurate."

I'd visited Oat + Olive enough times to know the route and the timeframe. With it being a Friday night and traffic being questionable, the extra two minutes made sense. It was usually a ten-minute drive. Hopefully, Collin didn't extend it with his precise, impeccable driving skills.

He opened the door behind us and waited for me to climb inside of his car. Once I was snug, he closed the door behind me and galloped toward the driver's side. I reached over and opened the door to ease his transition.

Miguel's track was heightened in volume as we set out toward the secret spot that I'd been visiting for a few years now. It was one of those that not everyone shared with too many of their friends so that it wouldn't get turned the hell out. My family frequented the spot monthly, but tonight I was tackling our favorite alone – with the exception of Collin.

Comfortable in the heated seats, I closed my eyes and enjoyed the silkiness of Miguel's voice as he sang about his love being a sure thing. If I wasn't witnessing two strong and healthy relationships play out in front of me, I'd call the song total bullshit, but I knew that everything he was singing about was possible.

My parents had been together for forty-two years. Since they were babies, pretty much. All these years later they were still loving each other as if it was the first year of their relationship. They'd been honeymooning since the day they'd been married. Each year, choosing to vacation to celebrate their union.

Luca and Ever reminded me so much of them. Their love was new and fresh, but it was evident it would stand the test of time. The two loved each other unconditionally, to the point that it pained anyone who was single to see them. They were prime examples of everything you wanted in a partner and from a partnership. There weren't any roles or responsibilities dedicated to one gender or one person in their home.

As a couple, they made sure their home and children were cared for. Everyone played a part in the success of their marriage and parenthood as a whole. Whether it was cooking, cleaning, combing hair, or taking out the trash. Whatever needed to be done was done without hesitation or question. Anything the one could do to make the other's day a little better or easier, they did.

I admired that. I admired them. When my person came into my world, I wanted that. I wouldn't settle for anything less than it, either. Every day I was seeing what was possible – thanks to my parents and my brother – so there was nothing a man could tell me to convince me otherwise.

"We're here," Collin announced.

So lost in my thoughts, I hadn't noticed we'd stopped or that we'd reached the valet attendant. As another attendant pulled my door open, my cell rang. Checking the caller I.D. I noticed it was Ever trying my line. I silenced the call as Collin intertwined his hand with mine, guiding me toward the door.

I'll call her in the morning, I thought as Collin slowed to a creep when we neared the door. Like Luca and Laike, he wasn't a fan of lines. He'd get the quickest access his money could buy at any venue. It was one of those things that I liked about him that reminded me of my brothers.

I paid little attention to the doorman that Collin was bribing as I tried unlocking my phone to text Ever and let her know why I'd pressed ignore. She was already calling me back. I ignored the call a second time as Collin pulled me into *Oat + Olive* by my hand.

"He said we can reserve a spot if someone is already sitting where we want to sit and they'll have them find another place to crash," Collin yelled over the music.

"Yeah. I'm aware. I've already reserved a table," I informed him.

"Oh yeah?"

"Yeah. It's this way." I began tugging him in the opposite direction while unlocking my phone to text Ever. When I accessed our message thread, there were three dots inside of a gray bubble bouncing.

"It's the same one we alwaaaa—" I dragged just as my phone pinged with a new message, and my eyes batted to be sure that I wasn't being deceived.

Luca's handsome features all raised as they formed

a full-faced smile. Laike's brows raised as he looked at me for an explanation. And, Ken...

Ken?

I dropped my head into my chiming phone, face recognition unlocking it immediately. Ever's words were simple but rang loud in my ears. She'd tried to warn me, but the cat was already out of the bag by the time I read the messages.

He's home.

Ken is home.

"Who the fuck you with, Lyric? Care to introduce us to your boyfriend?" Laike was the first to speak.

"He's my friend."

"Whatever the fuck he is, who is he? Matter of fact, nigga who are you?" Laike turned to face Collin and asked him instead of me.

"I'm Collin," Collin responded, extending a hand that was left hanging.

Not even Luca shook it. Though his sentiments were much different from Laike's, I knew that until he figured Collin out, he wouldn't indulge. He'd only observe. Hopefully, Collin passed whatever test Luca was preparing to give him. Laike, on the other hand, Collin probably wouldn't ever pass that test. He was convinced that there wasn't a man alive that deserved me. I'd started to believe him before therapy saved my life.

"I'on like this nigga," Ken stated immediately, sucking his teeth in the process.

His words caused me to snap my head in his direction though I wanted to avoid his gaze at all costs. I wasn't expecting to see him. The months seemed to have flown by since I stopped marking my calendar after he'd left me hanging. I knew that February was the month he'd be released, but he had been the last thing on my mind since I'd embarrassed myself by sending him that message. He tilted his head with hiked brows and dark, hooded eyes.

He's high, I concluded. *And why the hell does he have to look this fucking good?* I gritted my teeth at the realization. Prison had been kind to him – very fucking generous.

His eyes never left mine, causing me to crumble inside. My knees weakened as I tried to focus on not falling face first on the floor. I wanted to scream and run out of the nearest exit, but I was determined to stand my ground. Ken had basically left me on read. His opinion had no grounds.

"Well, good thing you're not the one who is dating him, right?" I sassed, utilizing every ounce of boldness I could muster. I was literally shaking in my boots, but he'd never get access to such classified information.

"Give the nigga a chance," Luca commanded.

"Who?" Laike inquired.

"I'm good, fam," Ken responded.

"I reserved this table," I told them.

"We know," Luca stated, tilting his glass until the

contents of it filled his mouth. I could bet he was sipping Hennessy. I needed to warn Ever this time.

"Pull up a seat," Laike insisted, making sure I understood Collin and I were part of their tribe for the night.

Fuck, I sanded my teeth with the grinding that I couldn't help. It was a habit as a kid that I'd gotten rid of by the time I was in seventh grade. For it to reappear so abruptly was astounding. I wanted it to stop already.

"If I wanted to hang out with you guys for the night, I would've invited you out," I fussed, pulling out the chair next to Ken to sit.

There was no way I was allowing Collin to take the seat. I preferred it if he pulled up a chair next to Luca. He was somewhat safe over there.

As I rested my bottom in the chair, I could feel Ken's eyes staring daggers into my cheeks. I could also smell the fresh wood and amber on his skin. He smelled like a slice of heaven, one that I'd never have the opportunity to indulge, but I was okay with that, finally.

"Are you okay?" I leaned over and whispered in Collin's ear. "They can be a little overbearing."

"It's fine. I'm a big brother. I know how it goes. I can handle myself."

He had no idea, but I'd allow him to think he did. Luca was hell but Laike was hell on wheels. And, Ken, he was down for all the shit that Laike forgot to get them into. The trio was a train wreck waiting to happen. With them was not how I planned to spend my night, but I'd happily drink until I forgot they were even in the place to ruin my date.

"Let me know if it begins to be too much," I advised.

"Over here," Collin beckoned for the waitress with his hand in the air.

I watched Luca watch him as he watched the waitress making her way over to us.

"What will you be having, baby?" Collin asked, gently rubbing my knee.

"Grilled chicken pasta, a glass of water," Ken started.

"And a dirty martini, extra dry," Laike concluded.

Collin nodded, impressed with their accuracy. I cringed inside, suddenly hating that they all knew me so well. Prior to tonight, it was adorable. Now, it seemed downright childish. Since my birthday last year, I'd been obsessed with dirty martinis.

As violent as they were in my mouth, I just couldn't stop ordering them. They made me feel like the rich bitch that I'd always dreamt of being. And thanks to being my family's accountant along with a select few of their business associates, I had become her.

"She'll take exactly that, and I will have your parmesan chicken over the bed of rice with a side of broccoli and cobbed corn. To drink, I'll take a bottle of Opus One."

"Opus One? The entire bottle?"

"The entire bottle, sweetheart," Collin clarified.

The eleven hundred dollar wine he'd just ordered would cost him at least fifteen hundred dollars solely because we were at a bar where all the prices were increased by at least twenty percent of retail value. It only increased from there.

"Good taste," Luca commented, tilting his glass in Collin's direction.

"Okay. I'll start working on that right now."

His orbs were still on me. I could feel his eyes all over my body as my palms became clammy and wet. I'd clenched my toes to the point of pain – and was ultimately forced to release them. Every other second, I swallowed a new knot that formed at the back of my throat, refusing to get caught slipping or soundless when it was my turn to speak. It was detrimental to my pride that Ken understood he hadn't fazed me with his silence after I'd poured my whole heart out to him. The lack of reply stung for a bit, but I shook back.

"I'm going to the ladies' room while we wait for the food," I announced.

Sccccccrrrr.

Every chair at the table slid from underneath it, each man standing to their feet. With a shake of my head, I watched as they all looked at each other for a solution. Everyone had intentions of seeing me to the restroom, but I didn't need an escort. Not from the three amigos at least.

"I don't need an escort to the restroom," I assured everyone.

Still, no one budged as they waited for me to make a choice.

"Either you're choosing or we're choosing for you," Luca explained.

"Collin," I said lowly, pulling his hand in the direction of the restroom.

Silently, I rushed through the small crowd to get to the ladies' room. Once there, I was relieved to see that the line that was usually there wasn't. I rejoiced as I dropped Collin's hand and headed inside.

I secured the lock of the single stall restroom and unlocked my cell. Because Ever was one of the only people I communicated with, it wasn't hard for me to find her contact in my call log. She'd already called me twice, and I'd missed both calls.

"Hey," she answered.

"Hey. Are the girls asleep?"

"Yes. Everyone is sleeping, and I'm up getting some alone time. Did you get my messages?"

"Yes. I did, and–" I paused, running my fingers through my hair.

I began pacing the small restroom in an attempt to calm my raging heart. The walls felt like they were closing in on me as my temperature began to rise and breathing became a bit more difficult.

"Annnnnnnd?"

"He's here."

"He's where? Where are you?"

"Oat + Olive. And he's here... with Luca and Laike."

"Didn't you have a date with Collin tonight? How'd you end up with Luca and Laike?"

"I am on a date with Collin. We walked in and there they were, with the nerve, to be sitting at the table I reserved for us."

"Oh my God. They've met him?"

"Kind of."

"What? That's not fair. I haven't even met him. What did they say?"

"Laike hates him."

"Laike hates everybody."

"Luca is still observant."

"And Ken?"

"He said I don't like this nigga before we could even sit down."

There was silence on the line before Ever burst into a fit of giggles. As upset as I wanted to be, I couldn't help but join in. I had to laugh to keep from crying because seeing Ken made me want to. My emotions were getting the best of me, but I didn't have the courage to display them. He didn't deserve that.

"I'm so sorry, Lyric. I don't mean to make a mockery of your situation but Ken has no filter. Whatever comes to that head of his comes straight out of his mouth."

"And to think that's one of the things I love about

his black ass the most. UGH!" I groaned. Why is he here?"

"Maybe to celebrate his release? He did get out today."

"I knooooooow," whining, I agreed, "but, why here? They could've taken him somewhere else."

"Oat + Olive is kind of a ritual now. Face it."

"I'm falling in the same boat as you," I joked.

"You kind of are, though. The love of your life was just released, you two met up at Oat + Olive, and now you're in the bathroom. Maybe he will come snatch you up like Luca did me."

"Can you believe that when I told them I needed to come to the restroom, they all stood up at once? What kind of fuckery is this? And, that's not the love of my life. I gave him a chance and he blew it."

"Then, why are you in the restroom whispering on the phone to me instead of standing your ground out there? It's Ken. A family friend. You've been around him all your life. Why are you bothered, suddenly?"

"Shut up."

"I'm just pointing out the facts, Lyric. It's okay. Feelings don't just dissolve because you don't get a reply to a message. They sit and they fester, and they build even more. When it's time, you'll know exactly where to place them."

"He doesn't want me," I reminded her.

"Has he told you that?"

"He didn't have to. His silence did."

"You're reading too much into it."

"He didn't give me anything else to read, so he left me no choice but to draw my own conclusion."

"That's fair, but I think it's the wrong conclusion."

"Well, it's too late for all of that. Collin has been hinting at us making things official."

"It's only been what... a month?"

"Ma'am, let's not talk about timelines. If fate would've had it, you would've been pregnant with Luca's kid after the first time you two fucked. A month is enough time to decide if you want to make things official with someone you've been seeing consistently."

"So, yeah. You got me there."

"Mrs. Two years, two children."

"Be quiet!"

"I'm just saying. Anyway, I need to get back out there before they come looking for Collin thinking he's kidnapped me."

"Call me in the morning?" Ever asked.

"Yeah. I'll call you in the morning."

"I love you, and I know you've got this."

"I love you, too. Kiss the babies for me."

I cleaned my hands and made my exit. Collin was standing in the hallway waiting patiently for me. When he noticed me approaching, his lips curled into a smile.

"You ready?"

"Yes," I answered, taking him by the hand and leading the way again.

When we arrived at the table, our food and drinks had come.

"That was quick," Collin praised, obviously impressed.

"Would you like for me to open your bottle," the waitress asked. The bucket of ice sat in front of her and next to Collin.

"Please," he insisted.

It was always between pasta and wings for me. On a decent, chill night I would've chosen the hot wings over the pasta, but tonight was supposed to be date night. Oat + Olive's pasta had been on my mind all day long. Without hesitation, I dug into my helping.

lyric + kenn

I WASN'T sure if I was on beat and neither did I care. The liquor was flowing through my system, and I was having the time of my life. Collin stood closely behind me as I grinded my bottom into his slacks. I couldn't miss the knot that hardened as the songs continued to play and my ass continued grinding into him.

We'd traded our seats at the table with the three musketeers for two seats at the bar so that we could be alone. Between Laike's lack of couth and Ken's unwavering gaze, I couldn't catch a break. Though I didn't want to leave altogether, I had to put some distance between us all. The second I finished my serving of pasta, I demanded Collin and I relocate.

"You're barking up the wrong tree," Collin leaned over and whispered in my ear.

Turning around and wrapping my arms around his neck, I teased. "Am I?"

"Umm hmmm," he responded with a nod, pushing a few strands of hair from my face that had stuck to my clear gloss.

"I don't think that's such a bad thing."

I couldn't hide the smirk on my face even if I wanted to. Collin was everything one's mother prayed their daughter would find in a man. He was handsome. He was paid. He was nice. He was confident. He was ambitious. And he was thoughtful. So, I couldn't understand why my thoughts were consumed with the man that was a few feet behind us, eyes trained and unmoving.

"Not so much," he admitted.

"I like you," I confessed, "a lot."

"The feelings are mutual," he responded, pulling me in for a hug.

Unable to refrain from following the trail that led back to our table, my line of vision ended where Ken's began. His gapping eyes penetrated me as Collin tightened his arms around my body, lowering his hands until they caressed my butt.

Sometimes when your gaze lingers on me, I wonder if I'm imagining it or if you might actually feel the same way that I feel. Or anything even remotely close. How do you feel, Keanu? I'm desperate to know.

Closing my eyes, I tried ridding myself of the thoughts surrounding the message I'd sent months ago. To my dismay, Keanu's chocolate skin appeared behind my lids. The thong that was situated between both of my ass cheeks was instantly saturated with my creaminess.

"Ummmmmmm."

Forcing my eyes open, I stifled the moan that I'd imagined. Unfortunately, it had surfaced and now I was feeling slightly embarrassed because my body wouldn't let me believe that it was anyone but Ken's hands caressing me.

"You should spend the night with me," Collin suggested as I peered at an unmoving Keanu wishing I could solve the mystery behind those eyes of his.

The cup of brown liquid in his hand that was cooled with a few cubes of ice approached his lips before he took a sip. With his eyes, he unclothed me, skinned me, and then carefully cut through the surface of my bones to get to the core of me. Bare and unable to hide, I allowed him a view of my tarnished soul, the one that I would've offered him on a platter if I thought he'd accept it.

Feeling the stinging of my orbs, I tore away from his paralyzing peer. Oxygen filled my lungs as I inhaled deeply before exhaling. The feelings that I'd tucked away came rushing back at once. Willing myself to remain strong, I fought the chest-caving whimpers that threatened me with embarrassment and shame.

To cry for a man that had absolutely no interest in the heart I had offered him was pure foolishness. One wouldn't catch me participating. Not publicly, at least. Not tonight. Preferably not any other night.

"Did you hear me?"

"I didn't." Or, maybe I had but had forgotten what Collin had said.

"You should spend the night with me."

"I don't know. Maybe I should," I agreed.

Anything to get over him. If it meant getting under Collin, then I was willing to try. We hadn't reached that milestone in our journey, but tonight I was willing to pull back the curtains a little sooner than I'd originally planned.

"I think so," he insisted. "So let me know when you're ready and we can go."

"I'm ready," I pushed out, unsure of what I was saying or what I was doing.

"Then, let's get out of here."

"I have to let my brothers know that I'm leaving."

I dropped my hands from around his neck and he did the same with my waist.

"Of course."

Grabbing his hand, I pulled him in the direction of our table. It had been over an hour and two drinks since we'd left for the bar. When I returned, there was someone sitting in Laike's lap, keeping him entertained. Luca was in his phone, more than likely texting Ever. Ken, he gave us both his undivided attention as I began to speak.

"I'm going to get out of here."

"And go where?" Ken asked, straight-faced and expecting a response. When I hesitated, he turned to Laike and tapped him on the arm. "Y'all just letting sis roam the streets with anybody or y'all done did your due diligence?"

"I didn't even know the nigga existed, so I haven't had the chance to check into him."

"Bet," he confirmed with Laike. "So, again, where are you headed?" Ken sassed, daring me with his large, round eyes that were now visible. The weed had begun wearing off, obviously.

"Home," Luca shrugged, never looking up from his cell.

"Sounds about right," Ken agreed. "Have a good night, *baby girl*."

"Goodnight," Luca followed up.

"Call me in the morning," Laike finalized.

Snatching Collin's arm, I scurried from the table and didn't stop until we were out of the door. When we reached the parking lot, and not a second sooner, I released a long, shaky stream of air. With my fingers spread wide, I fanned the night skies with my hands – desperate to catch a breeze though it was far from humid or hot.

"You good?" Collin asked, concerned.

"I'll be fine."

"You listening to your people or are you coming home with me?" he probed, handing the yellow ticket to the valet attendant at the small podium.

"If I'm not home and they happen to check, there won't be a place on earth you can hide and not be found. This is all a test and the last thing I want you to do is fail. My brothers mean the world to me and their opinions matter. I've messed up once, and I refuse to do it again," I explained.

Nodding, Collin accepted my answer for exactly what it was as our wait began in silence. His Tesla appeared two minutes into our wait. Once we were inside and on our way back to my house, he lowered the volume on stereo.

"Just sitting here thinking about what you said back there a few minutes ago and how I've been feeling. I'm not worried about your brothers. They're looking out for you and doing exactly what I would. More women need more men in their lives that care for them like those men care for you back there. They just confirmed what I already knew. I'm not walking into any bullshit, and I appreciate that.

"For the past few days, I'd been feeling like I'm ready to take things between us to the next level. I'm ready to make you mine, officially. I just want to know if that's something you're interested in or if there are any reservations."

I'd known this moment was coming but now that it

was here, there was a lump in my throat so large that I couldn't get past it. I palmed my face, trying to relieve myself of the discomfort as my airway cleared.

"I've been enjoying our time together. You've made me the happiest I've been in years, but simultaneously, you're the first person I've dated in ten years. Aside from random hookups and a few first dates in which I only had one intention, you're the first real thing. I've fucked up before, Collin. And before I agree to something so altering – for me – I want to make sure that I'm making the best decision. This has nothing to do with you but everything to do with my baggage. I'm asking that you give us a little more time before I make the decision," sadly, I expressed.

Had it been a day prior, I would've agreed at the drop of a dime, but with Keanu's fresh cut, heavily melanated skin, and perfect smile sitting at the top of my brain, there wasn't room left to think of anyone at the moment. Not even Collin.

"This thing isn't one-sided and will never be. If you're not ready then it means we're not ready, and I'm not doing a good enough job gauging that. I thought I was onto something, but I was wrong."

But you weren't, I admitted. *It's him. It's always him.*

"I'll get there," I assured Collin while trying to convince myself, too.

"You will and I'll be right there when you do. Until then, we keep rocking." He smiled.

"I like that."

I did. I really admired Collin, his efforts, and his patience. He understood that our pace wouldn't be dictated by society's norms, but on our own terms. And tonight, there had been a wrench thrown in our path. Once I was able to step over it, we could continue. I didn't want to go into something knowing that my thoughts were preoccupied with something or someone else. It wasn't fair to Collin. It wasn't fair to me.

"Me, too."

The short drive to my home seemed to have shortened as I noticed we'd made it to my gate. Before exiting Collin's vehicle, I leaned over, pulled his face in my direction, and rested my lips on his. Their softness was rewarding, causing my cheeks to peak as I pulled back.

"What you smiling about?" he asked.

"What the future holds for us," I revealed.

"Oh yeah?"

"Ummm. Hmmmm."

"I can hardly wait."

"Me either."

"Get inside," he instructed, watching as I slid out of the passenger seat.

"Yes, sir."

The walk to my front door after I'd entered the gate went on for far too long. When I turned back, I found Collin still posted and waiting for me to open the door. I shoved my key in the door as Laike entered my thoughts. He had been promising to upgrade my lock to the same as he and Luca's but had been slow about doing so.

Asshole, I fussed, finally making it inside and closing the door behind me. I opened my threads and sent one to our sibling group message that included the three of us so that I could kill two birds with one stone.

Home, I shared along with a picture of my foyer.

Upgrade my lock! Asshole! I typed with precision and speed. I didn't have to specify my message. We all knew who it was for.

Fuck that lock.

Who is that lame ass nigga? He followed with, but I ignored.

That's why I'm Dad's favorite.

Fuck Dad, too.

And, Mom's favorite.

You're taking it too fucking far.

I'd agree, Luca replied.

Have a good night. I enjoyed seeing you.

Truth was, Luca was her favorite. She'd never admit it, but he was. Laike was so close to her favorite. It was almost tied. She loved her boys more than anything in the world. Dad was all for me. The boys were extensions of him, so of course he loved them, too, but his baby girl was his entire world. He'd proved it time and time again. His ideations had rubbed off on his boys. To them, I was everything. That's why I tried my hardest not to disappoint. I had too many men that

I loved looking for me to make healthy, wise decisions in every area of my life.

I love you, too, Luca.

Always.

Call me tomorrow. I'll install the system, Laike demanded.

You've been saying that for a whole two months.

I'm saying it again. Call me tomorrow.

Just come over when you wake up. I'll be here.

Aight. I'll be there around ten.

Bye.

You don't love me, too?

Bye.

Lyric Eisenberg.

I love you, Laike.

Always.

I shut down my phone for only a few seconds before reopening it after remembering Luca's sparse attention span before I'd left. It only meant one thing. Ever was awake and waiting on him to get home.

Are you awake? I messaged.

Instead of a reply, my phone rang.

"Hi, waiting on your brother to make it home. I promised him I'd wait up and he's holding me to it."

"I just left them and saw him preoccupied with that phone. I knew that it could only be you holding his attention like that."

"I told him to stop texting me and enjoy himself."

"Well, I'm here to tell you that he didn't."

"I know. Our messages gave him away. I always tell him that he needs a break from work and the girls but when he decides to, I can't get him off my line."

"He's addicted to his homelife, children, and wife. It's kind of a good problem to have."

"Yeah, but he needs time to himself. We will be fine."

"Try convincing him of that."

"I've tried. Anyway, what happened? I feel like needing to know the details of your story is half the reason I agreed to staying awake when Luca asked. That and this boy doing flips in my belly nonstop."

"Ken is fucking headache, and I don't understand how I didn't see it until tonight."

I made it upstairs and began undressing. A shower wasn't in my plans, so I began running the hot water from the sink.

"He's the type of headache you're trying to have."

"No, he's not."

I grabbed a towel from the basket of white wash-cloths and sat it inside the sink.

"Then, we wouldn't be having this conversation."

"You asked," I reminded her.

"Okay, and you could've declined comment, but we both know that's why you wanted to know if I was awake."

"I hate it when you're right."

Admittedly, she was hardly wrong. I dabbed a bit of soap on the rag before placing it against my bare skin. I cleansed my vulva and the surrounding skin carefully.

"Ummmm. Hmmmm. So, spill it."

"He was so mean toward Collin. When I told them I was leaving, he basically made the guys aware that I had plans of going to Collin's as if I'd told him that."

"Did he overhear you guys perhaps?"

"No."

I rinsed and repeated the same steps twice before allowing the water to wash away the soapiness of the towel. There wasn't much. Because I loved to allow my vagina to cleanse itself, I didn't interfere with its process often. I wiped with water, finally, and then hung the rag to dry. I hated putting wet rags in the clothes to be washed.

"He felt it," Ever replied. "Oooooh. You're in trouble, babe."

"He asked the second it came out of my mouth that I was heading out. He wanted to know where. When I didn't answer, he pulled Laike into his foolishness. Luca was planted in his phone, but made sure he put his two cents in."

"What did he say?"

"That I was going home."

I pulled the robe from behind my door and onto my body. The drinks were still in my system, slowing me down tremendously. Nevertheless, I began removing my makeup with the wipes from my makeup drawer. Laying down without applying my skincare was something I tried to never do, no matter how many drinks I'd had or how tired I was.

"Well, hey. To their credit, they want to make sure you're safe before you just start having sleepovers and stuffs."

"Are you on my side or theirs?"

"I'm team Keanu, babe, and that means I'm on the guys' side tonight."

"I should've ignored this call."

I tossed the two wipes I'd used to the side and grabbed another fresh white towel to follow up with. Once it was wet enough, I applied the hot rag to my face and began to scrub away at my skin.

"But you didn't."

Ding. Dong. My doorbell sounded, pulling me from my thoughts and halting the words I had for Ever.

"Was that your doorbell that I just heard?" she asked.

"I– uh. Yeah," stuttering, I responded.

"I can bet you Laike is coming to make sure you actually went home." Ever chuckled.

"What am I going to do with these two? I won't be surprised if Luca in tow."

"Luca is already on his way home. He just texted me."

"Of course... the only mature one out of the bunch," I hissed, marching down the stairs, slightly in a rush to be sure that Laike didn't wear down the doorbell. He had a key but for the sake of my privacy, he rarely used it. But on a night like tonight, I wouldn't put it past him.

When I reached the bottom step, the oxygen I'd collected on the way down exited my body and left me searching for more. My blood followed it, draining from me and leaving me clinging to life. As much as I wanted to blink, I couldn't, too afraid that I'd miss even the tiniest of movements that the man before me would make.

As black as he was, it should've been illegal for him to wear all black and looks so fucking good while simultaneously blending seamlessly with the darkness that surrounded him. I almost didn't recognize his frame, but the toothpick that hung from his pearly white teeth was my savior. It exposed his perfectly aligned teeth, halting me at once.

"Ever... I uh– I'm going to uh– call you back."

"It's him, isn't it?" she squealed in my ear, but I was so lost in my thoughts and his eyes that I had no words.

None for him and especially for her as we shared unwavering gazes that splintered my heart and milked my eyes for tears that I simply couldn't bring myself to shed, but inside, I wept. I wept. And I wept. Slowly, loudly. Uncontrollably, ridiculously I wept.

For my sanity and for my soul, I sobbed. Because no matter how much I tried to conceal it, forget it, dismiss it, the man before me held my heart in his hands. Whether he knew it or not, my body did, which was why I was drawn to him, unwillingly. Planting my feet on the floor, I tried my hardest to not move any closer no matter how magnetic our frames were.

"Ken?" I gasped, his dark figure sending me into shock.

"You love that nigga?" he asked, completely disregarding my panicked state.

Words failed me again.

THREE

keanu

SHE SAID NOTHING, pissing me the fuck off. I could feel my internal rage and distaste form for a nigga I barely even knew. He wasn't worth the energy of getting to know, but the fact that he was more than likely trying to conquer a heart that I wanted to myself forced my interest. Only because I wanted to know what he was doing to make her smile the twenty-six times she had since she walked into Oat + Olive. I thought I would've lost count around ten, but as the number grew, so did my disdain.

"Ken," she said my name, again, frustrating me.

"Keanu," I corrected. That's who she was interested in and that's who stood before her.

"What are you doing here?"

"You want me here, so I'm here," I stepped forward and didn't stop until we were nose to nose. Chest to chest. Mouth to mouth.

She's mine, I told myself.

"Why you talk all that shit in that message then fold on me?" I asked, chest aching at the thought of her not waiting for me like I'd waited for her all these years. "You love that nigga, Lyric?"

I needed to know. Waiting for her response had my jaws locking and my fists clenching. She didn't get to love anyone else. I was her only option. No one else existed as long as I did.

The air that she released from her lungs after holding it in so long, brushed against my lips. Her chest inflated, meeting mine as it rose and then it fell shortly after. The energy shifted as she prepared to answer the question I'd put into the atmosphere almost a full minute prior.

"No," she finally replied, pushing out the word along with another heavy breath.

Her chest rattled as her cheeks hiked and eyes lowered. The glossiness of them didn't go unnoticed. Nothing ever did when it came to her. I caught everything, even the tears that fell from her eyes as she tried turning to run away from me.

"Come here," I demanded.

Unable to control myself, I found one hand around her neck while the other untied the string that held her robe together. I leaned down and watched as her mouth slacked, opening and waiting for my intrusion. Infuriated that she was lending her time to another nigga while simultaneously aroused knowing that nigga could never fuck her or love her like I was going to, I summoned every drop of saliva I could.

Spuhhhhh.

I spat into her mouth, my dick hardening as the thickness slid down her throat and splattered around her lips.

She's mine.

My lower hand continued to roam upon the realization that she was pantiless. Her hairless pussy slipped through the slits of each of my fingers, its meatiness making my mouth water and pre-cum ooze from the tip of my dick.

"I missed you, too," I whispered to her, tightening the grip around her neck as her mouth fell open and legs widened.

"You don't give a fuck about me," she cried, softly, her voice weakening with each word.

Even she didn't believe the bullshit she was spewing. Had it been anyone else, I'd allow them to think that because it would be very true. But, not her. Not my Lyric.

"You're right. I give two fucks," I admitted, rubbing her bald pussy with my index and middle finger. Her head fell back onto the wall.

The tears that stained her face didn't resemble the ones I imagined she'd cry if our reunion went anything remotely close to what I'd planned. But I'd let her release them because secretly I felt as if she deserved them. I'd been tormented from the moment she walked into Oat + Olive with a nigga on her trail. I wasn't over that shit and wouldn't get over it in a matter of minutes. She'd understand the pain I felt sooner than later. When she couldn't walk a few steps without gapped legs and a prayer because I'd punished her pussy for hours on end, she'd comprehend.

"You didn't write me back," she whimpered.

"What the fuck did you expect me to say?"

"Something!" She found her strength, lifted her head, and looked me dead in the eyes.

"I'm here to show you better than I could've told you," I reasoned.

"I needed you then."

"But, I'm here now."

"And, I'm involved," she spat back.

"Then, why my hand in your pussy and not his?" I asked, slowly penetrating her with the same two fingers I'd massaged her clit with.

Her body raised as she gasped and clenched both my arms for support.

"Hmmmm?" I demanded a response.

"You left me hanging."

"Only so that I could tell you to your face," I admitted, pecking her pretty, pouty lips as I massaged her internals.

I hurt her. I hated that. I hated myself for allowing her to believe anything other than my truth. That wasn't my intention but no amount of words could accurately describe my feelings for her. She'd recalled the same night that I discovered my feelings for her. Prom night, the first time I'd ever felt a twinge of jealousy and it was for the nigga on her arm.

"Tell me— whaaaaaat?"

"That my heart, my pockets, my dick, my thoughts, my world belongs to you. I been yours, Lyric. I was only waiting for you to stake your claim."

As the words left my mouth, I felt a gush of fluid streaming down my fingers, wrist, and onto my arm. The never-ending flow heightened my adrenaline and forced a smile to my lips. Baby girl was pent up, and I was about to knock her shit down.

"Oh God."

"And, that's the only nigga you better call besides me from now on."

She continued to rain down on my fingers, her knees buckling and the features of her beautiful face knotting in so many different ways.

"Oh God. It won't stop." She worried too much. Always had.

"Shhhhh." With my lips, I silenced her.

If I was being honest, for the moment, I didn't want to hear shit she had to say. I heard her loud and clear three months ago. Tonight was my response. For every syllable she'd poured out her heart with, I'd stroke her pussy with my tongue, my fingers, and eventually my dick.

Lyric's flaccid body rested on me as the supply to her river stopped flowing. She was breathless as she clung to life by a thread. I wrapped her legs and arms around me and pulled her into my chest before turning and heading for the stairs.

"Hold on to me," I advised. Her weakened state made it a bit harder than to keep her from slipping from my arms.

"I can't," she whined, head hanging over my shoulder.

I placed a hand at her back and one underneath her bare ass, marching up the steps with her bouncing the entire way. Her home wasn't foreign to me. I'd visited countless times since Luca had come home. Prior, she was ducked off and unavailable to the world. But since he'd touched down, she'd been the butterfly I'd known since we were kids.

It was also Laike who'd shown me how to enter her crib without a key. He'd lost his a year ago, according to him, but knew how to maneuver the lock and get it to open for him. It was the main reason he was going to upgrade her security system soon. He'd mentioned it before we parted ways, but if he didn't within the next week then I'd install a new one myself. I'd entered her home far too easily using Laike's maneuver.

Her body hit the bed, indenting her comforter and making the ends lift. The robe that was once snug around her body was loose and threatening to fall from her shoulders. She was stunning, staring up at me waiting for me to lead her to wherever it was I planned for us to go.

"This isn't my bedroom."

"It's not your main bedroom," I corrected her, "but the one you love sleeping in when home alone because you're furthest away from the door and that comforts you... makes you feel safer."

It's me you're talking to, I thought. When it came to her, I paid attention to detail.

"You hurt my feelings," she confessed, spreading her legs exposing parts of her that I'd only dreamt about. And now that they were in my line of vision, I could admit that my dreams hadn't done them much justice.

"I'm sorry."

"For what?" she pushed.

"For whatever you want me to be sorry for," I replied as I pulled my shirt over my head.

Once it was completely off and I could see again, I

noticed her position had changed. Her legs had closed as she sat up in bed tying the string around her waist.

"What's the matter?" I stopped to ask, placing both hands in the front of my briefs. The comfort it brought me was unshakable. I imagined it was the same for someone who sucked their thumb.

"Just forget it, Ken."

"Keanu."

"Whatever the fuck you want to call yourself. Just forget it. Just forget I ever wrote you. It was a mistake. I'm still regretting it 'til this day and you being here is not helping. You should leave!"

"So what, you can cry yourself to sleep? Nah. I'm here and I'm staying because I know that's what we both want."

"Where did you park?" Her eyes bulged as she stood to her feet.

Gently, I pushed her back onto the bed and then placed my hand back into the waistband of my briefs.

"What does it matter?"

"I don't want my brother riding by and seeing your car outside."

"Not that it would be an issue if he did, but don't worry your pretty little head. I'm not parked in your driveway."

"Well, enjoy the walk back."

"I'm not leaving."

"I said forget the letter."

"I can't. Neither can you."

"It meant nothing," she argued, her words stinging.

"It meant everything," I admitted.

"Why are you here?" She softened, eyes watering.

"Why the fuck you keep crying, Lyric?" There was a very thin line between lovers and friends and it was blurring each time I saw tears in her pretty brown eyes. More than anything else, I wanted to know if she was well.

"Because you made me feel like a fool... even now I feel foolish."

"Why?"

"Because as much as I don't want to, I still want you."

"And you're going to keep wanting me. That shit doesn't just go away because you're upset or in your feelings. It intensifies. So, why are you willing to deprive yourself for the sake of pride?"

Lyric's pretty, yellow skin looked edible. Her big and light brown eyes, a distinctive characteristic of the Eisenberg crew, were as seductive as the curves on her frame. From head to toe, she was undoubtedly the finest motherfucker I'd ever seen. Not that new-aged fine, either. The one that reminded you of Halle or Megan Good. The girl next door seduction those two possessed was exactly what Lyric had and it was exactly what had drawn me to the girl next door.

"But why didn't you write back? Why'd you keep me waiting?"

"Because I didn't have the words for you, Lyric. I'm

no poet, baby. I'm a street nigga. I sell dope and tote guns. I'm not one to write words as engaging or as beautiful as the ones you wrote me. My presence tells a story of its own, no words needed. From the day that I got that message up until the moment that I saw you tonight, I thought about making it home to *you*. This visit was happening regardless of if I'd run into you or not. Because I thought you were still waiting for me, still marking your fucking calendar, and still preparing for everything you mentioned in your letter."

"I checked my email at least twelve times a day for a month straight. I was desperate to hear from you. To hear anything. I felt like you disregarded me. Disregarded my feelings. You popping up at my house won't get me past it so easily."

"Ok."

I was quickly reminded that Lyric was not as passive as most. When there was confusion, she sought clarity. When there was chaos, she sought order. When there were reservations, she sought a new path. When there was an issue, she sought a resolution.

"I hear you and I understand you, Lyric. Now that I know how my silence affected you, I will learn to meet you halfway. Is that a good enough resolution for you, love?"

"Do you mean it?"

"Yes, baby. I mean it." Referring to her as whom I'd already considered her for the last three months felt most natural to me, but it caused her brows to rise.

"Anything else, Lyric?"

"I feel so unsure," she acknowledged.

Leaning forward, I placed my hands on each side of the bed. With our lips only a few inches apart, I looked her in those doe-y eyes of hers.

"It's me, Lyric."

"It's you." She nodded, closing her eyes and then reopening them as if I'd disappear.

"It's me."

"My intentions aren't to be selfish," she reasoned.

I'd dealt with Lyric all my life. She was the center of everyone's world around her. I didn't have an issue making her the center of mine, too. In fact, it was what I was most excited about.

"You're not."

"So, tell me, what are you thinking? What do you want from me? I don't want to underdeliver. I want to be fair. I want to be considerate. I want to give you want you want," she rambled, her nerves beginning to sprout. Though the shit made her mad cute, I desired her comfort. She was safe with me.

"I want you to understand that you're safe with me."

"I know." She bowed her head briefly and then raised it again. "Anything else, Keanu?"

Hearing my government fall from her lips was heavy. I loved that shit.

"I'm going to marry you," I smiled, causing her to

smile, "and give you those kids you keep imagining for us."

"My brothers will leave you no choice. Two," she called out.

"Fuck both of them niggas. And, two," I agreed.

"Anything else?"

"Don't be sad." After a peck on the lips, I told her. "I hate when you're sad."

"My feelings are just hurt but at the same time, my heart can't phantom your presence. It's like, I can see you, but you're like really here." Those same cat-like eyes sparkled with tears before they fell onto her cheeks.

"I'm here," I confirmed, wiping her face.

"These are not sad tears, Keanu."

"I know." I did. I could feel it, feel the happiness she'd buried beneath her strife.

Silence entered the small space between us as we both worked to clean her face. Our fingers left evidence of her mental and emotional state, staining her skin red from stimulation and constant manipulation. In her fragility and disheveled state, she was still the prettiest girl in the world to me.

"Anything else?" she mustered with a titter after she'd gotten herself together as best she could.

Her eagerness to include my desires and eagerness to fulfill them hardened my dick. The next time tears fell from her eyes, I wanted it to be from the utter bliss derived from my uncompromising strokes.

"When I'm alone at night, and I begin to touch myself, it's you that appears behind my lids. I've wondered for far too long how well we'd mesh together, how my body must contour to your frame, and how we probably fit together like two puzzle pieces," I spoke the words from her message. "Show me how you touch yourself when thinking of me."

"Keanu." She shuttered.

"Scoot back."

Her legs weren't on the bed, but I wanted her to be comfortable. Attempting to find comfort myself, I pulled the loveseat that was a few feet away from the bed closer and removed the black Amiri jeans. Immediately after, I was planted on the velvet cushion watching as Lyric propped the pillows from the head of the bed up behind her.

"Keanu, I can't," she whispered, her cheeks flushing a crimson red.

"Be a big girl for daddy," I encouraged. "Show me what that pussy does when you think of me. Aight?"

"Okay," she answered, spreading her legs.

Her pretty, pink pussy peered. My eyes didn't leave it as I watched her fingers settle on her meaty lips. It was taking everything in me to remain seated, but I understood the assignment.

"Wider," I commanded.

Upon my request, Lyric spread her legs even wider until she was able to see me through the large gap she'd created. She closed her eyes as her right hand rested on her pussy.

"Open your eyes," I requested, slipping my hand into my briefs and freeing my dick.

When her lids reopened, they closed again immediately. Then, reopened again.

"Keanu," she begged.

"Eyes open and on me."

Dazed, she obsessed over my tool. I spat in my hand to lubricate it. Lyric's body jerked as the sound of my spit leaving my mouth penetrated the air.

"Oh God." She melted.

"Show me, Lyric."

Her index and middle fingers circled her vagina before disappearing inside of her. *Fuck*, I fumed, wishing it was me getting lost in her wetness. When her fingers reappeared, they were covered in her slime. She utilized the self-lubrication to glide her fingers over her clit.

Up and down.

Around and around.

Dick standing tall like a missile, I gripped the head and began massaging it while admiring the view. Lyric's eyes remained open but were so low that I could barely see anything but the skin on top and bottom of them.

Cum oozed from the tip of my dick though I wasn't ready to nut. Seeing Lyric skillfully satisfy herself with the thought of me circling her brain just had my head gone and me falling victim to an intoxicating stupor.

"Ummmmm," she moaned, caressing herself while looking back at me.

She held her pussy lips open with one hand and focused on her clit with the other. Every few seconds, she'd rewet her fingers, pulling nectar from her canal each time they reappeared. She was so fucking wet. I wanted to slide right in her shit, but it wasn't the time.

Nothing compared to my view. Nothing. Lyric's movements was like poetry in human form, each move she made forming a new line on the page. It was the best writing I'd seen in all my years.

Around and around. She worked her pussy like only she could. Her face scrunched and relaxed over and over, revealing her proximity to her mountain's top. She was almost there, and I wanted to take her the rest of the way.

"Oh my God." Her legs trembled as she came close to her peak.

"Stop."

Lyric's eyes widened as I stood from the chair I'd been perched on. When I made it to the bed, I pulled her legs until her ass was at the edge. I leaned down and took her tongue into my mouth, sucking it before setting it free again.

"I'm not going to fuck you, Lyric," I promised.

"Why not?" She breathed, passion in every particle of oxygen that exited her lungs.

"Because we're not ready."

I stood straight and rested the weight of my dick onto her wetness.

"Keeeaaaanu," she whimpered.

Once.

Twice.

Three times, I slammed it against her clit. Her gooiness stuck to my dick and formed slimy webs each time I lifted it.

Tat.

Tat.

Tat.

"Oh God."

Showing Lyric a bit more mercy than I initially desired, I began rubbing my thickness between her pussy lips. The head of my dick touched her clit each and every time. I reached up and palmed her right breast. It was the perfect size. With my thumb, I flickered the hardened pebble again and again.

"Put it in," Lyric begged.

"No." I stroked, not missing a beat. She was so fucking wet, and I was trying so fucking hard not to fall into the trap I'd set for myself.

"Put it in," she pleaded.

"No."

"Put it in."

"No." Stroke after stroke, her shit got wetter and wetter, driving me up the fucking wall.

"Please. I'm going to cum."

"No."

Before I could comprehend what was happening, Lyric's hand was around dick as I stroked, making it easier for her to guide me right inside of her.

"Ummmmmmmmm, I'm cummmmmmming," she announced, forcing my hand.

I pulled out of her instantly, overwhelmed by her warmth and softness. My dick exploded, cum shooting from the head and landing on her pussy, stomach, and chest.

"FUCK!" My legs locked as I milked my dick with the gushiness of Lyric's skin surrounding her vagina where I should've remained, but she had other plans. "Fuck."

Lyric reached down to assist me as if I needed any help from her. She'd disobeyed me. I should've slapped her fucking hand away, but it felt too good as it drained me of my cum.

"Why did you do that?" I asked, shivering from the gratifying orgasm she'd brought me to.

My dick was still hard, ready for another round of the thunder between her thighs, but I wasn't. Neither was Lyric. As much as she assumed she was, I knew she wasn't. The type of fucking I wanted us to do came with a lot of obligations, responsibilities, promises, communication, and energy. If she wasn't ready to give into that, then she wasn't ready for the dick that I had to offer.

"Do what?" She smiled, scooping some of my cum from her stomach with a finger on her other hand and placing it into her mouth.

My shit throbbed. I didn't understand how anyone could be so fucking pretty – and feminine, soft, and sexy and *forbidden*. Yet, there she was, massaging my hard dick and swallowing my cum.

"You know what the fuck I'm talking about."

I wanted to fuck her brains out and then fuck her again until she regained her common sense, but it would have had to wait. We would have to wait. As of right now, she wasn't ready for what I was ready for.

"This?" she asked, sliding me back into her pussy.

"Lyric," I gritted, wishing I had the strength to pull out but I didn't.

"Hm?" Innocently, with those big, button eyes that I loved, she quizzed.

"Why the fuck you do that?" I grilled her as I grabbed her waist and began my assault on her pussy. "There's still cum on my dick."

"Hmmmmmm." Ignoring me, she closed her eyes and tucked her bottom lip into her mouth. I didn't recall her ever being as defiant as she was tonight, and I hated her for that shit. She knew as well as I did that I wouldn't have the strength to pull out of her like I'd done before.

"Shit. This shit too fucking wet."

One that could definitely go round for round,

cumming back-to-back, and still be able to get my dick hard, I knew that it wouldn't be the case for Lyric. The way she was gripping me with her pussy muscles and trying to extract my nut from me, again, I wouldn't last more than three rounds with her at best.

Removing my hands from her waist, I stroked Lyric long and deep for all the times she wished I was. For all the times she'd imagined I would. For all the times she craved me. For all the marks on her calendar she'd made for me. For all the years we kept each other waiting. For all the times she wondered if the feelings were mutual. For every time she checked her computer hoping I'd responded to her message. For all the turmoil I'd caused her by not. For our past, present and future, I stroked her.

"Ooooooh God."

Her eyes rolled into the back of her head as I placed my palms on the back of her thighs and pushed them forward. I wanted to feel her guts. There wasn't a centimeter of dick that I didn't want her to have. She deserved all of it and I was going to see to it that she got it.

Her pretty feet dangled in the air, filling me with desires I'd never felt before. I leaned over, spread my lips, and sucked her big toe into my mouth. Her skin was tasteless, but somehow it satisfied my tastebuds.

"Keeeeaaaaaannnnuuuuuu!"

The sound of our connection smacked the air. Each thrust making a unique landing and sticking slightly due to her pussy leaking all over my dick and thighs.

Bhat.

Bhat.

Bhat.

Bhat.

"Fuck." I felt my knees weaken as my nut rose from my sack.

Bhat.

Bhat.

Bhat.

"Shit." It surfaced, slowly climbing up my shaft.

"I'm cumming!"

Bhat.

Bhat.

Bhat.

"KEANU."

Pulling my dick from Lyric's pussy, I plopped it on her vulva and watched as it spit up. This time, my semen oozed out and onto her skin. As she came down off her high, she reached down until her fingertips touched the cum on the upper portion of her pussy. She rubbed it around and around until there was a nice amount of it on her fingers. I waited, patiently, for her to stick them in her mouth, but she instead inserted them into her canal. When they reappeared, most of my creaminess was gone. With what remained, she used to lubricate her clit as she rubbed it in circles.

I lost it. Lost all sense of control. *Because, why? Why are you so fucking reckless?* I wanted to know.

Desperate to get back inside of Lyric's warmth, I slid in again. Third time's a charm. I watched intently as she played with her pussy as I stroked it, doubling her pleasure. The distorted look on her face let me know that she was mounting swiftly. I wasn't far behind.

"I'm going to cum. I'm goin–" she howled as her broken levee forced me out of her.

Grabbing my dick, I massaged it with the help of her pussy's saliva and watched as the gates opened, and she flooded the sheets beneath her. The sound of her personal sprinkler was music to my ears.

"Ahhhhh. Fuck. Ahhhhh. Ahhhhh!" she screamed as she squirted all over the bed, my stomach, my chest, and my dick. "Ahhhh fuck."

She bounced off the bed until her flow discontinued. Obviously exhausted, she tried catching her breath. Not giving her much of a chance, I slid back into her slipperiness where I planted my seeds in her garden.

"Fuck!" My body jerked as I unloaded inside of her, not giving two fucks about the consequences of my actions or hers at this point.

I pulled back, ejecting myself slowly while watching her pussy convulse. The internal heartbeat was my favorite to watch. It had served its purpose and pulled every drip of nut from me. I didn't have anything else to give.

"Ummmm," Lyric groaned.

Still watching her pussy jerk every few seconds, I held my dick in my hands. It was finally bowing out gracefully, until I witnessed the semen I'd just stuffed inside of Lyric sliding out and onto the bed.

"Stop," I demanded

Lyric knew exactly what she was doing. Disobeying my orders again, she continued to push my semen from her walls as I watched – unable to look away.

"You don't fucking listen," I told her.

"Then make me," she challenged.

I pulled Lyric from the bed and bent her over it. Mushing her face in the cum that she'd just gotten on the bed, I used my left hand to keep her head in place. With my right, I slapped her ass so hard that it immediately bruised. This time, I wouldn't be so lenient. This time, she'd be begging me to cut her loose but I wouldn't.

I slid into Lyric for the fourth and final time, hitting rock bottom in no time. She was in such a fragile state that she could only whimper silently from the deadly strokes I was hitting her with. Her legs were like noodles and the only thing holding her up was my right hand. She'd bitten off much more than she could chew.

"Maybe next time you'll shut the fuck up and listen," I advised, feeling my nut rise as she placed her hand on my stomach in an attempt to keep me from stuffing every inch of me inside of her. I slapped it away.

"This what you wanted, so take this dick."

FOUR

lyric

AS I OPENED my eyes in the blackness, doom consumed me. Regret crippled me and all that was left to do was stare into the darkness. Nothing made sense at the moment.

Keanu rested peacefully beside me while I laid silently in an uproar. My naked body clung to the sheet as my temperature rose and panic began to sit in. How my night had ended with Keanu's semen swimming inside of me when it had started with Collin, I had no idea.

What have I done? I asked myself, afraid to move a muscle. This wasn't just anyone laying beside me. It was Ken, my childhood friend and both of my brothers' best friend. If either of them ever discovered the night of passion that we'd just had, we'd be toast. While Keanu probably didn't give a damn, I cared. I cared a fucking lot. Too much, probably.

I glanced at the digital clock on the wall noting that it was 4:30 a.m. Time had flown. It felt like an hour ago when Keanu and I were showering and using all our strength to climb in bed. It was a task. A very difficult task because we were both beyond exhausted and drained from the multiple orgasms we'd had.

The way that he could cum and still keep going had blown my mind completely and kept me aroused far beyond my limit. That's why my pussy was still throbbing after what I'd endured the final and fourth round. He was a machine, one that I'd love to ride every chance I got but it wasn't that simple.

In fact, it would never be that simple. As good as his dick was, it would be a problem – one that I hadn't fully considered before sending him a message three months ago. Yet, as I lay beside him, it was all I could think about.

Oh, Luca. I'd let him down, again.

Laike. I cringed at the thought of disappointing him.

I can't. I finalized quickly. *I can't break their hearts*. I wouldn't. Neither of them deserved any more grief from my poor decisions when it came to love. I'd caused my family enough pain. I needed a way out, and I needed some retail therapy. It was going to take the best holy oil and a lot of trips to the mall to get over the dick that I'd just gotten. But, I could. I had no other choice, *except...*

Collin. I relaxed a little, remembering his offer. Shuffling at the thought of my newfound solution, I searched around for my phone. I bumped Keanu's firm frame in the process, causing my pussy to cream and my mouth to water. He was that good at what he did. I wanted him back inside of me, but my pussy was begging for a break and so was my head.

"Why aren't you asleep?" Keanu groaned, pulling me closer to him.

Just as I'd imagined, our bodies fit like two matching puzzle pieces. We were frustratingly perfect. I sighed at the realization of it all.

"What's the matter?" He yawned.

"We can't do this," I rushed out. "I can't do this."

"Man, take your ass to sleep, Lyric. It's already done."

"We had sex. That's it. Nothing is already done."

"We had sex. That's it?" Keanu scoffed.

"Yes."

"Keep talking crazy, and I'm going to put my dick in your mouth."

"Keanu, I'm serious."

"So am I. Lay your ass down. It's too early for this shit."

"I'm going to tell him yes," I blurted.

"Tell who yes? What are you talking about?"

"Collin. Last night, he asked if I'd be his girlfriend. I told him I needed time, but I don't. He's good for me. We're good for each other. I'm going to tell him yes."

Chuckling while releasing me from his hold, Keanu shifted in bed. He turned his back in my direction while hugging the pillow. He was extremely amused, somehow angering me. His nonchalant demeanor made my head throb and my girl downstairs followed suit.

"I'm serious."

"Ummm. Hmmm."

"I'm going to be in a relationship now. So, this, this between us, can't happen."

Whipping his body around, Keanu lifted his top half. I couldn't see him in the darkness of the early morning, but I could feel his eyes on me.

"You want a reaction out of me, so here's one. Here's a piece of advice for you. If agreeing to be his girlfriend makes you feel better then, then do it. But it'll never undo what has been done between us. As long as you with that nigga, stay the fuck away from me, aight?"

"See, that's why I didn't want to do this. I've been around you my entire life. What do you mean stay away from you?"

"I mean what the fuck I said," he gritted. "I'm not about to watch you go through life miserable and unhappy when the nigga you really want, the nigga you really love is willing and ready to give you the moon and the stars. I'm ready to give you what I don't even think I have to give but have every intention of learning to give. So, yeah, stay away from me. We still good but keep that shit far away from me."

"You're only proving my point, Keanu. We can't do this. You're telling me to stay away from you because I'm agreeing to be someone's girlfriend to save my family and us both some heartache?"

"Fuck your brothers, Lyric. I love them niggas dearly but when it comes to you, it'll be fuck everybody forever if that's what loving you requires. What about your heartache? Huh? What about what and who you want? Do you ever take that into consideration? Or are you always worried about the next motherfucker?"

"I've seen where my feelings can lead this family. I don't want that for them."

"Aight," he finalized with what I assume was a shrug.

"Alright?"

I wasn't sure why but I didn't want him to end the

conversation with that. I wanted him to convince me that we deserved a chance. I wanted him to keep fighting for what I knew could be the greatest love story ever told. I wanted him to forbid me from seeing Collin and any other man alive. He didn't. He simply fluffed the pillow and laid back down.

"Yeah. Aight."

"You don't have nothing else to say?"

"Play house with that as long as you want but if you give that nigga my pussy, it's going to be a fucking problem. *For both of you.*"

Frustrated, I fluffed the pillow underneath me, turned my back towards Keanu, and rested my head on it. My feelings were all up in the air. On one hand, I was madly obsessed and in love with the man lying next to me but on the other hand, I knew that our union would cause problems for my family. I didn't want that.

I felt the bed shift and a second later, I could feel Keanu's breath on my face. He hung over me, head dangling in the air. I waited for him to say something, anything.

"I love you, Lyric." His words pierced me, lifting small painful bumps from my skin. "I'm in love with you, Lyric. I have been for a long fucking time. Just been waiting to actually love you. There isn't a woman in this world that can say that I've ever loved them. I reserved that for you because only you could have my heart.

"Now that I'm here, you're telling me you'd rather give what's mine to the next nigga and that shit got me tight. I don't give a fuck about nothing and you know that. But you, I give two fucks. You're being unfair to me, but I wasn't built to beg a motherfucker to do shit they aren't willing to do on their own. So, if telling that nigga yes is what you want to do then do it. But know that you're simultaneously telling me no."

Scoffing, I covered my eyes with my hands and sighed deeply. This was far too complicated. There was no denying the fact that I wanted Keanu but neither was there any denying the fact that I wanted to make my family proud of my choices surrounding love for once. I had to redeem myself. Collin was my redemption.

"Lose that fucking attitude, aight? You're the one breaking my heart with this bullshit. I'm not breaking yours."

His lips landed on my top set as his fingers caressed the bottom set.

"You broke mine first," I reminded him, spreading my legs wider.

As exhausted as my body was, I couldn't resist him. The darkness concealed his face, but I felt him near. His fingertips grazed my skin as I felt his tongue on my right nipple. Then, my left. Then, my right again.

"You need to get on birth control."

He slid into me effortlessly. I craved him, making it hard to turn off my faucet with him near. He aroused me to the point of no end. His influence on my body was irrational. I couldn't imagine encountering him from this point on and not obsessing over how good his dick felt inside of me but I'd try my hardest. I had to.

"This is our last timmmmme."

"Not even you believe that shit," he countered, covering my mouth shortly after while stroking me long and gently.

This is insane. He was too damn good at this.

Lyric + Keanu

I RETURNED from the shower to find my bed empty and made. With my robe wrapped around me, I exited my second bedroom in search of Keanu. I kept my legs slightly gapped to relieve the pressure I felt below. I'd need a day or two to heal from his girth and skill.

"Keanu?" I called out after realizing he wasn't in the kitchen.

I checked every room downstairs, including the garage, but he was nowhere to be found. When I checked my front door and noticed the lock had been twisted, it hit me like a sack of bricks. *He's gone.*

It was almost six in the morning and the sun had started to ascend. Its glow touched my skin when I opened the door and looked around to see if there was any chance Keanu had decided to just get some fresh air. He wasn't there.

He's gone.

My heart twisted into a large knot at the realization, leaving me paralyzed and unable to move – unable to think and unable to comprehend. He'd left. *Me.*

I wasn't sure how much time passed before I stepped back into my home and locked the door behind me. Like the zombie that I felt like, I trekked up the stairs and into my bedroom. The second I rested on the edge of the bed, trying to calm my ragging heart, my cell phone rang in the distance. Somehow, I knew it was Keanu.

I rushed to the nightstand where it was. When I picked it up and saw Ever's name cross the screen, I squeezed my phone to the point that I thought it would break. With a low, deep groan, I fell back onto the bed with my eye to the ceiling. I'd never been so disappointed to see my best friend's number on the caller I.D.

"Lyric?" Ever's soft, swaying voice appeared on the line after I didn't greet her for a few seconds.

"Yeah."

"What's the matter?"

"I don't know," I admitted.

"Is everything okay? Are you hurt? Are you at home?"

"Everything is not okay and for some reason my

heart hurts. Yes. I'm home," I answered her questions one after the other.

"Do you want me to come by once San gets here for the kids?" she offered.

"No. I know you have a busy schedule today. I'll be fine," I assured her.

"I'll drop it all for you, babe."

"I know." I cringed.

She would and that's what I loved so much about her. While women found themselves having several friends to juggle, I only needed one. Ever was a Godsend and there weren't many in the world like her. She had my back and my front. If women weren't stepping like her then I didn't want them in my life. She was rare and she was mine. I loved that for me and for her because I had her covered, too.

"Talk to me."

"We had sex," I confessed.

After a gasp, the line went silent. I waited for Ever to get herself together before I said anything else. Before I was able, she responded.

"Wow. Okay."

"And not regular sex, Ever. It should be illegal for him to be so good at what he does. He doesn't cum once. He cums over and over and over. I've only seen that in porn, never in real life. He had me risking my livelihood, begging him to re-enter me each time he removed it. I didn't give a damn that there was still nut on his dick or if he decided to leave it inside of me when he came. I just wanted every crevice of my pussy filled to capacity with him."

"It sounds like the ideal night to me, so what's with the sadness?"

"When I got out of the shower about ten minutes ago, he was gone."

"Woah. Did he really do a hit it and quit it or did you say something to make him leave?"

"He didn't do a hit it and quit it," I explained, needing to give credit where it was due, "I just got so scared after last night and this morning. I'd go crazy over Keanu. If he's been giving out dick like that all his life, I'll go completely insane over that man. I will. I'll only end up breaking my brother's heart, again. Both of theirs. I can't risk that, Ever. Not for anyone and especially not for some good dick – no matter who it belongs to.

"So, I told him that I was going to agree to being Collin's girlfriend. He asked me on the way to my house last night. I told him I needed some time but after that night with Keanu, I don't. I've made my decision. Collin is the safest option so that is what I'm going with. Keanu is a threat to my body, brothers, and heart. I can't do this with him. Not freely and openly. Collin is different."

"You told him what?" Ever's voice raised, something it hardly ever did. In fact, I'd never heard her raise her voice in the decade I'd known her.

"I told him I was going to agree to being Collin's girlfriend."

"And you're wondering why you're hurt over there? Imagine how he feels right now. He came home to you, Lyric, risking it all as well. He risked his friendship with the two men that he loves dearly all for you to be ungrateful for his sacrifice and have the nerve to tell him that you're going to agree to be someone else's girlfriend. That's ludicrous. I hate to say this, but whatever pain you're feeling right now, you deserve it."

"Ever!"

"I apologize, but I'm serious, Lyric. Why would you do such a thing?" she complained, making it obvious that she was not agreeing with my actions.

"You're rooting for Keanu. I get that. It's why you see errors in my ways, but if you were to really think about it... like really. You'd understand why Collin is my choice."

"I'm rooting for you, Lyric. I'm rooting for your heart, and I'm only upset because I know where it belongs. Of course Collin is the better option on paper and maybe when it comes to the family, but none of that matters when the heart is involved," she reasoned.

I understood where she was coming from, too, but I wasn't willing to dismantle the family's dynamic for the hell of it. I'd grown some courage that I shouldn't have over the course of Keanu's stay and wrote him a message that should've stayed between Ever and I. When I wrote it, I hadn't thought about what would actually happen or how much it could change things for everyone. I was being selfish, but after having three months to think things through, I knew that it wasn't a risk I could take.

"The heart has gotten me into a lot of trouble, Ever," I reminded her.

"I understand." She sighed. "As much as I don't want to, I understand."

"Thank you."

"But the damage is kind of already done. It'll be too hard for you two to stay out of each other's bed now that you've both experienced what one another feels like. I couldn't imagine not being intimate with Luca after the first time we gave into our desires. It would be torture and an unnecessary evil that I wouldn't be able to face."

"That's exactly why I have to go ahead and take that next step with Collin. I've felt his dick. He is not half–stepping."

"Well, if that's what you think it will take, but I don't see it. Because, even if he has the size, does he have the skills?"

"When I find out, I will let you know."

"I just can't believe you told that man that." She released a long, hard breath.

"I can't believe he just left." I sighed, feeling the sadness from the top of my head to the bottom of my feet. "I want him back already."

"I'd tell you to get him back there immediately and

apologize but there's a small piece of me that really understands where you're coming from and won't allow me to encourage that. I will, however, keep an eye on you and see how well you handle his absence now that you've had Keanu in your presence. If it's not up to standards, I'm calling him myself to get him back over there. If you want to give Collin a chance before you give into Keanu, then do it. But don't think that I'm going to sit and watch you try to force something with another man because you're truly in love with another one."

"I won't do that. I promise. If Collin isn't for me, I won't force it. I promise."

"I won't let you."

"I'm sleepy again," I yawned, dragging the words much longer than necessary.

"Well, I bet you are," Ever chuckled, "get some sleep and call me when you wake up."

"Only if we're not talking about this."

"Then, we won't talk about this."

We ended the call after saying our goodbyes. I slipped into something a bit more comfortable and silky, knowing that I'd be out for a while. My body had been overworked and so was my pussy. We needed to recalibrate and it wouldn't be a small task, either.

lyric + keenu

THE EXPLOSIVE POUNDING on my door had awakened me from my slumber. I descended my steps in a drunken-like haze, rushing to see who was demanding my presence. When I stood close enough to the peephole, I could see Laike's frame situated on my porch, pissing me off to the max.

"Why not just use your key?"

"I'm trying to respect your little privacy or whatever and not barge in only to find that lame ass nigga in there."

Laike walked inside, looking around as if he'd find another human in my home other than myself.

"Laike, you care nothing about my privacy for the most part. Let's be very clear on that. As far as Collin goes, he's far from lame and you're going to have to start showing him some respect."

I followed behind him as he made his way into the kitchen. He was making it clear that it's where he preferred me. My brothers considered me spoiled, but it was them who I'd spoiled over the years. Whenever they came over early mornings, they'd get a hot, fresh, homecooked meal that would fill their bellies for at least a few hours.

"Says who?" He stopped, turned around and waited for my answer.

"Says me because he's going to be around for a while. He asked me to be his girlfriend."

With a roll of my eyes, I kept walking ahead of him. When I made it inside of the kitchen, he was still trying to comprehend what was being asked of him.

"I hope you declined," he muttered.

"I don't have a reason to," I told him as a matter of fact.

"You've been around your father and your brothers your entire life and that's the nigga you're choosing to spend the rest of your days with? Have we not taught you anything? Shit, has Laura not taught you anything?"

Sucking the skin of his teeth, Laike shook his head. The disgust on his handsome face didn't go unnoticed. In fact, it caused my stomach to turn as Keanu flashed before my eyes.

"What? You'd rather I get a man like you who can't keep his dick in his pants long enough to save our relationship and end up sad for a full decade like Baisleigh? She's just getting her life back on track after you ravished her fucking heart and soul. And, Luca, he was more of the same. The only difference is, he didn't lead anyone on to believe that they were his match until he was ready to get in the ring with them, for real," I reminded him. So quickly he'd seemed to have forgotten their history.

"She is my match," Laike confirmed, referring to Baisleigh.

"Then, why did you let her get away?"

"Just because we're good to each other doesn't mean we're good for each other."

"That's bullshit and you know it, Laike. If that's what you used to convince yourself that what you did to her was right, then you're sicker than I thought."

It was my turn to wear the disgust I felt on my face. I could hardly look Baisleigh in the face these days for the torture my brother had put her through. Willingly, she stayed hoping he'd get his act together. But after years and years of turmoil, he did what we all knew was best and forced her out of his life. He knew that he was the one mistake she was willing to make over and over if he allowed her to. Laike loved her far too much to continue to allow it so he put an end to it himself. Though it shattered Baisleigh, she picked up the pieces and kept pushing.

"I'm not trying to convince myself of nothing, Lyric. I know I hurt her. You don't have to keep reminding me. I see it every time I look into her eyes. I'm still dealing with that myself. She's gotten over it by now. I'm still fucked-up about it, but I did us both a favor by letting her go. I can live with that."

"You broke her heart, Laike."

"I broke mine, too."

"Like, really broke hers."

"And I would've kept breaking it if I hadn't let her

go. It was for the best. She deserved better. I couldn't give her that. Too young, too much money, and too many bitches ready and willing to do whatever I asked before the words could come from my mouth."

Perched on the stool at the island, Laike explained himself.

"So, you'd rather I get with a man like that? Huh?"

"Naaaa," he dragged as he said.

"Then, what are you saying because we both know I tried that route and it didn't end well for me – for anyone. Especially Luca."

Folding my arms, I stood next to him and waited for what was to come. You never knew what to expect from Laike. Luca was a bit more calculated and predictable. He was a very smart man so you could always expect him to move as such. Laike, he was just as wise as Luca. But the coolness and control over his actions that Luca possessed, Laike didn't.

He reacted – *and fast*. He and Luca balanced each other so beautifully. They truly complemented one another. Their knowledge was incredible, unbelievable even. Luca was patient. Laike was precise. Often times, I wondered if it was why he was so in love with archi-tecture.

"You need to get off that shit, Lyric," he hissed, sounding just like the older one of us three. "Stop blaming yourself for the next nigga's actions. It could've been a random nigga in the streets pushing the limits, and Luca would've done the same thing. If it was me that had pulled up, I would've done the same. Pops, too. Moms, too. So, let that shit go, sis."

"It's easy for everyone else to say but I'm good." Shaking my head, I unfolded my arms and dropped them at my side.

"What was the point of Luca paying all that money for that fine ass therapist then?"

He was always thinking with his dick. That was part of his problem. If he could just put those thoughts behind him then he'd be much better off, in love, and giving me more nieces and nephews to spoil.

"She served her purpose. The guilt no longer lingers like it once did, but that fatal night will always have a voice of reasoning in the decisions I make when it comes to men. That'll never change. If therapy didn't do its job, then I wouldn't be seeing Collin seriously."

"Oh, so you're seeing him seriously?" Laike cackled.

I punched him in his arm as I rolled my eyes.

"After today, I'll be his girlfriend and you're going to treat him with some respect."

"That's doable. I can respect the nigga but that does not mean that I have to like him. I don't and won't ever pretend that I do."

"Whatever, Laike. Just behave. That's all I ask."

"I can't make any promises." Shrugging, he lifted his brows and kept them high with big arches.

"Laike. Do I need to tell Mom?" I countered.

"All you do is snitch."

"Eggs, turkey bacon, and breakfast potatoes?" I asked, ignoring the little comment he'd made.

"Yeah. I want some oatmeal, too."

"Alright, greedy."

"I'll be in the front. I need to keep the door open a little while to get this system up and running. Put on some damn clothes."

Standing from the stool he'd been sitting on, Laike opened his arms for me to come inside. I obliged. Just like when we were kids, I loved hugs from him and Luca. They're love was almost all the love that I'd ever needed. It was the reason I was never pressed for boys when I was a kid or men as an adult. The love that I was showered with was more than enough to keep me from seeking validation from anyone I was involved with.

"I have on clothes, and my neighbors are too far away to even see what I have going on at my house. That's also why I have those tall ass bushes. For privacy."

Stepping away and releasing myself from his embrace, I reminded my big brother.

"I'm not thinking about your neighbors, Lyric. It's cold out here."

"Oh, right." I chuckled, nodding my head.

"Always ready to pop off. Take ya ass upstairs and get out of that thin ass silk. That's what I should be telling Momma about. Shit looks cheap."

"Well, it's not but you're welcome to buy me more since you have so much shit to say."

"Charge it to one of my cards. You've got all the numbers."

"Will do."

When I made it into my room and out of Laike's sight, I slowly shut the door behind me and placed my back against it. Sighing in relief, I released the breath that I'd been holding since he walked through the door. The comfort I'd always felt being openly and freely me had dissolved. For the first time, in the presence of one of the people I loved most in this world, I felt like a fraud.

Knowing that just hours prior, his best friend was slipping and sliding inside of me, leaving traces of him that could result in long term consequences without his knowledge was disheartening. And if I hadn't known it after we'd indulged, I now knew that I'd definitely crossed the line – the very thick one that I knew better than anyone not to get near. The thought was invasive, consuming my entire mind and body at once. I was immobile, crippled as I remembered what I'd done and how fucking good it felt doing it. The fact that I wanted to do it again and again was repulsive.

Get your shit together, Lyric, I chastised.

Inhaling, I reserved a pit of oxygen that I slowly exhaled seconds later. As I counted down from ten, I could feel my body and mind relaxing. My splintered nerves slowly rejoined as I centered myself.

My cell rang out loud as I came from under the agonizing stress my actions had placed me under. I rushed to my bed, finally mobile again. Seeing Collin's contact flash on the screen made my heart smile.

"Hey," I answered.

"Good morning," his baritone warmed the line as he greeted me.

"Morning."

"I was thinking about you on my way to this meeting. What do you say we go to lunch tomorrow?"

"Tomorrow is a little tight for me. What about Monday? Brunch, maybe?"

"Brunch sounds good."

"And, I was thinking about what you asked me last night."

"What about it? You don't have to decide now. Like you said, you need a little time to think about it."

"I've thought about it."

"And?"

"I want to move forward. I'd love to take this thing between us to the next level," I revealed.

"Lyric, you sure?" he asked, I could hear the smile in his tone.

"Yes. I'm sure. I've thought about it and made my decision."

"You just made me the happiest man alive, Lyric!"

"Did I?" My heart galloped in my chest. It made me happy to hear that I made him happy.

"Yeah. You did! Are you sure you can't squeeze me in tomorrow?"

"Not tomorrow but Monday for sure, Collin. I already agreed to some family stuff tomorrow. I can't back out of that, ever."

"Got it. I can't wait to see you on Monday, then."

"Same," I replied, looking forward to our day date on Monday.

"Talk to you later."

"Later."

I ended the call and held my cell to my chest in disbelief. After a decade, I was finally a girlfriend again. The realization of it all curved my lips up into a smile.

keann

TWISTING and turning my nose from one side to the other, I tried to break through the dryness and discomfort I was beginning to feel. The vent was almost directly above my head, pushing out heated air to keep my home warm. The large, floor-to-ceiling windows that allowed me to overlook the city of Channing that was beneath The Hills and beyond made sure that my home reflected the weather if there wasn't any inter-ference.

In the summer months, my home would be so hot that the floors would sweat if AC wasn't involved. In the fall and winter months, it would be too cold inside for anyone to function properly if the heating system wasn't involved. Though I was thankful for both, they easily dried my nostrils to a crisp sometimes, waking me from my sleep after experiencing too much discomfort. This time, it was more of the same.

"Shit," I fussed, lifting straight up from my pillow and covering one nostril as I pushed mucus through the other to rewet it.

Once my head and nose were both feeling a bit better, I rested my hands on my knees knowing that there would be no more sleep for me. The sun's light radiated through the windows but did nothing to keep anyone or anything warm. For the most part, it was useless.

The clock on the other side of the room read 10:00 a.m. I couldn't remember sleeping so late. Ever. Not even before my time in the joint. Nevertheless, I stretched my limbs and granted myself grace as I stood and headed for the shower.

I adjusted the temperature of the water before I started it by hiking it up a few notches. This morning, I wanted to feel the burn. Though I'd been released a day prior, today was officially my fresh start. Prepared was an understatement.

Unclothed and ready to step into the steam that came from behind the glass doors, I took a good look at myself in the mirror. With a shake of my head, I glared at the rustiness of my skin. It hadn't come from lack of moisture or extreme dryness. I dropped my head to get a closer look at her residue still clinging to my dick like she was clinging to my heart.

Lyric. It didn't matter what she'd said to me hours prior. I knew deep, deep down inside that this thing between us didn't end here – with me washing away remnants of her in the shower. It couldn't. I wouldn't allow it but if she needed time to play around with ole boy to figure that out then I'd allow it.

The steamy water cascaded down my body as I placed both hands on the shower's wall and bowed my head. There was one person I wanted to talk to more than ever at the moment. It didn't matter how old I got, I'd never steer from their guidance, love, and under-standing.

"Dear God, it's me," I began my prayer, "humbly before you, thanking you for my freedom and my emancipation. Because of you, I stand in my shower a free man. One that is no longer bound or limited by the system's beliefs of what he can or should be doing. For that, I'm forever grateful. I come to you today with an open mind and open heart, asking you again to forgive me for my sins, those of my closest friends, those of my father, those of my brother, and those of the people that I love most.

"Lead us, guide us, protect us, and continue loving us dear God for we are only human. As I stand here in need of your forgiveness, I'm also asking for your blessing God and your assistance. Dear God, I'm asking for you to light my path to Lyric's heart and hers to mine. Our hearts, may they beat rhythmically and in sync. I don't want to spend my days without her as I don't want to spend my days without you.

"Bring her home to me, mind, body, heart, and soul and I promise to never deter from the path that you create for us to walk together. Equip me with the strength and the ability to love her properly and be everything her heart desires. Equip me with the patience and discipline to wait for her while she sorts things out in her heart and head. She's confused. Give her the understanding she needs. Fill her with the knowledge and understanding she seeks. Help her to understand that she isn't choosing between me and her brothers. Help her to understand that I'm the better choice. Shit, I'm the only choice for her."

"We need each other. Today, tomorrow, next week, and every year after this one. Let her know that I got her. Always. Bless her. Bless me. Bless us. Amen."

My grandmother had us in the hallways faithfully every morning, my cousins and I, praying to the Lord. Not only did we confess our sins and ask for forgiveness, but we were encouraged to speak about the blessings we were expecting to receive. Mine was always the same. I wanted my mother, the healthy and clean version of her. I wanted her then and sometimes, I still wanted her. But the ideal of having her in my world got a little vague each year and didn't bother me as much now. Out of sight, out of mind. That's how I played that.

Feeling the heavy burden I'd been carrying since around five lifted from my shoulders, I opened my eyes and pulled my hands down my face to clear the water. It reappeared the second they dropped. I grabbed a fresh towel from the rack and placed it underneath the dispenser for some body wash.

Once there were two pumps in my palm, on top of the towel, I scrubbed it back and forth in between both hands until I was satisfied with the suds. I combed through the small selection of songs that I fucked with heavily but nothing stood out over the other. So, instead of going back and forth, hurting my head to make a choice, I called on Alexa for assistance.

"Alexa," I yelled, "play something I'd love."

"Playing *Pulling Up* by Meek Mill featuring The Weekend," she responded, bringing a smile to my face.

The irony of her choice was comical. Kissing the skin of my teeth, I began to wash my body from head to toe. Alexa was on the same shit I was on and all of that patience that I'd just asked God for was unnecessary now because I knew that when I was ready, it didn't matter who she was with or where she was, I was pulling up on her.

Maybe that's the nigga telling me not to wait. Pull

down on her. Patience must not be the answer he wants me to have 'cause why play this shit? Finally, he's on the type of time I'm on. Him and Alexa, I thought, scrubbing my nutsack.

The thought of her with the next nigga pissed me off, causing me to scrub faster and harder. *I'm shooting up her club every chance I get,* I confessed. If she didn't want to tell her brothers right now, I could respect it but sooner or later when her belly bulged from those tiny shirts she liked to wear, there wouldn't be any more concealing.

We could openly and freely love one another which was all I wanted. It caused for desperate measures, but I could live with myself for taking them. It was either that or play the background as long as she wanted me to. I couldn't. Not only was I not interested, but my loyalty when it came to the Eisenbergs ran deep.

Lyric + Kenu

THE TRACKHAWK ROARED as I added to the mileage with one destination in mind. *Dooley.* I'd been out a full twenty-four hours and it was time to see the woman that I'd given my heart to before I even knew I had one. She was the reason I hadn't been tossed into the system after my mother pushed me out with drugs pumping through her bloodstream. Then, her habit was manageable, but still a problem. After my birth, the nasty addiction grew.

I was born a crack addict and stayed in the NICU the first three months of my life as I was weaned and cared for by the nurses. When I was finally released, it was to my grandmother. She cared for me the first few years of my life. When her health started to decline, I was given to my aunt and uncle, who weren't blessed with the ability to have children. My life could've been shitty, but because of three people that loved me dearly, it was far from it.

With *Pullin Up* on repeat, I damn near missed my exit. My tires halted as I approached the light just off the expressway that led to my old neighborhood – where I'd gotten my first battle scars and the knowledge of how the streets operated. It didn't matter that my grandmother had gotten me out of them at an early age, I'd been bitten by the bug and knew that they were exactly where I wanted to be when I grew up.

While doctors and lawyers excited the people in class next to me at my private institutes, it was El Chapo, Pablo Escobar, the Ochoa brothers, Amado, and Liam Eisenberg. While the others, I'd read about in papers, see in documentaries, or watch their stories unfold on the news stations, Liam Eisenberg was close enough that if I just reached out I could touch him.

My infatuation with his world is what led me to his sons and our bonds formed from there. Though discreet, I could spot a Lord from anywhere. Liam wasn't any different. While his home life was the perfect disguise for most he encountered, I knew what lie beneath the surface.

The newly remodeled white bricked home that I stopped in front of sat between a blue one and a gray one that I'd acquired many years ago. They were rented to two cousins who weren't interested in putting Dooley behind them. My money was received on time, every time which came as a surprise to anyone that was aware of our arrangement. I wasn't a stranger to the rule – never doing business with family. But before anything, I was about my paper and both tenants knew it.

If they had a problem paying, I'd kick them out on their asses just like I would anyone else and without getting authorities involved. To avoid conflict, they emptied their pockets religiously and paid every dime owed each month. The money went directly to my Nanny. It was her source of income in addition to the social security she'd been getting for years.

Dressed in an Armani tee and jeans, I stepped out of the truck after disabling the engine. I stuffed the key into my jeans to make sure that I didn't sit it down somewhere and lose it. That almost always happened in Nanny's house. It was so easy for any and everything to come up missing.

"Ken here!" I heard as soon as I rounded the truck.

Deante, Nelly's boy, jumped up from his seat on

the porch and screamed. He wasn't a day over eleven and as wild as they came. He was a fearless young bull, reminding me so much of myself as a youngin'. Just like me, no one was putting out the fire that was burning inside of him.

Whatever he put his head to, he would become and he'd be a beast at it. His love for basketball, if he allowed it, would take him to the top. I knew it and so did everyone else around us. The only task was keeping him alive to see his dreams come true. As much as he was on the courts, he was in the streets. As often as I could, I was sure to talk to him about it.

"You staying out of trouble, young nigga?"

"Man, what's that?" He sniggered.

"Don't get fucked-up out here thinking you cool and shit. Keep your head in them books and your feet on that wood."

"I been in the gym," he shared.

"Good."

"You got like twenty dollars you can spot me?"

"Only if you promise to pay this shit back when you make it pro!"

"Ahhh. I see what you did there."

"And, I see what you be doing. Don't let these streets keep you from giving your mother and brothers a better life. They deserve it."

I dug into my pockets and pulled out a hundred from the knot of them that was folded inside. His eyes glowed when he realized he'd be getting much more than a twenty.

"Give Tay and Renny twenty. You get sixty. I want my shit back, too," I reiterated.

"I got you," he agreed.

If paying to keep him off the streets was what I had to do, then I was more than willing. If anything ever happened to either of her boys, Nelly would never recover. Tay was too young to know much of anything. Renny wasn't interested in the streets. He was still finding himself and had recently realized he was into humans with the same body parts that he had. We'd all known it was coming and was happy that he could finally free himself from whatever shackles or shame his preference held him hostage with. He was only twelve, a year older than Deante.

I left Deante where he stood and headed up the three steps that led to a concrete path, stopping right in front of her door. So much about my Nanny's home had changed since the remodel, but it still felt the same. It still resembled home, even with the new upgrades.

"Knock, knock!" I yelled as I swung the door open and walked in.

As expected, I found my old lady posted on the couch with a cup of coffee in hand and the remote in her other. Slightly, she turned her head until she noticed my figure headed in her direction. The toothless smile that she displayed was utterly unfair, clenching my heart and soul simultaneously.

Excitedly, she rested the coffee cup on the small, portable table in front of her and stood to her feet with a quickness that I didn't know she could muster. Her skinny legs marched toward me and it wasn't before long that our bodies were crashing into one another. Her head nestled in my chest as my arms wrapped around her, encasing her in my frame.

And just like that, we remained for umpteenth seconds. Neither of us in a rush to dismantle our connection. Neither of us interested in releasing the other. So, we stayed. I could feel the wetness of her face on my skin after it had broken through my shirt. Her fragile frame shook as she began to mumble words that were beyond me and my understanding, but I was certain they had something – if not everything – to do with the man upstairs.

After what felt like two laps around the sun, we parted. Nanny wiped her tear-stained face with the back of her hands as she looked me up and down. It was her way of making sure I was in good health – mentally, physically, and emotionally. I was. Almost.

"My baby!" She clapped her hands together after she stepped out of my embrace. "What's the matter?"

"What you mean, old lady? I'm good."

"Oh, Keanu, save that for someone who gives a shit about the front you like to put on like you're just this tough booger. I know your heart and it's uneasy right now. So, tell me what's the matter?"

"Can't I just be happy I'm out and trying to adjust to being a free man again?"

"Oh that little slap on the wrist was nothing for you. I'm sure you did that time with a smile on your face, son. I know you. Your aunt might've kept you, but I raised you. I'm no fool. Don't insult me," she fussed, sitting down and grabbing her coffee.

"You think you know everything," I teased.

"I do when it comes to you and that damn Kale. You ate? Don't look like it."

She was a handful, but I loved her, nonetheless.

"No ma'am. I have not eaten."

"Ma'am? Boy, if you don't shut that mouth up of yours."

She hated to be referred to as anything other than Nanny, not even ma'am.

"I haven't eaten."

She stood again, this time much slower.

"Lock that door over there. I don't want nobody coming in behind you."

"You want me to yourself, huh?"

"I damn sure do, now lock that door and close my storm door."

She was selfish with me. Whenever she had the chance, she'd put everyone out of her home to spend time alone with me. Sometimes, Kale didn't even get a pass. It wasn't a secret that she was my confidant. Our time together was the only time that I was able to unveil. My armor was left at her doorstep every time I crossed it. I could stand tall or I could crumble before Nanny and when I walked out of the door she'd see me as the same man as I was when I came through the door. Most times, an even better man.

I locked up and closed her door as she'd requested and then followed her into the kitchen where she removed a carton of eggs from the fridge. Inwardly, I rejoiced. *Cheese eggs.* I'd choose them over any dish you put in front of me and Nanny knew it.

"Now, what's eating away at you? I can see the sadness in your eyes, Keanu, so don't bullshit me. I'll come across your head with this skillet."

She wouldn't. I knew it. She knew it. But I also knew that lying to her wouldn't end well, either.

"She wrote me while I was away," I admitted, causing her to turn all the way around from the stove in my direction.

"Are you serious?"

She knew, though no one else did. Long before a letter and long before my one night in heaven, Nanny knew. For that, giving a name wasn't necessary.

"Halfway into my bid."

"Around your birthday?"

Glory be to God, her memory was as sharp as a sword's end.

"On my birthday."

"And said what?"

"How long she's been in love with me and how much she fantasizes about a life together."

"And, what did you say to her in return?"

"Nothing."

"Nothing?"

"Nothing."

"Keanu, have I not taught you shit?" she hissed, shaking her head as she placed a dollop of butter in the skillet. "If that's what's got your panties in a bunch, then good for you."

"Why you tripping with me?" I hunched my shoulders in question.

"Because, the girl finally shows some interest in you, finally lets her guard down and confesses whatever love she must have for your frail ass and you just leave her hanging. No response, nothing. That's insane, Keanu. She'll never trust you enough to do anything remotely close again. You did a great job fucking that up, son. Shit."

"Calm down, old lady."

"I am calm."

"I saw her."

"When?" Her neck snapped in my direction again. With a raised brown, she waited for a response.

Her skin was as black as mine with hints of cocoa. Her hair was long and still so pretty even in old age. It passed the middle of her back, falling just above her waistline. She kept it plaited in four large braids almost every day. Sometimes, Nelly put the hot comb to it for her a few Sundays out of the year for church, but other than that it was plaited up.

"Last night."

"I bet she wanted nothing to do with your ass, too."

"She was with a guy."

"Oh, this is better than my soap operas." She chuckled, "Good for her. Go Lyric."

"Who's side are you on, Nanny?"

The fire in my chest rose as she continued to cackle.

"I'm on love's side and you messed up your chance acting like I didn't teach you any common sense. How stupid must you be to ignore that girl like that and not expect her to keep it pushing. She's probably still feeling like that was the worst mistake of her life, right now. Probably wish she could take back every word. Probably wants nothing to do with you now."

"She has no other choice."

"Bullshit! What makes you think she doesn't?"

"'Cause I made her go home."

"And she did like a fool?"

"She did."

"So, maybe that's where she wanted to be anyway."

"I went over."

"Keanu, I thought you said she was with a guy."

"I don't care who she was with, Nanny."

"Oh, so now there's urgency once you see that she's moving on. Men are just pathetic. All of them."

"I didn't know what to say to her then. In my

defense, I'm not good with words. Not those kind. I'd rather my actions speak for themselves."

"You could've told her that. Hell, told her something."

"I told her everything she needed to know last night."

"I'm sure you did, Keanu. I hope you kept that little thing of yours in your pants. Don't go disrupting that girl's life like you don't have any home training."

"I didn't keep it in my pants. That's why she has no other choice but to have me in her world, now. She shouldn't have given me inside."

"You sound stupid!" she spat, cracking four eggs in the pot.

"All you cooking a nigga is some eggs?" I laughed, knowing it would piss her off even more.

"You better be lucky you getting that with all this mess coming from your mouth."

"Wow. Okay." I nodded, knowing that she was in her feelings and wouldn't be giving me shit but some eggs. I was just praying she added the cheese.

"You're going to have to do more than get her little coochie wet to make her forgive you for what you did, Keanu. I imagine you've figured that out too and that's why you're over here looking like you just lost your best friend."

"I kind of did. If this goes south, I'll lose three of them at once."

"It doesn't have to go south, but you're going to

have to do a lot of making up to make it right. Didn't you say she has someone?"

"You know I did," I replied, catching her drift.

"Aw, yeah. You have plenty of work to do."

"She told me after we'd spent the night together that she was going to agree to be his girlfriend."

"And what happened next?"

"I gave her something to remember me by, and then I bounced when she got in the shower to wash my scent off her body."

"You left? You didn't try to talk her out of it?"

"Nah. Lyric is mine, Nanny. She knows there's no escaping me. Whether it's today or tomorrow that she gives in, I don't care. As long as she does. I've waited this long. What's waiting another month or two."

"Hmmm. I'm glad you're so confident, but it might just be longer than that."

"Can't be."

"What makes you so sure?"

"Because around that time she'll be sick every morning and will have missed her period at least once."

"Get out, Keanu!" she yelled, pointing toward her door.

"Nanny, I need my eggs."

"Nigga, you don't deserve eggs," she claimed.

"I thought you said you wanted a baby from me before you leave this earth."

"I ain't finna leave it, yet. I've got time."

"Tomorrow isn't promised," I reasoned.

"To me it is. God said he'd give me ninety-eight years, and I believe him. I'll see your kids have kids, son. Why'd you do such a dumb thing like that?"

"I wouldn't call it dumb, but you have your opinion just like I have mine."

"It's not dumb," she toned it down a bit. "I just want you to do the right thing by this girl and whatever situation you two might've put yourselves in last night. This isn't just anybody, Keanu. This is Lyric. You still have Laike and Luca and their parents to consider."

"I'm willing to go to them today and run down my intentions, but she ain't ready to be with a nigga."

"She's scared!"

"We're both about to do something that neither of us have ever done before. I have my fears, too."

"But have you messed up in love before? So much so that it harmed the ones you love, too?"

"No."

"That's why you can't understand her sentiments. Give her some time, but don't give her too much space. I have a feeling that this one will get away if you let her."

"I promise I won't. Now, can you please add some turkey bacon to my eggs, please?"

"I shouldn't, but I guess I can."

"I love you, though, Nanny."

"I love you, too, son."

lyric + kenu

WITH A STOMACH full of Nanny's food and a heart full of gratitude, I climbed into my truck on my way to the next destination. The orange gas light glowed as my engine howled, reminding me that my tank was low, however. Just before closing the door all the way, a small hand with pink painted nails pushed it open again.

"Twenty dollars, Ken?" Renny folded his arms, bringing humor to the moment.

"And what's so funny?"

"Shit, Renny," I lied.

"You must don't like my nail color?"

He brought his hands to his face to examine them.

"Na. I don't," I admitted.

"Why not? What about my fit?"

He stepped back to show me the short ass top and baggy pants that he wore. His hair had been colored, too. It was a lighter color than I was used to seeing on him.

"It's cool." I shrugged.

"Okay, then. So, why you hating on me. Laughing and stuff?" He propped a hand on his right hip.

"I'm just happy you're happy, Renny. But them nails need a fucking color change. That shit too loud."

"Okay, well if you'd give me more than twenty dollars, then maybe I can get that change you're speaking of."

Reaching into my pocket with a sigh, I handed him one of the hundreds from my knot. His high-pitched squeal left me in tears. Everything about my little cousin was changing before my eyes, but his freedom was the most precious thing.

"Get the fuck away from my truck sounding like that," I insisted, grabbing the handle of my door.

His voice deepened immediately. "Don't play with me," he demanded.

"See, that's that bullshit, Renny." Unable to contain my laughter, I shook my head and wiped the tears clouding my eyes.

"At the end of the day, I'm still a boy," he admitted.

"Good, and I need you to know that you'll always be a boy. Be who you be and do whatever the fuck you want but don't ever try to be anything other than that. We could never compare. Ever. Not to them, anyway."

"Period," he screamed, high-pitched and with so much emphasis.

"Get the fuck away from my truck, Renny. I'm going to need stitches fucking with you, my nigga."

"Bye. Thanks for the coin."

I closed the door after he'd moved out of the way, made sure that my Bluetooth was functioning properly, and pulled off. The gas station was my next stop before heading to Edgewood. It was Saturday, and I knew that my aunt and uncle were somewhere enjoying the start of their very short weekend.

Three blocks away from Nanny's crib and closest to the expressway, I pulled into 24/7, the gas station that never closed its doors. Rain, sleet, or snow, it was open twenty-four hours a day, seven days a week. It was a multi-purpose store that fixed cell phones, cooked dinner plates, served as an arcade, and was a one-stop shop for all the hood's necessities.

Without disabling my engine, I stepped out of the truck. On my hip, my pistol was perched, safety off, and ready for any amount of drama that anyone decided to bring to me. I stalked across the parking lot that was littered with chicken boxes, plastic wrapping, and cigarette butts in pursuit of the door.

Once I entered, the bell above my head sounded to let the employees know that they had a new customer. Every neck in the building turned in my direction. Waistlines were released from lethal clutches as greetings erupted from every end of the establishment. It wouldn't be a secret, now, everyone would know that Ken was home.

"Look at this black ass nigga!" Hammer yelled across the store as he closed the door to the fridge.

"They done let this nigga back out on the street!" someone else confirmed.

"My nigga walked that shit down with a smile," Hammer replied.

"What's good?"

"My man," Jerry, the store's clerk, said.

"Jerry motherfucking Berry," I responded, placing a fist up to the glass while stuffing my other hand into my pocket to retrieve some money.

I still couldn't understand why his parents had named him Jerry with a last name like Berry. That shit would never sit well with me, and I let him know it every time I saw him.

"You need to get that shit changed."

"I'm an old man now. Who cares?" He shrugged.

With a shake of the head, I slapped a hundred-dollar bill on the counter and pointed out at the black Hawk that was still running in the parking lot.

"Got you."

"Be easy, Ham."

"You already know, nigga."

I exited the building as the bell sounded again. When I made it to the truck and shoved the nozzle into the tank for the gas to begin flowing, I pulled the wrapper from the apple flavored *Now and Laters* that I'd swiped on my way out of the door. A kleptomaniac at heart, I couldn't help myself. Jerry knew what was up and if he was a smart man, he'd put it on my tab. I knew he wouldn't though.

With my fire clutched, I waited until the premium gas filled my tank. I wouldn't worry about the three dollars that were left. I slid back into the cool truck and opened another piece of candy. Before I could unwrap it, the sound of water and a squeegee hitting the windshield startled me. I looked up to find a fragile, hooded junkie in front of my truck.

"Aye. Aye. Na. Get that shit off my truck," I demanded after rolling down my window.

"Okay man. Okay man." Even the raspiness of her voice couldn't conceal her gender or identity.

Sighing, I ran a hand down my head, ending at my neck where I squeezed in a desperate attempt to contain my emotions. Before I was granted the strength to roll the window up, she appeared, placing her filthy hands on the interior.

"I can— I can get in with you and handle my business. You know. Whatever you want. I'm good with this mouth." She grunted, fidgeting all the while. She couldn't stay still for even a second.

"I need some money, man. I'll do whatever, baby."

Ignoring her advances to perform tasks on me that was unacceptable and inappropriate, I reached into the same pocket that I'd been reaching into all morning and pulled off four hundred. Her head was still bowed and her eyes were still fixed on the ground as I handed her the money.

"Oh. Oh, man. Oh man," she stared at the money I'd just handed her, never lifting her head to see exactly who it had come from or show any signs of gratitude.

My heart, my full heart, crumbled into twelve million and fifty-eight tiny shards of brokenness that were irreparable. Encounters weren't often but each time, they left me in worst shape than the last one. As my life progressed, hers continued to decline. No matter how much money I had acquired over the years, none of it was enough to buy back the woman I'd heard so much about as a child.

The one that stood before me resembled nothing of the one in the photos that lined my grandmother's walls. Gone was the long, flowy hair. It was replaced with matted, grays that could use good shampooing. The healthy weight was replaced with bones. The beautiful smile was no more. There were only gums and missing teeth. The ones that remained were stained beyond repair and were ready to fall out any day.

"Don't spend it all at once," I suggested, pulling at the gear before burning the rubber of my tires while racing out of the parking lot.

As I tried collecting the fragmented pieces of my heart when I hit the expressway, the blurriness of my eyes subsided. It didn't matter how much older I got or how many times I encountered her, seeing my mom in the predicament that she was in tugged at my heart-strings. It left me speechless and altered my mood instantaneously.

One would quickly or easily say that it was as simple as picking her up and taking her to a rehabilitation center, but shit wasn't that simple with addicts. Until they were ready for help, there was nothing you could do to help them but toss them a few dollars every once in a while so that they didn't have to risk their lives to get it themselves.

My mother wasn't ready. Not yet. She wasn't tired enough. My grandmother had placed her in several centers. My aunt had placed her in two. I'd even tried pleading with her years ago to allow me to help her. Not only did she not recognize me, but she declined every effort I made to get her the help I knew she needed.

So deep in my thoughts and completely satisfied with the silence around me, I didn't notice I'd made it to my destination until I saw my aunt and uncle standing next to my truck knocking on the window. I didn't have to spell it out for them to both know what was on my mind and what I'd just encountered. The weariness in my aunt's eyes exposed her concerns and the revelation of my truth.

"You're home!" She smiled, sadly.

"Y'all headed out?"

"Yes. We're due at Paula's in thirty minutes, sweetie. Are you okay?"

"I will be."

"Where'd you see her?"

"24/7."

"How is she?" my uncle butted in.

"Same shit, different day."

"Did you at least give her a few dollars to hold her over?"

"Four hundred. Hopefully, she uses it to get a room for a few nights and rest."

"She will. I'm sure she will." My aunt sighed, always the optimist.

"Can we have this homecoming tomorrow? Maybe? Please. I'm so sorry that we have to run."

"Nah," I assured her, "it's cool. I wasn't planning to hold y'all long anyway. Tried to catch y'all before y'all started your weekend."

"Tomorrow," my uncle voiced, placing a thumb in the air.

"Tomorrow," I repeated with a nod of my head.

"I love you, Keanu," my aunt told me.

"I love you, too. See you tomorrow."

"If you need us, call us," she ended with.

"You already know I will."

I watched as the two made their way to the open garage where their cars were parked. Releasing a thick, heavy stream of oxygen, I pushed the entire gas station ordeal behind me. I wouldn't allow it to ruin my day. I couldn't. So, instead of sulking, I dead the engine of my truck and stepped out.

After a few feet, I'd reached the only porch in the neighborhood that was just as familiar to me as mine. Before I could knock on the door, it swung open, and out popped Liam. his lengthy frame mimicked his sons' and mine, of course. His long arms wrapped around my body as he pulled me closer, forcing my head onto his shoulder with one hand while patting my back with the other.

"Welcome home, son!"

Exuberance was evident in his tone and mannerism. Though I was widely uncomfortable, I relaxed in his arms knowing that within them I was safe. He was as close to home for me as it got. So, if he wanted to hug me until I turned blue in the face then I'd let him have that moment – as long as he released me before I took my final breath.

After I was finally set free, I couldn't contain the contentment in my bones. The Eisenbergs did that for me. While I loved my aunt and uncle for who they were and how much they loved me, I never felt like I belonged with them. I was a hood nigga in the sheep's clothing they purchased for me religiously.

It wasn't until I came across the street that I felt like I'd found my tribe. I didn't have to watch what I said at the dinner table, hide my true interests in drug lord documentaries and investigations, pull my pants up to my waistline, forget the dialogue I'd learned in Dooley, or be anything other than myself.

"You look good," he complimented.

"I feel good, Pops."

"Good. Good. You ran into them knotty-headed boys of mine yet?"

"You know I have."

"What about our baby girl?"

Ran into her. In her. Through her. Yes, *sir*, I wanted to admit.

"Yeah. Last night." *And this morning.*

The words were at the tip of my tongue, but out of respect for Lyric, I swallowed them. The taste was bitter and foreign. I'd never bitten my tongue or swallowed my truth for anyone, but it was whatever when it came to her.

"Good. Good."

"Where's the lady of the house?"

"Out spending my hard-earned money already."

"Let's not act like she doesn't have her own to spend," I teased.

"Oh, we all know she does. What you got on your agenda today?"

"Shit. Making my rounds, checking on my properties, and handling a bit of business."

"Sounds productive. How is Kale?"

"Kale is much better, but I'm sure you already knew that."

There wasn't much that got past Liam Eisenberg. Once he set his sights on Kale, he wouldn't let up until he was certain that he wouldn't get himself into more trouble. That's how I slept so well every night when I was down. I knew that with the Eisenbergs still on the streets, Kale was in great hands.

"I did. He's doing good up there at the school."

"Yeah, he's doing what needs to be done."

"That's all that matters."

"I'm going to get out of here, old man. Tell Ma Dukes I stopped by to see her. I'm sure I'll catch her in these Channing streets soon."

"Especially if you plan on doing any shopping." He chuckled.

"Right."

"Be easy, son. I'm happy you're home."

"Appreciate that," I mustered before taking the small set of steps that led toward the winding path.

SIX

lyric

"MAYBE WE COULD GO some place for a few days to spend some time together – one weekend you're free."

Fuck, I groaned inwardly, still unable to rip the plastic open and retrieve the content of it. It was content that I desperately needed and couldn't go even another few hours without. In fact, I was hoping I wasn't too late already. The seventy-two hour window was slowly closing and the small talk that Collin was making was disrupting my train of thought.

"Lyric. Baby, did you hear me?"

"I'm sorry. Uh. Yeah. Sure."

"Yeah? We should get out of here. Where to?"

Wrestling again with the stubborn plastic in my hand, I nodded. "Umm. Hmmm."

"Lyric, baby you don't have a clue what I'm saying, do you?"

"I really have to go relieve my bladder. Sorry."

Discreetly, I tossed the entire package into my oversized Chanel and pulled it up on my shoulder. Before Collin could get his next set of words out of his mouth, I had disappeared down the hallway. I crept into the bathroom and locked the door behind me. Finally alone, I removed the packaging from my purse and stared at it intently to see what the hell was stopping me from getting inside of it.

"Looks normal."

The wrestling started again as I tried to force my way inside. Frustrated with my failed efforts after a few seconds, I tried determining the best course of action. Asking Collin would be absurd, but I wasn't against the idea completely. Desperate times called for desperate measures. The only other option was asking someone in the kitchen of Maple Berries Brunch House that we were visiting to lend me a knife because instead of their food, I was having a Plan B for breakfast.

"Ugggggggghhhh."

Bzzz.

Bzzz.

Bzzz.

My phone buzzed in my bag.

Bzzz.

Bzzz.

I rummaged through the purse to find the newly cased iPhone. Because I hated clutter and unnecessary junk inside of my bags, it was easily located. Ever's name danced across my screen, prompting me to answer.

"Why is the Plan B package so difficult to open?"

"I have no idea because I've never had the pleasure of taking one. I'm five babies in."

She included Dylan, always included Dylan, and I loved that about her. He wasn't forgotten and never would be. Not with a mother like Ever. Lucas was her first boy since Dylan, and I was just as happy for her to hold him in her arms as she was. In so many ways, he was her redemption.

"Well, I don't have that luxury seeing as though I was definitely ovulating when I slept with both of my brothers' best friend. It's a risk I'm simply not willing to take."

"Better you than me, love, but try squeezing both

sides until the little part that they hang on the shelves opens. Then, you can stick your finger through it and pull it apart."

"Of course you have all the answers. Thank you," I praised her.

"Of course, babe. Where are you?"

"At Maple Berries with Collin. I promised him brunch Saturday morning, so we're here grabbing breakfast."

"Yet you're in the bathroom wrestling with a Plan B package?" She chuckled, finding my situation comical.

"Hey, you're laughing a little too hard," I warned, trying my hardest not to join her.

"You're just prolonging the process, love. It's going to happen one way or another. Whether it's this year or next or the one after that, you'll have some pretty brown babies running through your home soon enough."

"I'm not having that man's children, Ever. Please get whatever idea you have about that out of your head."

"I see that you're in the business of convincing yourself because you're surely not convincing me of anything."

"Thanks for your help, Ever, but I'm going to end this call."

"Oh, for once I'm not right?"

"Goodbye!"

I ended the call before she could taunt me any longer. I hated that her words felt so true, but the challenge to make her a believer intrigued me beyond satisfaction. Soon enough, she'd understand that the entire Keanu phase had swiftly ended, no matter how long it had lasted prior.

The little shimmy she'd suggested worked like a charm. I was able to safely remove the pill without harming myself. Once I'd secured it in my bag, I used sanitizer to clean my hands before stepping out of the restroom.

When I made it back to the table, Collin was still waiting for me and so were the two waters we'd asked to start with. I slid into the crushed velvet booth, smiling to reassure Collin that everything was well, although I felt like I was falling apart.

As a woman who prided herself in having it altogether, I felt as if I'd lost control of myself the moment I shared my most intimate thoughts with a man who didn't give two thoughts about mustering a reply. Not even a few words but had the audacity to show up to my home, and I allowed him. Not only did I allow his presence, but I allowed him to fuck me into a rage that forced me into a relationship that would possibly save me from embarrassing myself in front of my family again.

It wasn't ideal, but it was my reality. So was the fact that Collin was a great man. He deserved me, and

I damn sure deserved someone mentally stable and financially suitable for my lifestyle. I didn't feel a single regret after agreeing to be his girlfriend because I knew he'd handle my heart with care. The only thing I was afraid of was being able to reciprocate his energy and give him all that he was deserving of.

With the glass of water in one hand, I popped the pill into my mouth with the other. It was small and easily glided down my throat with the assistance of the water that had been waiting for my arrival. Collin's throat cleared in the distance.

"Are you alright? Is everything okay?"

"Yeah," I answered with a nod, "everything is fine."

"Then, why are you taking medication?" He wanted to know.

"Preventative measures. But I'm fine. I promise."

"Okay. If you're not feeling well, we can reschedule."

"It's fine, Collin. I don't want to reschedule. Here is exactly where I want to be right now, with you."

"Music to my ears. I ordered for you already if you don't mind."

"I don't. So, what am I having?"

I put the entire Plan B fiasco behind me as I adjusted my posture and straightened my body. With my chest piercing the air and my head held high, I felt a bit more control of the moment as I waited for Collin to run down the order.

"A chicken and cheese omelet with a side of breakfast potatoes and fresh fruit."

"Look at you," I boasted. "You've got me all figured out, huh?"

"Not quite, but I'm trying."

"A man that pays attention to detail... I like it. I like it."

"It's the least I could do, right?"

"If you say so."

"Now, about this trip," casually, he revisited.

"Where are we going? When? And for how many days?"

A trip sounded like the perfect solution. With everything going on around me, I could use the break. It had been over a decade since I'd left the city with anyone other than family or Ever, but I was willing to let my hair down for once.

"Ahh. I was thinking of Aruba and in the next sixty days? I have a shitload of important dates coming up, but I have a week break coming up in about thirty-eight days."

"You know your schedule too well," I tittered. "I don't even know what my schedule looks like next week so definitely not next month."

"It's the only way I function. Otherwise, I'll lose my shit. My calendars are set forty-five days ahead of time at all times. I always know what's coming up so that there are no surprises. Now that I have a lady in my life, that's important. I can block off early morning meetings and start my weekends on Friday now, so that you never feel neglected and time is always carved out for us to get to know each other better and help this thing we're starting to grow."

"I like the sound of that."

"So do I."

"So, saaaaaaay, about a month and a half from now you want to go to Aruba?"

"I do."

The waitress returned with hot plates in her hand. She sat my food in front of me and then Collin's in front of him. Conversation ceased until she disappeared again.

"I'm ready to make fond memories with you," Collin revealed before forking his benedict.

The smirk that rested on his handsome face confirmed my assumptions, making the flesh of my walls cream. Keanu's round, curious eyes and dimples flooded my memory. Instantly, my eyelids sealed themselves and my chest hiked. Pebbled were my nipples, tingling as they brushed against my top.

"Ummmm," a moan seeped through my lips.

I clenched my walls, milking them of the goodness he'd thankfully left behind. Because if I didn't know any better, I would've sworn he was trying to wring me of everything I had to offer so that I wouldn't have it to produce for the next. *For Collin.*

Give that nigga my pussy and it's going to be a problem, his words were vivid as they rushed to the forefront of my thoughts. I could hear the seriousness and pain that radiated from his body as he delivered them.

"Lyric?" Collin pulled me back into our reality, one that didn't include Keanu.

As quickly as my walls began to salivate, the moisture they produced dried.

"You good?"

"Yes, babe. I'm fine," I confirmed with a nod.

Silence fell over us as we both dug into our food, making light conversation in between. Divine was the food. I absolutely loved the effort put into the aesthetic of Maple Berries Brunch House, but I was most appreciative of the fact that the food matched it. It, too, was perfect.

"I need to get to this meeting across town," Collin announced after finishing his second glass of water.

"And I have some work I need to get to as well." I sighed.

Admittedly, I wasn't ready to leave and neither was he. Reluctantly, we both cleaned our hands and faces before standing to leave. Collin left five twenties on the table, though our meal was no more than fifty. His generosity reminded me of Luca's and Laike's. Much of him did, no matter if neither of them saw it just yet.

"Call me later?" He pulled me into a hug as we stepped outside.

"Of course."

Standing to the tips of my toes, I placed my lips on

his. The small peck quickly evolved into a beautiful symphony with our tongues as the closers. With hiked breaths and an overwhelmed nervous system, I balanced myself after pulling back from Collin's embrace. He was divine, without a doubt, but no matter how much, he simply wasn't *him*. But he felt good, good enough for me to forget that *he* existed, even if only for a little while.

"Later, Lyric."

"Later, Collin," breathlessly, I replied, watching as he dashed down the pavement as if he was in a hurry, suddenly.

lyric + kenu

"THIS IS GOING to be the hardest shit in my life!" I screamed, barging into Ever's bakery shop. Because I had the code to her door, access was always granted.

"Hello to you, too!" She laughed.

"What's so funny?"

"Nothing." With a shrug, she disappeared into the back.

I should've gone home and dug into the pile of work that was waiting for me after I left Collin, but my irrational emotions had led me right to my best friend. Being in her presence had its perks. Ever was always in control of herself and her emotions. I couldn't remember a time other than when her children's well-being was at stake that she ever lost it. Even then, she was calmer than any mother of missing children that I'd ever heard or seen in my life. She handled the situation a lot better than I could've, which was why it was her that I was following to the back like a lost puppy.

"This is just so difficult. You don't understand."

"I don't. Because we both know that it doesn't have to be. You're making it this way."

"Collin is a good guy."

"A great guy, Lyric. But he's not *your* guy."

"Ever."

"Until you get that through your skull, you'll make these visits. And, after a while, I'll have Laike change the code because I'll be tired of your sulking."

"So, you'd really lock me out?"

"And talk to you from the other side of the door until you get your act together. Yes, I would."

"Wow, some type of friend!"

"The best friend. Your only friend. And you know I love you too much to see you being crazy," Ever reminded me.

"I know. Are those fresh out of the oven?" I asked, reaching over and grabbing one of the snickerdoodle cookies from the sheet before she could stop me.

"Well, I'm sure glad I always make extras."

"Me, too." I sniggered, tossing my head back as my laughter evolved.

"But seriously, are you okay?"

"I'm fine, Ever. Just all over the place a little. I'll get it together, though, and I promise not to burden you for much longer with my antics. This shall pass."

"It will and you'll never be a burden, Lyric. I've never been one to you, so don't even go there. It's harmless conversation, a listening ear, and some sound advice. It's the least I can do for all that you've done for me and the girls. I'm at your mercy for the rest of my days. You literally saved our lives. Your whole family," Ever expressed, putting the lid on a large bowl of sugar.

"Awwww. I love you so much, especially when you're pregnant and emotional."

"I'm not emotional."

"Then, why are you wiping your tears away?"

"Because I'm just thankful, Lyric. Every day, I'm filled with so much gratitude that it just spills from my eyes. I'm happy. Too happy. So happy that I'm just waiting on something to come disrupt that happiness."

"Nothing will. He's gone and that man he brought with him is gone. Nothing is going to steal your happiness this time. I promise, babe. I know because I have to catch up and your happiness has to wait for me to do that."

"Yeah?" She smiled.

"Yeah. Give me a few months, and I'll be right there with you. I can feel it."

"Me, too."

"Uggghhh. I have to get out of here and go do some

work. Seriously, I have no desire to leave, but I know the longer I stay the harder it will be to leave."

"That's true, so go get busy instead of watching me be busy."

"See you later, babe." I wrapped my hand around her neck and kissed her cheek, then swiftly pulled away.

"See you later," she returned.

With my head held a little higher and feeling a bit more in control over my emotions, I trekked through Ever's bakery and out of the door. Before I slid into my truck, I finished off the cookie that I'd stolen. It was delicious, per usual. There hadn't been a single creation of Ever's that I'd tasted that left me disappointed. The girl was good at what she did. That wasn't a secret. All of Channing knew, which was why she was extremely busy all the time.

lyric + kermi

MY SOLITUDE WAS UNMATCHED. I loved being alone. It's where I thrived for the most part. As I stood over the stove, plating the garlic mashed potatoes, steak, and creamy-cheese broccoli, I savored the silence that it afforded me with.

Instead of the dinner table, I opted for a seat on the couch so that I could continue to binge Blacklist. It had quickly become my favorite show and with eight seasons on Netflix, I knew that I had a while to go before I'd completed it. And once I did, season nine would be waiting for me.

Red's mind was impeccable. He was the smartest man I'd ever watched on screen. The way he thought twelve steps ahead of everything and everyone was impressive. If there was anyone who reminded me of him, it was my father. They were both wise beyond their years and always ahead of the crowd.

I rested my bottom on the plush, tan sofa that I melted into each night for two hours while watching Blacklist. I was sure not to consume too much at once because then I'd have nothing to watch once I was off and done dealing with numbers for the day. Besides, television wasn't exactly something I enjoyed watching for hours on end. It was mainly the reason I didn't have cable and could always keep up with my remotes.

Ping.

My cell alerted me of a text message once I was comfortable and ready to dig into my food. I felt around the couch in search of it, not bothering to take my eyes off the television. It wasn't long before my fingers were wrapped tightly around it as I pulled it up to my face. Collin's name was beside the message icon. I tapped it without hesitation, wondering what he was thinking at this hour.

You at home?

I am.

How about I come join you?

Though I'd loved his company any other time, now wasn't it. That had nothing to do with Collin and everything to do with my solitude and desire to get through my show without someone attempting to talk my ear or my drawers off. I simply wanted to be alone, which was another concern of mine when it came to getting back into a relationship. I loved my solitude far too much.

Still working. Sorry.

It's all good.

What are you doing?

Thinking about you. I was thinking dinner later this week.

Sounds doable. Let me know when, what time, and where we're going.

I will, tomorrow, once I've finalized the plans.

Okay.

I'll let you get back to work. Talk to you tomorrow.

Have a good night, Collin.

I will.

As soon as I read the final text, I tossed my cell over onto the couch and dug into the pile of garlic mashed potatoes I'd been craving. From the second they hit my tongue until they flowed down my throat, I hummed.

Ummmmmmm.

The broccoli was next to go. Before I was able to

truly dig in, my phone disrupted me again. After placing my fork on the plate and my plate on the side table next to the couch, I scooted over a bit to retrieve it from the spot where I'd thrown it.

"Hello," frustratedly, I greeted the caller.

"You should sound a little better than that when answering the phone for your favorite brother," Laike grilled me.

"If it was my favorite brother calling, then I would have."

"You just like your fucking daddy," he fussed. "You and that nigga a hater."

"Yet you love us all the same."

"Admittedly, I do."

"What is it, Laike? I'm watching my show."

"You, watching a show?"

"Yeah. I'm really into Blacklist right now."

"You cook something?"

"Yeah. You hungry? I can fix you a plate if you plan to stop by."

"Hell yeah. I'm not even ten minutes away."

"You live in The Hills, too, Laike. You're only ever about ten minutes away." I chuckled.

"Not always, but I'm on my way."

"Okay. I love you."

"Always."

With a heart full of gratitude, I reluctantly paused the television, grabbed my plate, and made my way back into the kitchen. Having either of my brothers over was always a treat. Though my parents rarely visited, their presence felt like an occasion as well.

I piled garlic potatoes, broccoli, and the biggest of the three pieces of steak I'd cooked onto his plate. It was still hot, so I shoved it into the microwave to maintain its warmth until he arrived. My bar area was my next stop. I gave the bottle of Hennessy a spin before dumping five shots into the blender, measuring them with the gold shot cup that Ever had gifted me. It came with an entire set from Target.

Frozen sliced strawberries, peaches, mangos, and crushed ice were all dumped into the blender one after the other, followed by a splash of fresh pineapple juice. The mixture only took a few seconds to combine, ultimately creating a fluffy, cold, and very tasty combination.

"Ummmmm," I hummed, licking the spoon.

"Give me some," Laike begged from the other side of the kitchen, startling me.

"Shit, you nearly gave me a heart attack."

"Damn," he praised after grabbing the spoon and licking the rest of the frozen beverage from it.

"That's kind of nasty," I joked.

"How?" he questioned.

"You have no idea where my mouth has been."

"Man, gone on with that shit. Where's my plate?"

"In the microwave."

"Bet and make me whatever that shit is. Put a little more liquor in my shit, though," he instructed.

I halfened the mix and added a pretty healthy shot to what was left before blending it for a few more seconds. Once his was ready, I carried them both into the dining room where he was making himself comfortable. I raced back to the kitchen to get my plate and noticed it was already gone.

"I heated it up for a few seconds," Laike shared once I realized he'd already brought both plates to the table. I hadn't even noticed when I'd dropped the drinks off.

"Thanks."

I sat across the table from Laike, who immediately dug into his food before asking, "What's new? Anything you want to share with your bigger nigga?"

I'm madly in love with your best friend, I desperately wanted to confess, but the words just wouldn't emerge.

"Collin and I are official."

"Anything else?" Laike shook his head, ready to change the subject already.

"Why don't you like him?"

"I don't know the nigga enough not to like him. But I don't like him *for you*. There's a difference."

"Why not for me?"

"It just doesn't seem... right? I don't know. I just imagined you with someone with a bit more finesse about himself. This nigga is a square if I've never seen one before."

"He is, but he's a good person."

"Is that all you require?"

"Are you insinuating I'm settling?"

"I don't have to insinuate shit. I'm telling you right now that you are."

"I don't think that I am. Safety and settling are very different. I'm just being safe."

"Them blue collar niggas be on some foul shit, too, Lyric. Don't let that shit fool you. Niggas be low down, down low, conniving, abusive, and all the rest of that shit. Just because he wears a suit and doesn't tote a Glock doesn't mean that he's to be trusted. It ain't about the career the man has. That doesn't determine his character. His actions do."

"I agree. Collin's actions have been nothing but outstanding."

"Wasn't Chauncy's in the beginning?"

He cut deep, reopening wounds that I'd patched up over therapy and the duration of our brother's sentence. There wasn't a follow-up for his statement. I didn't have a rebuttal. Silence was my only defense because we both knew that he was accurate, and he meant well – although his statement was brutally honest.

"Listen, all I'm saying is don't settle on our account 'cause we're coming behind any nigga and any broad that dare to fuck with you," he continued after a few seconds.

Laike shrugged as he sipped from his cup and then dug into his garlic potatoes. Nodding, I took the hint and continued eating the food that was left. I knew that everyone meant well around me and wanted what was best for me. It was just difficult recovering from such a huge blow, it didn't matter how long ago it was. What everyone else saw as a simple task, for me was much more complicated. I wouldn't apologize for my hesitancy or my choices. I'd made enough bad ones already.

SEVEN

keanu

LEANING AGAINST MY RIDE, I listened to the most beautiful sound ever known to a hustler. The sound of the hood. From the children running around to the mothers calling for them because the streetlights had come on and it was time to come home.

From the random, unrelatable words that some of the prostitutes chanted as they walked up and down the street, hoping someone would stop them to the whispers of the nightlife insects as the sun set. From the chatter of the niggas that lined the block to the cries of the babies with empty bellies or tired eyes.

From the sound of the corner store's bell to the screeching of tires up and down the pavement. From the giggles of the women that walked past the niggas that lined the block wishing one would pay them some attention to the continuous slamming of car doors.

I loved it. I loved it all. Dooley is and would always be home. It flowed through my blood and wouldn't stop, not even after I was underneath the dirt. It balanced me. I appreciated Huffington Hills for the knowledge it instilled in me, making me a downright, dirty dog in the streets. And not the filthy kind one would consider but a genius. A mastermind. One that could outsmart, outrun, outlive, and outshine any nigga that ever walked Dooley's streets – including the politicians and police. Though I was a nigga from the hood, I was blessed with the same education as presidents and the people that appointed them.

My aunt and uncle only accepted the best of everything for me, bringing sheer balance to my world. As well as I could eyeball a bad batch, I could solve a trigonometry problem just by looking at it. I was the best of both worlds.

Glancing at my phone, I happened to catch the moment the numbers after the nine hit fifty. It was going on ten and the urge to call it a night reigned supreme over all else. I stretched my arms as I stood straight up, my knees locked and a grunt evaded my body. *A nigga getting old as shit*, I thought as I tapped the button on the fob to start my engine.

Just as I opened the door, I heard a familiar voice on side of me.

"Can I go with you, Ken?" Deidra, one from around the way, asked while stopping near the door that I'd just opened.

"Nah. Keep going where you were already going," I suggested.

"I was going right here," she informed me, rolling her neck in the process. Her brown skin and silky hair were flawless – always had been.

"To ask a question you already know the answer to?" I chuckled, sliding into my truck with one hand on my steering wheel.

"You're fresh out, Ken. I'm sure no one has swooped you up yet." Folding her arms, she frowned and tilted her head as if I owed her an explanation. I didn't but Dee was aight with me, so I gave her one anyway.

"Somebody already beat you to the punch."

"Who, so I can find her and beat her ass," she asked, looking around as if the person I was speaking of was near.

"She's not out here, Dee." I chuckled.

"You just keep breaking my little heart," she groaned, overly dramatic as she always was in conversation with me.

"Better yours than hers, baby girl." With my right shoulder, I shrugged.

"Oh, this one must be special."

"The most special," I admitted.

"Well, maybe better luck next time, huh?" She was still hopeful, but there was no use for the small glimmer she was holding onto.

"There won't be a next time. There's an entire block full of niggas. Take your pick," I reminded her, pointing at the corner where there was a cluster of niggas kneeling and playing dice.

"You're my pick."

"I'm not available, baby girl."

"For how long?" She chuckled. "Almost everything has an expiration date when niggas like you are involved."

"Not this one. This one doesn't expire."

"Awwwww shit, Ken," she whined, puckering her pretty brown lips that I wouldn't have minded seeing wrapped around my dick. "She really got you bent like this?"

"Bent!" I agreed with a nod.

She did. I wasn't trying to hear shit from anybody about it, either. As much as she didn't want to admit it, she was bent, too.

"See you around, Dee."

"I guess." She sighed, walking away from my ride defeated.

Dee was thorough. I'd known her since we were

kids and year after year, she shot her shot. I wasn't mad at her, but I wasn't the nigga for her. Neither were any of the niggas I'd pointed to. I knew that and so did she.

Deidra was a diamond in the rough, one that didn't belong in Dooley but didn't quite know how to get out. She wanted me to be her ticket, but I couldn't be. I was already spoken for and had been for far longer than I'd like to admit. Some nigga someday would be lucky to have Deidra in their world. I just wasn't that nigga.

"You gone, nigga?" Tron walked past as he asked.

"Yeah."

"Streetlights on, got to get home, huh?" He found himself amused.

"Something like that."

The slamming of my door rattled the truck a bit, causing it to shift from one side to another. I tapped the start button while simultaneously pressuring the brake. Once the truck acknowledged its official start, I placed it in gear and pulled forward, slowly and carefully just in case a kid decided to risk their entire life chasing a ball into the street or rolling down a hill on their bike.

lyric + kervn

THE DARKNESS of my home was welcoming, but the silence... the silence was eerie. Because for the first time in my life, it wasn't enough. It wasn't enough to welcome me. It wasn't enough to satisfy me. It wasn't enough to keep my heart from drumming in my chest as I pushed past the living rooms, dining room, theatre room, bathrooms, kitchen, bar, pool hall, and onto the balcony with the sickest view of my city.

It just wasn't.

Even as I pulled the blunt that I'd rolled on the way home from behind my ear and lit it, contentment just didn't find me. I inhaled, gathering the smoke in my lungs and letting it linger for a bit as I closed my eyes. Exhaling, I reopened them and watched as the smoke that once filled my lungs, ventured into the chilliness of the night shortly before disappearing.

I want a family. My inner thoughts surfaced long enough for me to admit it. My appetite for unconditional love and adoration almost felt unreal. Foreign to say the least. I was ready to love and be loved on.

The children, the headaches, the empty pockets, the holidays, the tooth fairy. The sports. The crying. The hollering. The births. The dates. The vacations. The smiles. The messy home. The diaper changes. The lack of peace and quiet. The crowded bed. The lack of sleep. The laughter. The love. The family. I wanted it, and I didn't want to wait any longer for it.

"Ha," I chuckled as I made my way back into my home, "all because of a fucking message."

The realization that a message I'd received months prior had been the seed of my current thought process;

I couldn't contain the laughter that erupted as I poured a glass of Remy from the bar area.

"And I didn't have enough fucking sense to just write back. Anything," I chastised, shaking my head before tossing the first shot back.

Another followed quickly after because I knew that as pissed off as Lyric had made me a few mornings ago, it was no one's fault but mine. Her hesitancy was my issue, not hers. She'd removed her armor and shown me her vulnerability, only for me to hand her my ass to kiss. While my selfishness and thoughtlessness convinced me that I wasn't good enough with words or didn't have enough of them to express my feelings to Lyric, I forgot that she'd done that for me.

She'd ripped off her shield and conjured the strength to share her deepest secrets and most intimate thoughts with me. Yet, I fed her silence. And to know that I thought it was better that way was sickening, forcing me to pour a third shot. My ignorance wasn't acceptable. It wasn't until I'd seen the hurt on her face and the trembling of her body when I touched her that I understood that.

Pissed because she wasn't willing and ready to accept me, yes the fuck I was. In all honesty, I had no right. I'd somehow found comfort in ignoring her for three whole months. Yet, I wanted her to fall to her knees and worship the ground I stood on when I was ready and in front of her.

What about when she was ready? The question replayed in my head.

All of my life I'd selfishly involved myself with women, and while I considered this taking a different approach with Lyric, I'd finally come to the realization that it was all the same. Reassurance was a priority for her. It was one of those things that she needed to feel loved, respected, and admired. To this day, I hadn't reassured her of shit. For three months while I sat behind the wall, I'd done the opposite.

Had I at least written anything in return, we'd be much further in our journey. And when I got out, everything I was now expecting from her wouldn't just be a figment of my imagination. It would've been my reality.

I felt queasy knowing that I'd bombarded my way into her world and barged into her home demanding things of Lyric that I didn't have the right to. My entitlement was repulsive. The way I'd invaded her space, kissed her lips, and fucked her as if both our worlds were ending. It was beautiful chaos. It made me sick to my stomach. She didn't deserve that. I didn't deserve her. Not, yet.

I needed to wait my turn. I needed to wait until she was ready again. I'd fucked up royally and though the rejection stung like a motherfucker, she was well within her rights. Lyric had done the legwork for us both, but I'd put us back at square one by leaving her heart on the platter to rot and dry.

I didn't deserve her. While I never felt like I did, my actions proved it. That didn't stop me from still wanting her and still needing her because I knew that I could be whoever she needed me to be. For her. Because I was hers. Forever and always.

But she doesn't trust me. Not Keanu, at least. Ken, the family friend she trusted but Keanu... no. Before anything else, I wanted to work on gaining that trust. Lyric would love me forever. I'd give her no other choice, but I wouldn't force us into anything she wasn't ready for. In due time, we'd be one. I knew it. She knew it. It was inevitable.

Just like any other nigga, I was ready to earn my spot in her life. Because once I was in her world, there would be no exiting. Then, I wouldn't have to fantasize about all the places in my home where I would love her body down. I'd be able to do that shit.

After tonight, I thought as my dick hardened. After tonight, I'd take my time with Lyric. As slow as she wanted this thing to go, I'd take it. But, first, I needed my dick wet and she was the only one I wanted at the tip of it.

Plus, I missed her. As spoiled and bratty as she was, her energy was pure. I wanted that in my world. It didn't take a rocket scientist to know that it would take a little coaxing to get rid of the attitude I was certain she had with me, but I'd work through it.

"WHAT THE FUCK I'm supposed to pick?" I grunted, lowly, circling the large section of flowers over and over.

The long display of botanicals that I'd been passing for years finally had my interest piqued. Though there were many different species and colors, nothing had popped out, yet. Nothing I'd looked at immediately screamed Lyric's name, either. She was a simple girl and one that lived a life almost completely absent of color.

Over the years, I'd noticed that she preferred browns, tans, black, and occasional grays. I couldn't recall the last time I'd seen her in a color that wasn't muted. It worked for her though. Contrary to what one might have believed, she wasn't as bland as the colors she wore – neither was her life. Lyric was complex. Hell, after knowing her forever, I was still trying to figure her out.

Bingo. The cream-colored, large bulbs sticking out from a bucket that was near the center of the display caught my attention. Instead of grabbing one bouquet, I grabbed the four that were in the bucket and made my way to the counter.

Order flowers. The thought occurred to me as I

neared the register. Though Lyric was appreciative, she was accustomed to the finest of everything, and grocery store flowers weren't exactly her speed. They'd serve as an apology for ghosting her the other morning, but I wouldn't make it a habit of grabbing $24.99 flowers on the whim. Eventually, she'd call me out on the shit. That's just how Lyric was.

It wasn't long before I was bobbing my head to the Hov track and hitting the corners in The Hills. The scenery was unmatched and to know that there were black and brown faces that resembled mine living in every home that I passed was enough to put a smile on my face. Poverty was handed to them all but it wasn't enough. Just like me, they'd strived for more and attained it.

I quieted my engine as I turned on the suburban street that reminded me of my own but with smaller homes and yards. Every one of the Eisenberg offsprings lived in The Hills; Laike, and Luca living a bit further up than Lyric. She was right in the middle of her parents, who lived in Edgewood, and her brothers who didn't live very far from me. A six-minute drive either direction and I could reach both of their homes.

Lyric's home sat comfortably behind greenery, a gate that had recently been installed, a perfectly mani-cured lawn, a lengthy driveway that slightly spiraled, and underneath constant surveillance. She was tucked in safely by her family. They made sure their little gem was well-protected.

The black Hellcat that sat in her driveway wasn't surprising at all. Since Luca's incarceration, Laike and Lyric had developed an even tighter bond. Now that Ever was in the picture and Luca was preoccupied most of the time with his growing family, the bond was even tighter.

Though it took a bit of convincing on my end, I decided not to interfere or blow Lyric's cover. I didn't give a damn about revealing to Laike or Luca that I was interested in Lyric. However, her wishes to reserve that bit of information put me in a tight spot. So, until we came to an agreement, I'd keep her secret.

I continued down the street, watching in my rearview mirror until I hit the next. The gas station was four and a half miles away, giving me plenty of time to kill. Completely out of backwoods, I wanted to grab more and fill my tank for what felt like the eighth time in the last three days. It was official. My truck was a gas guzzler.

Unlike any of the stations across Dooley, the GasCo that I pulled up to was free of clutter, stragglers, and loitering. But as clean and as quiet as the lot was, I didn't trust it. Leaving my truck running like I had the freedom to in Dooley was off limits, so I silenced the engine and locked the truck after I'd exited.

"Welcome to GasCo. Let me know if there's anything I can help you with. I'm Lisa," the attendant greeted with a smile.

"Lisa, let me get that box of backwoods behind you, mommas. Toss a lighter on there too. The good kind. Then, let me get eighty on the truck out there."

I didn't feel like checking the pump, but I was certain she could see it.

"The entire box?" she questioned with raised eyebrows.

"That's what I said, isn't it?" I nodded.

"Okay. The entire box it is."

I placed two hundred dollar bills on the counter, grabbed the lighter, backwoods, and a pack of candy from the countertop and headed out of the door.

"Your change?" Lisa yelled after me.

"Keep it," I tossed over my shoulder.

Without haste, I began filling my truck up again and loaded it with everything I'd gotten from the store. While the numbers on the display continued to rise, I slammed the door behind me and opened the box of cigars.

Click.

Before I was able to get the knotty buds into the grinder to break them down better, the pump sounded. I never broke stride, tossing a final knot of the greenish, purple bud into the gold grinder. From one side to the other, I twisted it until there weren't any more lumps. The aroma continued to flood my vehicle as I reopened the grinder and emptied its contents into the flattened backwood on the armrest.

In under a minute, I had a perfectly rolled blunt

before stepping out to hang the pump up. Once I slid back into my ride, I fumbled with the icons on my phone's screen until I reached the Pandora app. Choosing Hov's station was an easy decision. It was the most common since I'd started using the app years ago. It was almost always first on the list.

Love Happy. The tune filled the speakers, surrounding me as I bobbed my head and lit my blunt. I wasn't one to admire couples or ever make anyone my goals in life. Yet, I was fucking with whatever he and his woman had going on. Both were getting to the paper, ducked off, and minding their fucking business. Any nigga could appreciate that in life. I'm one of them.

Slowly, I crept down the streets of Huffington Hills, taking the scenic route rather than going straight to Lyric's place. Waiting Laike out wouldn't take long. He never stayed anywhere too long. So, when I spun the block and ended up in front of Lyric's home, it wasn't appalling that he'd already burnt out.

Blunt still in hand, I parked and stretched my limbs on the way out. I wasn't sure if it was a good thing or a bad one that I knew codes, secret entryways, and troubleshooting tactics for every Eisenberg residence. Sliding into Lyric's gate unnoticed was as easy as it was to get into her home nights prior.

Boooom.

Boooom.

Boooom.

I knocked at the door upon realizing the upgrades to her system. As soon as Laike had the chance, I wanted to make sure that he scanned me in. I wouldn't push the issue and raise suspicions, but I'd make sure he did so sooner than later.

Stepping back, I waited for Lyric to show face. Hearing the latches behind the door being removed and the locks turning, my adrenaline hiked a bit. I pulled from the blunt between my fingers, immediately feeling a calmness that was most familiar to me.

The door swung open at once and there she stood. As beautiful as I remembered. As angelic as I'd imagined. As pretty as could be.

"Hi." She sighed, a faint smile tugging at her lips.

She didn't have any fight in her. Her defeat was obvious. Apparent on her pretty face. For that, I was thankful, because I didn't have it in me, either.

"Pack some shit. You're coming home with me tonight."

My words flowed as did the smoke that I'd inhaled just before she opened the door. Tilting her head to the side, she stood in place. Unmoving. But said nothing. Her silence was loud, alarming almost.

"I don't want to fight, Keanu," she responded, running a hand over her face.

The stress lines that appeared on her forehead stiffened my heart. The last thing I wanted to do was bring chaos to her world. My only job was to make it a better place for her to live in. If I couldn't do that, then I didn't need to be around.

"Then I won't fight you, Lyric."

Still, she remained in place. Her eyes on me and mine on her. I wasn't sure what she was searching for but I hoped she found it. After what felt like forever, she stepped back and allowed me into her space. I couldn't help myself, pulling her into me immediately, using my foot to close the door behind us.

"What are you doing here?" she asked, head tucked into my chest.

"I missed you," I admitted.

Putting a bit of distance between us, she looked up at me in disbelief.

"I did," I emphasized.

Silently, she turned and headed for the stairs. I was quick on my toes, following behind her as she climbed them slowly. When I caught up to her, I slowed down as well.

"You don't trust me," I grumbled, knowing exactly why she hadn't admitted that she'd missed me, too.

"Do you blame me?"

"I don't."

"Good. I thought we said we aren't fighting tonight?"

"We're not."

"Good, because I can't. Not right now."

Exhaustion was apparent in her voice. Letting her be for the night quickly came to mind, but I shoved the thought to the back of my head once we reached her room. I expected her to start pulling out drawers and opening cabinets in the bathroom, but she did none of the such. Instead, she walked into her closet and grabbed an LV tote. When she made it threshold where the bedroom transformed into a space for a portion of her clothing, she stopped.

"I agreed to be his girlfriend," she informed me.

Nodding in understanding, I pressed my back against the wall and grabbed the back of my neck. She wanted to be upfront, and she wanted to be honest with me. I could respect that. Sighing heavily, I lowered my head before lifting it again to meet her eyes.

"You're mine, Lyric," I reminded her. "No matter what you told that nigga."

I could see it from across the room, the gnawing of her bottom lip as her eyes closed and then reopened. As if the words that were about to fall from her mouth was painful to conjure, she groaned slightly.

"I know."

There was nothing left to be said. I walked over to where she stood, grabbed the bag from her hand, and exited her bedroom. As I took the stairs to the first floor, I could hear her behind me. Slowly, hesitantly, she followed my lead. It didn't matter how she did it though, as long as she did.

lyric

AS I FOLLOWED Keanu down the stairs of my home, my heart was torn. There was no place in the world I'd rather spend my night than in his arms, but I'd just made things with Collin official, and I knew that he didn't deserve what I was willing to put him through for the sake of Keanu. As much as I tried to fight the feeling, it was one that I just couldn't evade.

Dinner with Laike had put so much into perspective for me. He was right. I was settling for what I thought would guarantee safety, hoping that my happiness wouldn't be sacrificed. It wasn't Collin that I craved. It was Keanu. It wasn't Collin that filled my dreams as I slept. It was Keanu. It wasn't Collin that my body desired. It was Keanu. The first chance I got, I'd share with Collin that I was sadly mistaken when agreeing to be his woman.

Keanu's boldness was exasperating. When we stepped outside, and I noticed his truck in front of my house, my nerves began to separate.

"Keanu, can we be a bit more discreet? Please?"

"This is your secret, Lyric. Not mine. I'm a grown ass man, and I'm not hiding from a fucking thing."

"It's not hiding," I reasoned.

"I didn't pull up when Laike was here. That's as good as it gets with me, love."

"Thank you."

Keanu opened the passenger door of his truck and waited until I was all the way inside before closing it behind me. He tossed my overnight bag in the back, right behind me. It wasn't until I heard the ruffling of paper before he sat down that I noticed the flowers in his hand. They'd been waiting on the passenger side, wrapped in brown kraft paper with the most decadent aroma.

"For me?" I hummed, accepting the bundled bouquets he was handing me.

"For you," he said before rolling down the window

and getting rid of the end of the blunt he'd been smoking.

Even in the darkness, I could see the beauty of the arrangement. Just like Keanu and I, they were fresh. I stuffed my nose in the middle of the bunch, inhaling and then exhaling.

Tiny bumps raised on top of my skin as I closed my eyes. This beginning wasn't exactly ideal, but it was ours. I wasn't sure what would come of it, but for the first time since he'd touched down, I was willing to try. When I found the strength, I would tell him just that. But for now, I simply wanted to savor the moment. Savor us.

"Thank you, Keanu."

Taking a second to glance in his direction, I voiced my gratitude. I couldn't remember the last time I'd received flowers from anyone that didn't share a last name with me. I'd almost forgotten how good it felt.

"You're welcome, Lyric."

I didn't miss the sparkling gold in his mouth as what appeared to be a smile altered the features on his face. *He's so darling.* His crisp line and thick lips made my lady parts tingle. I'd always thought Keanu was handsome, but as I stared at his side profile, I was beginning to believe it to be an understatement. He was astounding. Unbelievably beautiful. It was inexplicable. He was inexplicable.

Beyond his handsome face, his heart matched.

That was the beauty in it all. I knew it because I'd been around him all my life. Admittedly, I wanted him to have mine for the rest of our lives.

"What?" he asked, noticing I was still staring.

"Nothing," I said, lowering my head with a smile on my face.

"What is it, Lyric Eisenberg?" He chuckled, reaching over and pulling my face in his direction. He divided his attention between me and the road we were on.

"I'm just so happy you're home."

"I'm just happy I had you to come home to," he replied.

"You know..." I hesitated before grabbing his wrist and running my fingers along his hand.

Physical touch. It was my heart's language. The act spoke to me, directly and intentionally. Feeling Keanu's skin against mine was as close to caressing my heart as one could get.

"I've felt crazy all these years. I've loved you for so many moons and so many sunsets. And not the love that friends possess for one another. A different kind of love and a yearning that could only be described as one a lover has for another. But it made me delirious. Knowing that we weren't possible, no matter how I might've felt."

"Never knowing that I felt the same?"

"Never knowing you felt the same."

"Since you were like, shit... prom. I think that's when I knew, too. I wanted to be the one on your arm. The nigga you was with, I still want to kick his ass 'til this fucking day."

Tittering, I leaned into his open palm. "What do you want from this, Keanu? From us?"

"The best, Lyric. I can't give you that if you don't let me. I want to properly date you and give you every reason in the world to fall for a nigga. I'm not trying to use my position in your life and history to solidify my spot. I wish to earn it. That entitlement shit I've been on, tossing it. Keanu is the nigga you want and the nigga I want to give you. This sneaking around and shit that we're doing, I'm not with it. And you settling for bare minimum, I don't like it. Require of me exactly what you do of the rest of these niggas. I know you, Lyric."

"You've been bleeding them dry for years, turning their pockets inside out. Not letting anybody slack or think they can relax on your watch. I want to stay on my toes, too. Take you to these fancy ass restaurants you love, buy whatever makes your heart happy, and take care of any and everything I'm able to for you. I want to take care of you, good care of you. I want you out of your people's pockets and in mine. Your brothers have done their jobs. I want to make you smile on a daily basis, give you the entire fucking world because you want it."

"I want a family, Lyric. I've got my people, but I don't have a fucking family. I'm trying to create that with you. The shit my nigga on, I'm on, too. Sitting my ass down with the right woman and building my legacy. I'm a very simple man who has never wanted nothing more than some fucking money. Now that I'm sitting on seven figures, it's time to aspire for something greater. What's greater than family? What's greater than peace? Quiet? Happiness? That's what I want from this. That's what I want for us. I want forever."

"I'm forbidden fruit, Keanu," I admitted as our eyes met.

"I've had a taste, already, Lyric. It's too late. I'm here to stay."

I didn't have the words to follow. Only feelings. Big ones. Ones that made caused a wave of emotions to overwhelm me as my heart began beating erratically. The painful gulp that I swallowed got stuck in my throat, making it difficult to remain still. Seconds passed before it subsided, and I heard Keanu speak again.

"Is you with that shit or what?"

Nodding, I agreed. "Yes."

"Then, stop standing in our way."

lyric + keanu

I'D SEEN the inside of Keanu's home a few times. Maybe twice or three times at the most. It was fairly new to him as well. He'd only been at the specific location for the last two years. Laike had been generous enough to design his home, too. It was already in progress before he'd finished up Luca's place.

Though I'd been inside, everything seemed different when I walked in. I wasn't sure if it was the fact that I was seeing it for the first time as a counterpart and not a friend or if it was because it was truly different from the last visit. Whatever the case, I loved it.

"Everything seems so different," I told Keanu as he took my coat. The black, fur-lined garment was my go-to and was always waiting in the coat closet behind the door, making it easy to grab on my way out.

"Because it is."

"So, I'm not crazy after all?" I asked.

"You're not crazy after all," he reassured me. "Luca replaced everything inside. Did he not tell you?"

"He didn't." Luca hadn't told me a thing.

"Which means he paid someone to do the job and leave him the fuck alone," Keanu chuckled, taking a look over his shoulder and back at me.

"I'm pretty sure that's exactly what happened," I agreed.

"Nevertheless, I'm fucking with it." His broad shoulders hiked and then fell.

"Everything is gorgeous."

"Yeah? Anything you'd change?"

"Nothing jumps out at me. I love the vibe. The dark colors that are blended seamlessly with the muted tones. I'm a sucker for the muted tones," I admitted, walking through the wide space behind Keanu.

When we finally reached the bar area, he paused.

"Can I make you a drink?"

"Sure."

"Any specific?"

"Surprise me.'"

I watched as he began pulling out the contents of the bar. After he'd chosen two additives, he turned to me and smiled.

"You said surprise you. Close your eyes," he insisted.

Closing my eyes, I smiled. The man that I was witnessing before me wasn't the one I'd known my whole life. The one I'd known since a kid barely showed those dimples in his cheeks or those gold teeth in his mouth because he hardly had anything to say or anything to smile about. The one that I'd known since a kid also sported the most unchanging, serious mug on his face day in and day out. He was kind to the women he loved, ones like his aunt, grandmother, my mother, and I. But that was as far as his kindness stretched, much like my brothers.

I waited and waited, in the middle of the floor with

my arms folded in front of one another. The silly smile that I wore on my face didn't falter. Though it felt so stupid plastered on as it was, it felt just as good.

"You know... I've been wanting to get you here since I first read your message," he stated. I could hear his footsteps in my direction. He was on his way to me, closing the distance between us.

"Yeah?"

"Yeah."

"Now that you have me here, Keanu, what will you do with me?"

I felt a glass up to my lips, prompting me to open my mouth. I sipped from the glass, allowing the fruity mixture to slide down my throat. It was delicious.

"I'm going to fuck you on every surface suitable, in every corner that's available, and in every position you could imagine."

I pulled my eyelids apart and stretched them to the limit. His smooth, dark skin was so close that I could reach out and touch him. I wanted to, but first, I wanted to address the obvious. Before I was able to respond to Keanu's admissions, he'd placed the cup to my lips again. I opened my mouth, swallowing a huge gulp of whatever he had mixed for me.

"Then, once I'm done with you in the morning, I'm going to take you home so that you can think of what you're going to tell your ex because as of this moment, you don't belong to him. Shit, you never did."

"Keanu," I started to protest, but he cut me off.

"Do you understand me?"

With furrowed brows, I nodded. He just couldn't help himself. The entitlement he promised not to utilize, he was.

"What's the issue?" He noticed my hesitancy.

"You said you'd earn your spot in my life," I reminded him.

"I plan to, but I'm terminating his first," he explained.

The glass was up to my mouth a third and final time. I finished my drink and heard the glass collide with the counter nearest me seconds later. I watched as Keanu walked back to the bar, poured himself a shot of something brown, then toss the contents of the small glass into his mouth. He repeated the same steps twice more before grunting.

"Ahhhhhh," he bellowed as he turned in my direction.

It was as if the more alone time I spent with Keanu, the more I noticed about his beauty. For instance, the thickness of his brows and the thick line that traced his large lips. It was so defined and so perfect.

"I missed you, too," I finally admitted.

Tilting his head to the left, Keanu exposed every gold tooth in his mouth. My pussy thudded at the sight, salivating with each thump. I wasn't sure what God was trying to prove when he'd made Keanu, but he'd made his point. Vividly.

"Oh yeah?"

"Yeah," I responded, feeling utterly exposed although I was fully clothed.

Somehow, I felt as if he could see through it all. Underneath the designer fabrics, I was translucent. Straight through me, he could see.

The space that he'd put between us was quickly obliterated. Keanu's hands were underneath the cheeks of my ass, and I was being lifted into the air in the blink of an eye. Through the house, he glided as if my weight was that of a feather. When we reached the steps, his hesitation startled me. When he turned around and headed back into the kitchen, he confused me. But when he laid my body down on the island that sat in the middle of the floor, I understood.

Every surface. This was number one.

He said nothing as he tugged at the flap of my tan leggings, rolling my body to each side to get them over my ass instead of asking me to lift up a bit. He slid them down my legs with ease once he'd gotten them from underneath me and then tossed them to the side.

The thong that matched the color of my leggings covered my hairless pussy. I could see the internal struggle as Keanu decided whether he wanted to remove them, too. When he pulled the waistband of them in his direction, I knew that he'd made his decision. This time, though, I lifted so that he could pull them down with ease.

He spread my legs until my knees hit the countertop. Its coolness made small, fine bumps appear all over me. My body shivered in response, but the second Keanu's fingers parted my lips and his thumb located my stiffened pearl, heat consumed me. My eyes closed as my body submitted to him. He was in control. However he wanted me, he could have me.

"Eyes on me," he requested.

I obliged, pulling my lids apart and setting my sights on him. What a beautiful sight he was. He was the definition of perfection. Everything about his presence was addictive. Staying away from him was impossible, and I wasn't sure why I'd even tried to trick myself into believing I would. I couldn't.

Not with the way he'd handled my body the night of his release and surely not with the way he handled me. There was something about a roughneck with a good heart that checked every box for me. I'd been around them my entire life and wanted one of my own, now. Keanu was him.

"I don't like being alone anymore," Keanu said, breaking the silence, "I want you here with me whenever I call and whenever you feel like it. This home is yours as well as it is mine now. Understood?"

I nodded, too caught up in the way he effortlessly pleasured me with little energy and plenty of skill. His thumb circled my clit over and over, forcing me to close my eyes. His movements stopped. A low, ungrateful moan fell from my lips.

"Keanu," I begged, opening my eyes as I did so.

"Eyes on me," he demanded.

"Okay," I whimpered under my breath. "Okay."

As he'd requested, my eyes remained on his as his head lowered inch by inch until it was just above my exposed pussy. Not breaking contact, Keanu encased as much of my meatiness in his mouth as possible, suckling on my flesh as if it was the sweetest thing he'd ever tasted.

"My God."

The words fell from my mouth as I felt him dip his thumb into my wetness.

Once.

Twice.

A third time.

And, then, without warning, he slid it into the most forbidden crevice of my being. I tensed immediately but softened as he flicked he focused solely on my nub, assaulting it with his tongue.

"Ummmmm," he moaned, eyes still on mine.

He wasn't playing fair. I knew it and so did he. My orgasm didn't stand a chance. It surfaced almost instantly. I was near shame, the way my body began to convulse and my legs violently shook underneath his spell.

"Fuck!" I screamed. "Fuck. Oh, fuck. I'm cummmmmmmmmm—"

Quickly, Keanu lifted and utilized his right hand to dive into my pussy. Upward, he angled his middle and index fingers as he shoved them into me without remorse.

"Oh God. Oh fuck!"

The ringing in my ears grew loud enough to silence everything around me. My lids hurt from squeezing them so tightly together as my body began to spasm. Breath caught in my throat, I fought for more oxygen in my lungs while climbing higher and higher. When I reached my peak, I felt myself rise and fall from the island, bouncing as my fountain blessed Keanu with an overflow.

"That's it. Good girl. Good fucking girl," he praised. His words were so consuming, drowning out the buzzing that had drowned out everything prior.

Left in a puddle of my own potion, I tried reviving myself. My pussy had to be left on life support as I focused on regulating my breathing before I passed out of exhaustion and overwhelm. I placed a weakened hand on my chest as if it would make the difference. After a few seconds, the wooziness I felt had subsided and my breathing was as good as it would possibly get.

When I reopened my eyes, Keanu's handsome face appeared. The smirk that shifted his lips to the left of his face was agonizingly cute but caused me to cringe at the realization of its reasoning. He was basking in his success. He'd unraveled me – again.

I wasn't sure when my body began to regain its strength, but there was something about that damn smirk on Keanu's face that put a rush on it. When I was able, I climbed from the island, pushing his hand out of my way when he'd tried to help.

It made no sense for him to make me cum so viciously, so violently, and I wanted to pay his ass back for it. The shirt that I had on was soaked in the back – from the bottom to the middle. The embarrassment that I felt peeling it from my body shouldn't have been so intense, but it was.

Keanu would have to pull me off him for the rest of the night because I wasn't letting up until he begged me. I would pay him back, if it was the last thing I did before I closed my eyes to go to sleep in his arms.

"You good?" he asked, chuckling in the process.

"Shut up. I'd rather you not say anything to me," I confessed, rolling my eyes.

He'd done me dirty. The level of vulnerability that he'd unlocked with whatever combination he'd managed was my issue. I felt bare. Unveiled. Exposed. Uncovered.

Can you see right through me? I wondered. It felt as if he could and I hadn't been in such a position in... never. I'd never been here. The terrain was new and it was frightening, forcing me to attempt to put a guard up that I wasn't even equipped with. I was bare. Physically, emotionally, mentally, sexually. I'd been stripped.

I felt his hand around my neck and his tongue on the side of my face. Like the animal he was, he licked me from my lower jawline to my left brow. The moan that erupted couldn't be suppressed.

"Keanu."

The hand that was once around my neck, he placed on my chin and forced my eyes in his direction. My mouth hung, waiting and ready for whatever words he was hesitant to give me. I was hungry for them, hungry for him.

There was no doubt in my mind that I wanted him and all to myself. I craved his existence. I couldn't wait to fall so dangerously in love with him that the thought of us not being pained me to my core. The type of love that I felt was brewing between us couldn't be matched. One that would go down in Eisenberg history as either my greatest victory or my legendary demise.

Spahhh!

In my mouth, on my face, and on my neck, his spit flew. My deadened pussy alive, again.

"Ummmm." Swallowing the tasteless saliva, I smiled.

"You shut the fuck up. I'd rather you use them lips to suck my dick than talk shit."

My knees bent forward as I lowered my knacked body onto the ground. The black sweats that he wore, I pulled down along with me. His briefs followed the leader. Keanu didn't have to tell me twice.

"Ummmmm hmmmm," I dragged, watching as his dick sprang from its holding cell and into the air.

Keanu's long, thick fingers wrapped around his dick, massaging the tip as he looked down at me. When his hand slid to the base of his dick and he began swatting the air with it, I moved closer so that I wasn't left out of the equation. His meatiness slammed against the side of my face.

Once.

Twice.

Three times, he slapped his dick across my cheek. I could feel every ridge, every vein, and every groove. It was perfect, just like him.

"Open your fucking mouth," he demanded.

I'd waited for this moment for so long. Now that it was finally here, I couldn't contain myself. I looked into Keanu's dark eyes with my bright, brown ones as he grabbed my hair and forced me to. He sat his long, thick and extremely black dick on my tongue, making my wildest dream come to fruition.

Unable to conceal my deepest desire, I slapped his hand away from the back of my head and shoved his dick down my throat as far as it would go. Not even the pricking of my eyes or the pool of saliva that formed in my mouth could stop me from trying my hardest to fit every inch. When I couldn't take any more of him, I gagged. Keanu was forced from my throat as was the trail of slob that followed him out of my mouth, but still connected us as it dangled from the tip of his dick to the tip of my tongue.

As I tried my hardest to catch my breath, I felt him fill me, again. He showed no mercy on me, drawing snot from my nose as he reached the back of my throat again. In and out, Keanu fucked my mouth as if he was trying to make it cum.

"Is it everything you imagined? Big, black, and down your fucking throat?"

He didn't expect me to answer. Couldn't be expecting me to answer. Not with his pole shoved into my mouth, nearly blocking my airway completely. My only focus was breathing, keeping the snot from my nose from running down his dick, and keeping the tears that began to fall from my eyes to a minimum.

My pussy was soaking wet. I could feel the sliminess as I clenched my walls with each thrust of Keanu's hips. I couldn't wait until he was inside of me, fucking me just as he was fucking my mouth. Just like I wanted his semen down my throat, I wanted it smeared across my walls. I didn't have to wait long, either, because the second I grabbed his balls and massaged them between my fingers, his legs weakened.

"Fuck." He shuddered.

Knowing that I had him right where I wanted him, I worked the muscles in my neck and used my other hand as reinforcement. He needed to be drained, and I wouldn't stop until he was. He owed me this nut.

"Shit."

His body stiffened as his legs locked. The warm fluid squirted from his dick and into my mouth as he pulled out. The remainder landed on my lips, but quickly joined the rest after my tongue swiped my lips to collect all that was left.

Keanu's labored breathing was the loveliest sound I'd ever heard in my life. The smell of defeat lingered in the air as we both gazed into each other's rounds. The smirk that had appeared on his face moments earlier had vanished. I sported one much similar now. It was my turn to bask in my victory. But just like me, Keanu wasn't having it.

"Stand the fuck up, Lyric." His raspiness was captivating.

His large hand wrapped around the center of his log, and he began massaging it slowly with eyes still on me. Unfortunately, my gaze had drifted and his lovely piece was now the center of my attention. As he stroked his dick and closed the small gap between us, my pussy began to cream. Cum oozed from the tiny hole at the very tip of his tool, hitting the floor and going to waste. There was a place for that and it wasn't the floor. It was inside of me, whether in my mouth or buried deep in my tunnel, I didn't mind.

"This shit ridiculous," Keanu fussed, looking down at the mess he'd made.

"You're making a mess." A smile crossed my face.

"This is your fault, Lyric. Shit, I can't stop cumming," he groaned, still stroking his dick as cum continued to ooze from it.

"You're wasting my nutrients. Put it inside of me."

"Bend that shit over," he instructed.

I did and held onto the island for stability. I'd be needing it.

When Keanu slid into me, it was as if our universes aligned. The openness and vulnerability that I'd felt moments earlier returned. I was naked again, and not just physically. Bare. Uncovered.

I could feel our souls tie. Slowly, intensely, Keanu thrusted his hips and stroked me from behind. His arms dipped beneath mine and grabbed both of my breasts. He lifted me up until I was standing, almost completely erect.

My hands landed on top of his as I tilted my head so that his could fall down onto my shoulder. His strokes were so precise. All that could be heard throughout the space was both of our gratifying whimpers and the sound of my wetness.

Keanu had entered me with semen pouring from him, but I couldn't help but be a bit greedy. I wanted more. I deserved more. My greed led me to request it, shamelessly.

"Cum inside of me."

"You want this shit inside of you?"

"Yes. Please."

"You want to have my babies?" he asked.

"Yes!" I bellowed as he picked up the pace, separating us and forcing me to bend over again. His strokes intensified. The smacking sound our bodies made sent me on a thrill of my own.

"You feel so good," he breathed. "Too fucking good."

"Cum inside of me," I begged, not interested in the consequences of my actions.

"Be mine," he requested.

"Yes."

"Say it."

"I'm yours," I admitted, wholeheartedly. "Tell me you're mine."

"I'm... I'm yours," Keanu confirmed as he fell onto my back, attempting to catch his breath. "Fuck!"

NINE

keanu

FOR TWO DAYS STRAIGHT, I locked Lyric up in my home for us to fuck, fuss, listen, and love one each other. Undoubtedly, it was the best two days of my life. Getting to know Lyric on a more intimate level was a treat, one that I'd always known existed but never imagined discovering.

Together we cooked, cleaned, slept, and showered. I didn't know a damn thing about cooking full dinner proportions or deep cleaning your home. But watching Lyric add her feminine touch to the home that I already thought was immaculate solidified my belief that she belonged there. She made everything so much better.

Before going away, I'd spent almost a year and a half in my house, getting acquainted with the new space. I actually thought I had finally transitioned it into the home I'd craved for so many years. However, Lyric's presence put that thought to shame. It was her. She made my house feel like home.

I'd awaken to her two mornings in a row, feeling like the king of my castle. Prior to, I felt like a simple man who'd awaken up to tackle another day. The two nights that I laid down in bed with her, in preparation for a good night's rest, I slept like a bump on a log. I slept so hard and so good that the only things that woke me was the smell of her cooking breakfast and the feeling of her lips wrapped around my dick.

She didn't play fair. Lyric weaponized her pussy and the shit was lethal. I made a mental note to watch myself with her in the near future. She'd use her pussy to get anything and everything she wanted out of me and if I wasn't careful, I'd let her.

It was the antidote to my insomnia. That pussy put me to sleep each night without a problem. It was my alarm in the morning, waking me up from my slumber and helping me get a start on my day. It was my afternoon snack and dessert after dinner.

As I cruised through Dooley, on my way to The Hills, it was the motivation I needed to make the long drive without falling asleep behind the wheel. I was both hungry and exhausted from such an eventful day. The lack of sleep I'd gotten the night before was weighing me down.

Lyric had been away from my house for a full day and a half, but I refused to lay down another night without her. She was my sleep-aid. With her at my side, my worries were casted aside and all that was left was light snoring and fond dreams of us two.

She's my slice of peace, I realized. *And, I love her for it.*

While many had to wait for the moment they fell in love with their significant other, I'd had the luxury of loving mine since we were kids. We were simply allowing our love for one another to evolve far beyond its current state, and as the minutes passed us by, it was happening right before our eyes.

I cut my trip down by a few minutes, too exhausted to mind the speed limits and other traffic laws Channing had put in place. Corner after corner, I turned until I made it to Adeline Avenue where Lyric's home was nestled between a bunch of greenery. Just like any other house in The Hills, there weren't many that lined the block. The yards were all spacious, just like the homes, which didn't leave much room.

As I pulled up to Lyric's dwelling, the Tesla that sat near the front of her gate was baffling. I silenced my engine and stepped out of the truck without hesitation. Naturally, my hand grazed my hip, making sure that my Glock was in reach. I was through the gate and walking across Lyric's driveway in ten seconds flat. By the time I reached her porch, I could hear the lock being turned while simultaneously noticing that I was not alone.

"Ken, isn't it?" Collin turned, extended a hand, and asked.

Turning in his direction and acknowledging his presence would be a waste of breath and time on my end. I wasn't interested. So, instead, I kept my sight aligned with the door as I waited for Lyric to open it.

"Collin," she greeted with a smile, stepping toward him with outstretched arms.

He inched closer but wasn't quite fast enough. I filled the gap between the two as I watched Lyric's smile fade. Baffled, she dropped her hands at her side and took a step backward.

"Keanu," she gasped.

"Why the fuck you want to play with me?"

"I'm not... I mean. I don't," she explained.

"Is everything alright?" Collin interrupted.

"Not if you don't get the fuck off her porch."

"Collin, sorry. This is all just a misunderstanding. I'll call you."

"No. she won't," I assured him.

Every step forward I took, caused Lyric to step backward until we were both inside of her home. I could feel my blood boiling as I shut the door behind us. Lyric said nothing. She perched a hand on her hip and stared up at me as if I was the one who was on some bullshit.

"I'm not here to play games, Lyric, neither am I going to share you with another nigga. Not by any means."

"I'm not asking you to."

"Then, why was he here?" I pointed at the door behind me.

"For dinner, Keanu."

"Dinner? The nigga was here for..." I stopped mid-sentence, pulling a hand over my mouth as I shook my head. "Dinner?" I chuckled, slightly amused.

"Yes. I figured the least I could do was feed him before I broke the news to him."

"What news?"

"The news that I decided I'd rather fuck and fall in love with my lifetime friend than be with him. That news, Keanu."

"Does this," I asked as I pointed between us, "bother you? Hmmm?"

"While it feels like the greatest thing to ever happen to me, it simultaneously feels like my doom."

Offended by her honesty, I asked, "Why? Why does this feel like your doom?"

"I don't know, Keanu. Maybe because I feel like I'm letting the people I love down again."

"Then, let's nip it in the bud right now so that you're not feeling so burdened, huh?"

I shoved my hand into the pocket of my sweats, bypassing the small pieces of candy I'd collected throughout the day and grabbing my cell. When it was close enough to my face, it unlocked automatically. When I accessed my call log, both Luca and Laike's contacts appeared several times.

"What are you doing, Keanu?"

"What you're too afraid to do. There's absolutely no reason you should feel burdened by this shit. Until you let your people know what's up, you'll feel this way. I don't like it. You're not giving us a chance to survive. Our foundation is being built off a lie. It's not fair to me and it's not fair to you either. You deserve to be loved out loud, Lyric. Not in private."

"Please don't do that. I'm begging you," she pleaded.

With a shake of my head, I squeeze the phone in my hand until it began to hurt. The lack of faith that she had in me – in us – was disheartening.

"I agree with everything you've said, but to my credit, I've never and will never bring anything to my brothers' attention until I knew that it would be some-thing more than just lust and infatuation or whatever. They didn't learn about Chauncey until we'd been dating for three months. They only met Collin because we happened to be the same place at the same time. Otherwise, they wouldn't have known anything about him for another few months. Just give us some time, Keanu. It's only been a few days. Give me time to adjust. Give us time to make sure that we're destined for more than an unbreakable bond that we built over the years as friends. That's fair. Fair to you and to me. It's just shitty, but it is fair."

Loosening the grip on my cell, I allowed her words to sink in. They made perfect sense, but there were two people that I loved like blood that would be affected by the decision we were making and that just didn't sit well with me.

"Please."

She closed the gap between us, rubbing my arm as she repeated herself.

"Please, Keanu."

"When you're ready to grow the fuck up and allow me to be the nigga you deserve, hit me up. Until then, we're putting this shit on ice."

Without waiting for another word to fall from her pretty lips, I turned my back and headed for the door. I knew that if I stood and watched her crumble or more words to flow, I wouldn't have the strength to leave. Lyric was magnetic and trying to pull away from her was the most complicated thing I'd ever done in my life. I just couldn't. So, making it to my whip was progress that I was appreciative of.

The smell of rubber was prominent in the air as I mashed the gas with one thing in mind – getting the hell out of dodge. Pooh Shiesty pumped through the speakers, intensifying whatever feeling I was struggling with at the moment. As I bobbed my head to the sick beat, the blood I'd drawn from gnawing on my inner jaw sat on my tastebuds.

Sixty miles on the suburban streets of Huffington Hills wasn't normal activity for me, but this wasn't a normal night, either. It was one that I'd thought would end with skin-to-skin contact, forehead kisses, heavy breathing, and moon bathing. Instead, it would be ending with smoke-filled lungs and drunken slurs. It wasn't ideal, but it was reality.

lyric + kevin

I MADE it inside my home and to my bar in a flash. The brown liquid burned my throat on the way down. Once it reached my belly, it reminded me of the hunger I felt while on my way to The Hills. The smell of garlic and roasted meat that came from Lyric's kitchen was still fresh on my mind. I could taste the food she'd prepared on the tip of my tongue, and I wasn't even sure what it was.

She even cooked for this nigga, I fumed. Making my way to the kitchen had never been more difficult. I rounded the bar and crossed the threshold with the taste of blood in my mouth, and as quickly as I'd gone in, I wanted to leave. There was so much to eat, too much almost, but everything needed to be cooked.

With my stomach touching my back, I didn't have time to cook shit. I didn't want to cook anything, either. Lyric had already done so. I wanted whatever the fuck she was having, but I settled for a cup of noodles that I planned to drown in hot sauce.

I filled the cup with water and placed it in the microwave on top of a few paper towels to soak up the water that boiled over the top. By thirty second increments, I increased the time on the microwave until four minutes appeared. It might've been easier to just tap the four for a quick start, but I was so accustomed to doing it the way I had.

While my noodles were warming, I sparked one of the four blunts I'd rolled before leaving the house, knowing that I wouldn't have the energy to do so when I returned. I had too much ripping and running to do for the day, which I knew would leave me exhausted. Though I hadn't expected to pull up on Lyric and ole boy, that only added to my exhaustion.

I took the steps two by two, ready to undress and get a bit more comfortable for the night. My buzzing cell vibrated against my leg in the pocket of my pants. I removed it, took a good look at the screen to find an unsaved number dancing across the screen. Though I hated answering calls from unsaved numbers, since the incident with my brother, I was a bit more inclined to.

That unknown caller had saved my brother a life of

turmoil. Hadn't I answered it then he might've been the one going to jail that night, the minute he left the block. The police were waiting in the cut and had seen us pulling off the block. Though Kale had left days prior headed back to school, I was still worried about him. I always worried about him.

"Yeah," I answered, finally reaching my bedroom where I began to strip.

"Keanu, can we—" Lyric began to speak.

It wasn't until then that I realized I'd been all up in her mix and hadn't even secured her digits. Calling her while she was away from me all day didn't cross my mind because the minute I started missing her, I went to get her. Too bad, she was preoccupied. The thought occurring again pissed me off a little more.

"How'd you get my number?" I interrupted, cutting her off from whatever she was about to say. There was no doubt in my mind that she'd be upset by the question I'd just asked but that was my intention.

"Keanu, are you serious right now?"

When I didn't respond, she understood just how serious I was.

"I took it from Laike's phone earlier today when I found myself missing you. I planned to call you tonight."

"Call me? Yeah? Before or after you had dinner with that nigga?"

"Can we not do this?"

"We're not," I assured her and ended the call straightaway.

As I adjusted the temperature for the shower, a sigh escaped my lips. Showing Lyric tough love wasn't easy and neither was it a preference of mine, but it was necessary. When she rang my line again, I quickly silenced the call and shed the rest of my clothes.

Before stepping into the shower, I accessed the call log and saved her number with a simple black heart. A smile crossed my face as my head fell back in laughter. I'd never been on no corny shit, ever, but using an emoji for a contact for the first time made a nigga feel good. She was just that... my heart.

"Alexa, play *Brain Dead* by Moneybagg," I called out as I stepped into the shower.

The water penetrated my skin, relaxing me instantaneously. A little more stress rolled off with each bead. I quickly washed my body from head to toe and brushed my teeth. With Lyric on the other side of The Hills, that the hot water was the only assistance I'd get for a good night's rest.

I made it down the stairs for another drink, a towel wrapped around my waist and one in-hand. I patted myself dry with the smaller one. The sound of the beeping microwave caught my attention, reminding me that I had something inside. One bare foot in front of the other, I headed in its direction. When I popped it open and saw the cup of noodles inside, I cringed.

FUCK. The rumbling of my stomach commenced.

Simultaneously, my alarm system chirped, notifying me that someone had entered my home. With Kale at school, there could only be three other people bold enough to walk through my door unannounced.

I made my way to the kitchen's exit and stood. One by one, I counted the footsteps as they neared me. The closer the sound got, the higher my numbers raised. Second after second elapsed before the figure finally rounded the corner. Once she got a glimpse of me, her movements stopped. There was still so much space between us as we both remained quiet, glaring at each other.

This woman, not only did she hold the keys to my home in her perfectly manicured hand, but she held the keys to my heart in them, too. As I stared back at her perfect skin and perfectly contoured frame, there was no denying it. She was the end of the road for me. She was my final destination, and I didn't give a damn how many detours or other paths I took, I'd always end up here. With her.

It infuriated me, how easily I knew it would be to forgive her in the future. Her innocence as a kid, I'd allowed to follow her up into adulthood and seemingly the relationship we were starting to build. It was Lyric. My Lyric, and she meant no harm. She never had. Her heart was always pure even if it seemed as if her actions weren't. She always meant well. There wasn't a doubt in my mind about that.

"Please don't be mad with me," she spoke, dropping her hands at her side and allowing her keys to dangle from her index finger.

Unable to respond, I turned and headed for the stairs, again. I was ready to lay down and didn't have an ounce of fight in me. If Lyric knew what was best for her, then she'd join me.

When I made it up the stairs without hearing her footsteps behind me, it was to my surprise. When the beeping of my alarm sounded, letting me know that my door had been opened and closed again, my heart sank into the sock that I had just pulled up on my feet. In a haste, I pulled the black briefs over my ass and headed back downstairs.

Lyric leaving wasn't an option. She'd come and she'd stay. I'd been missing her all fucking day and now that she was here, the thought of going to sleep alone was too much to consider. I didn't want to do that, wouldn't, even if I had to pick her ass up and put her in bed myself. She was sleeping beside me. She had to.

When I made it to the front door, fully prepared to run out in the Channing cold to chase her down, it opened again. In walked Lyric with three large bowls stacked on top of each other, balancing them between her chin and two hands. Too relieved to even extend a helping hand, I watched as she kicked the door closed behind her. Our eyes met, revealing the thoughts that had crossed my mind without me even saying a word.

For a brief moment, Lyric stood in the same spot with her eyes on mine, reassuring me that she had no plans of going anywhere. For the first time, I knew just how much the validation she sought from the ones she loved meant to her. My troubled heart was finally at peace, lulled by a simple look. A glance.

"Come on so you can eat," she tossed over her shoulder.

I followed behind her like the lovesick puppy that I was. When she reached the kitchen and saw the microwave was still open with swollen noodles inside, I wanted to run and hide. I was so consumed with thoughts of her that I'd left the noodles in the microwave long after they were done while I was upstairs enjoying a shower and ignoring her calls. Her eyes danced between the noodles and mine.

"Noodles?"

"While you were thinking about stuffing the next nigga, yours was starving. So, yeah. Noodles." I shrugged.

"Oh, Keanu," she chastised, stepping closer to me, "I never took you for the jealous type."

Her index finger grazed my skin as it hooked the waistband of my briefs. The perfume that she wore bounced from her skin and into my nostrils, tickling the hairs inside of them. She smelled like money and rightfully so. Lyric was one of the most high maintenance women I'd ever seen in my days, her mother was the other.

There were literally only two of them. Even with all the money that Luca was stuffing into Ever's accounts, she still didn't possess the same aura as the two women she was around most often and it was simply because they weren't new to money. Their money tree was old and it was deeply rooted.

My dick stiffened as my jaws locked. As much as I'd love to bend Lyric over the table and feast off her for the evening, I knew that explosive sex between us wouldn't always be the resolution to our problems – no matter how fucking addictive it was.

I swatted at her hand, causing it to fall from my waistband. There wouldn't be any fucking tonight or the next. She wouldn't have the pleasure of even seeing my dick until we figured this shit out. Her pussy would only trick me into believing that we were okay when we weren't.

"What is it, Keanu?" She sighed, making her way back over to the counters where she was preparing a plate for me. I didn't give a damn what she had cooked, I wanted some of everything. My stomach was touching my back.

"I can fuck any bitch I want to in the streets. If that's the type of time I was on, then I wouldn't need you to make that happen for me. Pussy has never been an issue for me. I've been fucking since I caught my first body at thirteen. That's nothing for me, Lyric. Sex. It's nothing. That's why we're not about to use that shit as a means to fix everything that arises between us. It's not the solution. Love is. And that's what I'm aiming for. Is the pussy good? Fan-fucking-tastic."

"Best shit I done stuck my dick in but you know why? 'Cause of the love I've invested prior to even taking it there with you. 'Cause of the mental and emotional connection that we had long before I was bending you over and eating you out. That's the connection I want to keep building on. That one right there. The mental, emotional one, and the physical will continue to progress. You having that nigga over, that's not what's up. You could've took that nigga to a fucking park or a bar to break his heart, not on my territory, Lyric.

"Real shit, how would you feel right now if when you walked in, I was entertaining someone I was fucking with for the last time? Hmm? How'd you feel if you walked in here tonight and there was a woman at the table having dinner with me for the last time? On the same table I've fucked you on. Walking across the same floor your knees were on as you sucked the nut from my dick.

"Having drinks from the same bar that you've rearranged and put your own spin to? Eating from the same dishes you've washed, rearranged, and plated food you've cooked for us on? Hmmm? How would that make you feel? Me giving another woman access to territory you've marked for... the last time?"

"Awful," she admitted.

We both headed for the dining room.

"You feel me? Ain't no fucking last time, Lyric. Let that nigga down on the curb or at the fucking gas station for all I care. At your house, smiling in your face, and jeopardizing your safety... that ain't it. Not everyone can brush that shit off their shoulders like that. We both know this shit."

"I know," she replied, sitting my plate on the table in front of me. "I just wanted to tell him face-to-face why I've chosen to end things with us so swiftly. I feel awful for even agreeing to be with him and then turning around and choosing not to be."

"Shit happens, Lyric."

"I know, it's just that... You wouldn't understand."

"And, I will never try, either. But what I need for you to understand is that when I'm in the picture, I'm not dealing with another nigga. If that's what type of time you're on, this ain't going to work."

"It's not what I'm on, Keanu."

"Then, make me a fucking believer. Eight. Eight o'clock tomorrow our plane leaves the hangar. It was supposed to be the surprise I shared with you tonight but fuck it. Do whatever you need to do to prepare for a weekend of sexless intimacy. That includes doing your due diligence and letting that nigga know what time it is. Whether you're there at eight or not, it's wheels up. I'll send you the information by noon."

"Where to?"

"Away," I answered, stuffing my mouth with the moist chicken that was on my plate.

Lyric took the hint, not asking another question because she knew there wouldn't be an answer for it.

Together, we shared silence as we polished our plates. When we finished eating, I helped Lyric shut down the kitchen and then headed to bed while she showered. The comfort she flooded my home with was as close to insanity as it got. If she'd just act right, we could be on the same shit forever.

Once Lyric was out of the tub, I watched as she slathered lotions and oils onto her skin one inch at a time. She took so much time to care for herself that I knew she'd be the perfect mother. Because I knew it was probably what she wanted most, I couldn't wait to give her a crib full of minis that looked, acted, and dressed just like her spoiled ass.

After she'd finished her nightly routine, she made sure the lights were out throughout the master suite. She climbed into bed with her back toward me. Feeling as if she was too far away, I pulled her closer until her body touched mine. I cupped her chin with my free hand and pulled her face in my direction.

"You better not cry, either," I warned before kissing her lips and then turning her face back around.

As soon as I let her go and wrapped my arms around her waist, the sniffles began. Lyric was a bonafide crybaby, but she was my crybaby. She hated chastising, and I hated feeling like I was always chastising her, but there was so much shit we had to work through and sweet talk wouldn't cut it.

TEN

keanu

I CHECKED my phone for the tenth time as I sat in the overly comfortable seat on the left side of the plane. It was the spot that allowed me to see the movement beyond the space I occupied. From where I sat, there was a view of the small set of stairs that were still extended, waiting for my guest. My leg bounced on the floor as I waited impatiently for her to climb them.

7:56p, my phone read.

No sign of Lyric. Not one.

I opened our text thread again, going back to the second message I'd ever sent her from my new phone. The first was simply the flight details and hangar number so that she wasn't confused and stuck trying to find me when she made it.

Eight, the message said, reminding her of the time that I was expecting her. Just as she'd neglected to reply to the flight details, she'd neglected to reply to the last message. However, she'd read it. According to the read receipt, she'd seen the message at **5:34p**.

Worry lines creased my forehead as I hovered over the button that would initiate a call between the two of us. My intentions weren't to seem desperate, but in a sense I was. Though I needed the vacation to unwind after six months in a cell, it wouldn't be a successful one without her. Now that she was in my system, spending time out of the country without her was something I wasn't quite interested in. Physically, I'd be there but mentally, I'd be at a faraway place.

Where are you, Lyric? I thought, staring at her contact. The black heart on the screen was tempting. I watched as the time went from **7:56p** to **7:57p**. Then, **7:58p**. At **7:59p**, I couldn't stand the thought of leaving without her and finally gave the call icon a push.

The familiar sound of an iPhone ringing erupted in

the silence, and when I looked up, I found Lyric looking down at me. Her eyes fell to my phone and then rose again to meet my eyes. She didn't understand the magnitude of her presence, and I wasn't sure if I'd ever be able to explain it.

"Hi," she greeted me with a smile and tearful orbs.

"Hi," I returned, finally resting the worry lines of my face.

Lyric chose the seat across from me as her own. She lowered into the seat with her eyes still on me. Leaning forward, I swiped away the tears that had yet to fall.

"Thank you," she whispered.

The door of the plane closed and those steps that I'd been watching had finally disappeared. With both of her hands clenching the seat, Lyric prepared for takeoff. As the crew began speaking over the intercom, all around me faded into black. All that was left was Lyric's face. Her gorgeous face with brown eyes and lips that I loved to kiss. And then there was me. Just her and I.

Remembering her childhood anxiety of flights although she loved hopping from one to another, I extended my hand for her to grab. Once she looped hers into mine, I pulled her in my direction and onto my lap. I wrapped my arms around her, assuring her that she had nothing to worry about. Once we were finally in the air – cruising, that's when I felt the wetness from her eyes against the cloth of my shirt.

"Crybaby," I joked, pulling her deeper into my chest and kissing her forehead.

"I love you, Keanu," she cried harder.

"'Til death," I responded, finally able to close my eyes and relax.

A state of tranquility consumed me because she was now in my arms. It wasn't long before her light snoring induced a peaceful slumber of my own. Neither of us opened our eyes again until the plane's wheels were back on the ground.

Lyric + Keanu

EVERYTHING WAS PRIVATE. The villa. The pool. The jacuzzi. The showers that were just outside of our dwelling. The view of the water. The deck. Everything. It was as if we'd stepped off the plane and onto our own island where I could love Lyric out loud and without restrictions. That's exactly what I planned to do.

The rest we'd gotten on the plane, hours and hours' worth was enough to have us both energized long after the tour of the villa we'd call home for the next two days. So when we were alone again, we both decided that showering and finding somewhere to have drinks and fill our bellies was the best course of action.

So that I wasn't tempted, I stayed far away from

the window and glass door that led to the shower as Lyric handled her business. I was determined to keep my dick in my pants the duration of the trip. My only goal was strengthening our mental and emotional connection so that we'd both have something concrete to present to her people when the time came.

A month. That's all I was giving her. That's all the time she had to gather herself and share her secret with her brothers. Otherwise, we'd have to say goodbye to one another. I wasn't prepared to live my life in secrecy, and I wouldn't allow her to do it, either.

"She got nine or ten niggas. I might rob ehh one," I rapped along with Gotti as he spit over the beat.

"Matching APs rocking Prada."

Unpacking both our overnight bags, I bobbed my head to the beat. I'd advised Lyric not to bring too much because I had every intention of hitting all the shops she loved and emptying my pockets for her. She could have whatever the fuck my money could buy.

"Ninety-nine opps but where yo shooters at. What y'all shooting at? I got ninety-nine soldiers and I can feed ehh one. All the guys that got a bond, I done freed every one."

When the music stopped and the beat was no longer thudding on the Bluetooth speaker, I looked over at my phone. Nanny's name lit the screen. Without hesitation, I picked it up and slid the little bar over to answer.

"Old lady."

"Whatever. Will you be spending that trip alone or did she come?"

"Come on, Nanny. Stop playing with me. You know she came."

"Hmmm. I was kind of hoping she didn't," she admitted.

"Are you serious right now?"

"Dead serious. I hope she gives you a run for your money."

"Why would you say something like that? I thought you loved me?"

"I do, but your head too damn big sometimes. Somebody needs to humble your ass for once."

"She 'bout it," I confessed.

"I know she gone be the one to do it. I know she is. And I'm going to be watching from the sidelines every time."

"I'm about to hang up on you, old woman."

"Hang up on me and that'll be the last time you see your fingers."

"You're threatening me and you're all the way in Dooley, Nanny. And you wonder where I get this tough shit from."

"Oh, hush. I got to get off this phone. I've got shit to do."

"Oh, now you're ready to get off the phone?"

"I am. Have a good time. Be safe and tell Lyric I'm

sending my best wishes. Also tell her that she's not too good to bring her high yella tail by here and speak," Nanny fussed.

"Aight," I replied, finally resting on the bed, "I love you, Nanny."

"I love you, too, son. I'll talk to you when you get back."

"Bet."

I ended the call and the music began playing through the speaker. When I stood from the bed and began putting away our clothes in the drawers, the volume decreased slowly, drawing my attention away from the task at hand. When I looked up and saw Lyric standing near the speaker, I couldn't hold back the smile that appeared on my face. Not even if I'd tried.

"Hi," she said to me, a hand on her hip.

The polished Lyric had been stripped. I was left with a bare face, curly hair, glossed lips version of her that I loved even more. As I gazed from across the room, I silently prayed to God for the strength to keep my hands to myself and my dick in my pants as I'd promised. The shit would be hard. Literally and figuratively.

"You're gorgeous, Lyric."

"I feel naked."

"Because you are," I reminded her, tilting my head toward the towel wrapped around her body.

"Not that, silly. My face."

"It's most beautiful this way. Let it stay until our trip ends."

"I don't know, Keanu." She shied away.

"For me, please."

"Okay, but no pictures."

"Why not?" I chuckled. "It's our first trip together. Why wouldn't I start my training as the perfect photographer now and get a head start?"

"The perfect photographer?" She tossed her head back in laughter. It was the most precious sound I'd ever heard.

"Yeah, the nigga responsible for all of your fly ass Instagram pictures that you love to post."

"How would you know, Keanu? You don't have a single social media account, never have."

"Laike. Shit, Luca. Kale. They keep me updated on what's going on. I've seen a few of your pictures over the years."

"Did you like them?" she questioned, toying with her fingers as she waited for my response.

"As a matter of fact, I did."

Not wanting to keep her waiting long, I answered. Of course I liked what I'd seen. I loved them, to be honest.

"I loved each and every one."

Lyric paused, allowing her eyes to roam our space and then return to me.

"Did you unpack us both?"

"Yes. Your things are to the right and mine to the left. I grabbed this for you," I told her, pointing at the cream, strappy cotton material. "I figured you'd want to be comfortable."

"I do," Lyric agreed. "Thank you so much. I would've gotten us unpacked."

"So could the host, but I preferred it be me. I'm going to jump in the shower while you finish getting ready."

"Are you wearing that?" She pointed at the t-shirt and above-the-knee shorts. The weather in Maldives was warm, a far cry from the Channing winter.

"Yeah."

"Umm. Hmm. I see why you wanted me to wear that dress. You on your corny shit, I see. You want to dress just like me."

"Shit, why not?"

The warmth I felt rushing through my frame wasn't due to the elevated temperatures outside of our villa. It was solely because of the woman standing in front of me and all her beauty.

"Goodbye, Keanu. Go bathe. I'm ready for frolicking in Maldives and spending every red penny in your pocket." She sighed, sitting on the edge of the bed where I'd left her body lotion.

"That won't be an easy task, Lyric. That's a lot of fucking red pennies."

"Doesn't hurt to try, right?"

With a shake of my head, I left Lyric alone in the villa as I headed for the shower. So that she was still entertained, I left my cell phone behind as well. The volume was lowered, but she could still hear the music very well.

lyric + keanu

"LAST ONE," I warned, watching as Lyric took a sip of the drink our waitress had brought over.

She'd had four mixed drinks, a new one each time, and two shots. One was a celebration for our union and the other was for the 'No Sex' pact we'd made. We knew that it wouldn't be very easy but keeping our hands to ourselves was necessary for what we were both trying to achieve.

"Last one, baby. I promise."

Sober thoughts. That's what I had been getting from Lyric all night through her drunken haze. What was supposed to be a quick bite and a drink or two after our facials had turned into three hours of long, progressive conversations that we both needed to officially break the ice.

Though it was her third time referring to me as anything other than Keanu or Ken, it still made my heart speed in pace and the corners of my mouth turn upward. *Baby*. I'd be that for her because that's exactly what she was to me. *Baby*. The simple word meant everything coming from her.

Slouched in my seat, I found straying away from Lyric's frame far too complicated of a task. The sun was retreating and the beauty of its setting served as her background. Unintentionally and effortlessly, she commanded the attention of everyone within a twenty foot radius. She was the moment.

"Truth or dare," she broke through the silence.

"Truth," I responded, eyes never leaving her smile.

She was toasted. Her glossy, suckable lips made my dick hard underneath the table. Just the thought of how well she used them and how they sounded when wrapped around my shit had me wondering if we would really see the end of the trip without tearing into one another.

"No fun," she whined, taking another sip of her drink.

"Truth, Lyric."

"Am I your final destination?"

Liquid courage. She'd been surviving the entire evening off of it, and I didn't have any complaints. I wanted her to reveal her true feelings and desires when it came to us and if that meant allowing her to drink a few fruity mixes until she found the courage to do so, then so be it.

"Yes. Yes you are. I don't want nobody if it ain't you. I won't accept anybody but you. It's you, Lyric. It's you or nobody."

"Do you cum like that for everyone you've ever been with?" She asked a second question though she was only supposed to ask one.

"It's my turn. I think."

"But answer the question first," she insisted, taking another sip.

"Why? Why would you want to know that?"

"Because it would make me insanely jealous if the answer is yes, but I still want to know."

"No."

"No?"

"No. I've always known that I can keep going after I nut once, but I've never wanted to. One was enough for me until I ran into you."

Visibly relieved, she sighed. "I feel like I'm crazy for you or at least I will be. Deranged. You know. All in. Unstable when it comes to you. Madly in love. You have the potential to take me there."

"I've already arrived. I'm just waiting for you, baby girl."

"Ask me."

"Truth or dare?"

"Dare."

Taking a second to place my words, I rubbed through my facial hair. Lyric's glossy orbs peered directly into me as she waited for me to say something. Anything. Not until I was ready did I return the smile she wore and shared my thoughts with her.

"I dare you to let me love you out loud, without restrictions and without consequences. I dare you to let me be the nigga for you... forever. I dare you to do that shit."

"What do I get in return? For letting you love me unrestricted and without consequences?"

"Me. Happiness. Peace. Love. Endless supply of funds. And some minis looking just like you, running around the crib."

"Yeah?"

"Is that enough?"

"If you'd stopped after *Me*, it would've still been enough," she responded, tilting her head and smiling in the process. "Everything else is a bonus, especially a few baby girls."

"Is that what you want? Girls?"

"Yes. What about you?"

"Girls, because I had a feeling that's what you wanted. Honestly, as long as they're from you, I don't care."

"But, we're having girls. My heart says so."

"Then, girls," I agreed.

"I love you, Keanu," Lyric confessed, teary-eyed.

Leaning forward, I swiped her tearful eyes and replied, "I know."

"Not like, just love you. But, like *in* love with you," Lyric emphasized.

"And the feelings are mutual."

"Then, tell me. Tell me you love me. All I ever get

is always and whatever else my family thinks of. I want you to tell me."

"I love you, Lyric. I'm in love with you, deeply, wholly, and unconditionally. I love you."

"Yeah?" She nodded with furrowed brows and a pain in her expression that I felt from afar.

"'Til death."

"Are you afraid of losing our friendship if this all crashes and burns?"

"It won't crash and burn."

"But if it does?"

"My love for you will remain unchanging. I loved you before the message, Lyric. I'll love you forever after. If partnership isn't in our deck of cards, then we can always fall back on our friendship. That's the beauty of this."

"I don't ever want to lose you. No matter where we stand, I want to know that you're always at my side like you've always been."

"I'll be there. You know this."

"I'm exhausted," she rushed out with a sigh.

"And I think that's it for you." I pointed toward her cup. It was still half full, but she was done. It was time to call it a day.

"It is. We have such a long walk. I don't even want to think about it."

"Then don't," I told her as I stood to my feet and grabbed her belongings. I stuffed everything we'd brought with us inside of her large Fendi bag and bent down in front of her.

"What are you doing?" She chuckled.

"Waiting for you to climb on."

"On your back?" Lyric was utterly amused.

"On my back."

After a few seconds, reality sunk in and she knew that this was far from a joke. If she didn't want to walk, she didn't have to. I felt the weight of her frame as she climbed on and got comfortable. Once I was fully erect and standing tall, she kissed the side of my face.

"Can you take us a picture and a video? I want to send it to Ever."

Someone knows. The thought relieved me in ways I didn't know was possible. I wasn't sure why I'd imagined Lyric was holding onto the secret herself without letting anyone in. Ever had crossed my mind, but I wasn't sure. She'd mentioned her in the letter, but nothing about her had surfaced since our first night together.

Before taking off, I dug into her purse and retrieved her phone. I held it up to her face so that it would unlock. When it did, I obliged. I took an array of photos of Lyric and me. As the video began rolling, I thought it was awfully cute the way she began squeezing my neck, kissing all over my face, and screaming into the camera.

"I'm going to marry this man and give him chocolate babies. Girls. We're having girls."

Carefree. That's how I wanted Lyric at all times when it came to me... to us. The moment was so bitter-sweet knowing that Maldives and anywhere else I decided to take her would be the only time I'd get to experience this version of Lyric until we shared our relationship with the others.

"I love you, Keanu," she whispered in my ear long after the video had ended.

By the time we arrived at the villa, I wasn't surprised to learn that she'd fallen asleep. The heaviness of her frame was the first clue. The sound of the Indian Ocean and the plethora of drinks she'd consumed had lulled her right to sleep. She barely moved an inch when I peeled back the covers and laid her on the bed. Before tucking her in, I removed her dress. Sound asleep in only a silk thong, I left her so that I could blow one while watching the water.

lyric + keanu

"KEANU."

I heard Lyric's voice say.

"Your phone. It's ringing."

The time difference was on my ass, making it hard to even open my eyes after I began to hear the loud ringing myself. I felt the chilled piece of matter on my bare chest a second later. Appreciative that Lyric understood that I was completely out of commission and intervened, I spoke my first words of the day.

"Thank you, baby girl."

"Answer it."

"Yo?" I said into the phone after swiping to answer.

"Nigga it's too late in the day for you to be sounding like you still ain't rolled out of bed."

"Long fucking night," I admitted. "What's up, Luca?"

At the sound of his voice, I was up and now wide awake. I pressed my back against the headboard of the bed and wiped the sleep from my eyes. The fuzziness was clinging to my thoughts and making it hard to comprehend much, but I'd manage.

"Shit. I got some shit I want you to look into for me. Hit me when you wake up. I'll stop by the crib."

"I'm out of dodge right now. I'll be back in another day or two. Can it wait?"

"Yeah. It can wait. Needed to get out of dodge to clear your head, huh?"

"Had to change the weather, my nigga. Channing cold as that fucking cell right now." I chuckled, running my hand down my beard while watching Lyric as she watched me silently.

"I feel you. I'm trying to get out of here before Ever drops my little nigga. She needs the break."

"So do you."

"So do I," he agreed, "but she definitely needs it."

We'll get the girls, I wanted to offer, but I held

back. When the time came, hopefully we'd be able to. I loved those three little ones as if they were my own.

"I'm going to let you go, homie. Hit me when you touch down."

"Bet."

I ended the call with a sigh. Simultaneously, Lyric released a long stream of air. She'd been holding her breath the entire time I was on the phone. With a shake of the head, she smiled.

"Good morning."

"Good morning," I replied while stretching my arms straight above my head.

"Sorry."

"One month, Lyric. That's all you have. One month."

"One m—" she started but was cut off by her ringing cell.

She held it in the air and showed me the name on the screen before answering.

"Luca, what did I do to deserve this call?"

I couldn't hear what he was saying on the other line, neither was I interested. I used the time to get out of bed. When I stood and my morning wood tented my boxers, I immediately felt Lyric's eyes on me – on it. Those pouty lips of hers stuck out a bit more as desire filled her orbs.

I quickly reminded her of our pact with a shake of my hand. Then, I stuck it deep into my briefs and readjusted my hard. The sliminess on my fingers when I removed it turned Lyric's lips upward until she formed a smile.

I'd need to clean that up, and I'd need to lock the door while doing so because otherwise, the rest of it was going in her pussy for sure. There was no doubting it. If she came into the bathroom behind me, she wouldn't be leaving the same. A waddle, throbbing, and cum-filled pussy was the only way she'd emerge.

ELEVEN

lyric

I DIDN'T WANT it to come to an end, but I knew that it soon would. My body felt like puddy as it was kneaded, poked, rubbed, and caressed. I wasn't sure how much longer we had in our sixty-minute couples massage but I knew that it wasn't a lot. The masseuse had worked her way to my feet and then back up my body a second time. I was oiled to perfection and Keanu was... asleep.

"Thank you," the masseuses both said simultaneously.

"Thank you," I responded, immediately wishing we'd book at least one more massage before our flight was scheduled the next night.

I'd gotten countless massages in the States and countries I'd visited in my lifetime, but nothing compared to the one I'd just been given. It had put my baby right to sleep. He was dead to the world.

Before waking him, I sat across from him with my feet dangling from the bed simply admiring his dark, smooth skin. It was perfect, not a blemish in sight. Peacefully, he slept like a baby. The thought of disturbing him didn't sit well with me, but I knew that we had to get a move on it. We'd already slept the entire morning and almost all the evening. I imagined we both needed to catch up on our rest. Or maybe it was the fact that we were at peace in one another's presence, inducing disapproving amounts of sleep.

"Keanu," I called out to him as I slid back into the floor-length dress that I'd brought on the trip. He didn't budge.

"Baby," I whispered in his ear, nudging him as I did so. "We have to get out of here. Wake up, baby."

"I don't want to." He yawned, rolling over and pulling me closer to him. "Come 'er."

"Babe," I chuckled, "come on. Get up."

"I'm up. You're already dressed?"

"Yes, because we'd never make it out of here if I woke you before putting back on my dress."

"So, I can't slide in my shit right quick?"

"No. You can't. You made me promise so you have to keep your promise, too."

"This some bullshit."

"Your rules, not mine."

I stepped back and watched him stand from the bed he'd been laying on. His dick was as hard as it was when he'd awakened a few hours earlier. I wanted nothing more than to get on my knees and handle that for him, but we'd promised to keep our hands to ourselves. So far, we'd done a great job. Hopefully, we made it off the island without ripping one another to shreds.

"When we get back home, get ready to hand that pussy over on a platter. Soon as we hit the door to the crib, you're dropping them fucking panties."

"In that case, I won't wear any. And why are we waiting until we get to the house? There's an entire plane with nothing but space and opportunity."

"You're right about that shit. Don't even sit down. Head straight to the bedroom when we board, take whatever the fuck you got on, off."

"You don't have to tell me twice, love. But, for now, I need you to get your shorts and your tank on. I'm ready for you to pay for some of this pussy you keep referring to."

"Come on. I'm ready to see how much that shit worth, anyway."

Tittering, I shook my head from one side to the other. "It's priceless, boo. Ain't enough zeros in your bank account to afford this shit."

"Luckily, there's enough love in my heart."

"I guess, but unfortunately, I can't take love to the register and pay for my things so make sure you don't forget your wallet."

"You're your mother's child."

"Ummm. Hmmm. And my mother's child wants to stop for a drink before we go into town and visit the shops."

"Whatever you want, baby girl," Keanu replied, sliding into his shoes.

Hand-in-hand, we made our way back to the place that had some of the best drinks I'd ever tasted and food to match. We arrived, and as promised, I only ordered one beverage. The twenty minutes it took me to finish it off, we sat at the bar deciding which stores we would tackle and the order in which we would tackle them in.

When we hit them, we hit them hard. Keanu spared no expenses and telling me no simply wasn't in his plans. Anything and everything I held up, tried on, or stared at for too long, he added to his tab. By the time we headed back to the resort where our private villa was, we needed a minivan to accommodate us.

I fell onto the bed, completely exhausted from the

day's activities. I didn't give a damn about those bags or how they'd make it inside. Rest was the only thing on my agenda and that's exactly what I got the minute my head hit the pillow. The continuous sound of Keanu moving about our space was even better than nature sounds, putting me to sleep in minutes.

lyric + keanu

"HEY," Keanu called out to me as he rubbed the side of my cheek with the back of his hand.

"Hmmm?"

"Dinner is ready," he informed me, pushing my hair from my face.

"I'm so tired."

"I know. Would you like me to bring it to bed?" he offered.

"No. I know you were looking forward to dinner together. I don't want to be lazy or ruin your moment."

"You won't," he assured me.

"Can I have ten minutes to get myself together?"

"Of course."

"Okay. Help me up. I promise not to be long." I yawned.

"Ten minutes," he confirmed.

"Ten minutes. Did you miss me while I was asleep?"

"You don't even have a clue how much." Keanu smiled.

His cheeks rose and showed off those addictive dimples. They were the deepest, puffiest craters I'd ever seen, and they made him that much more handsome. Leaning forward, he placed his pillow soft lips on top of mine.

"Ummmm. I missed you, too."

"Then, hurry, so you can join me," he suggested, standing from the bed and pulling me up with him.

Once I was up on my feet, I stood on the tips of my toes and gave his lips another peck. Underneath his tough exterior, Keanu was the sweetest. And to top it all off, he was mine.

"Go. I'll be out in ten minutes."

"Aight. I'm going to spark a blunt while I wait."

"Don't let the food get cold."

"It's still under fire. See you in a few."

Before I tiptoed to the bathroom, he stepped forward and cuffed my ass cheeks in his palms. My thong disappeared in my pussy as the late night air brushed against my backside. Quickly lost in the moment, my fingers lowered until I was gripping a handful of his hard dick.

"Chill." He grunted.

"You started."

"You're right. My bad." He chuckled, dropping his hands and backing away from me.

It was then that I noticed he'd changed clothes.

The black Amiri fit that he wore made his... *his dick stand out*. I liked that. I loved that. In less than twenty-four hours, I'd be sliding up and down it. I could wait a little longer, I imagined. Because when the time came, he'd have to pry my pussy lips from around it. I was beyond prepared to milk him for every ounce of semen that was stored in his balls.

"You're handsome."

"Thanks, baby girl."

"Let me get myself together really quickly. See you in ten, babe."

Without a verbal response, Keanu nodded. He stayed put, watching my backside wiggle as I tiptoed into the bathroom, finally. Ten minutes. I wasn't sure how I'd upgrade my entire look in ten minutes, but I'd make it work. The perfect ensemble was already heavy on my mind so choosing wouldn't be an issue. Keanu had purchased so many options.

Because there wasn't any time for a shower, I settled for a quick wash up that only took two minutes of the ten minutes that I had. I fluffed my freshly washed lashes, lined my lower lash line, blushed my cheeks, and coated my lips with clear gloss. That was all the makeup I needed and all that Keanu would probably approve of on this vacation since he'd requested I stay bare-faced.

For my hair, I decided on a quick, low bun that brought more attention to my facial structure and features. The bun paired well with the thick, gold hoops that I'd picked up from a local boutique full of the prettiest, authentic accessories for men and women. We'd even gotten Keanu a gold anklet that I forced him to love as much as I did. He reiterated the fact that it wasn't his thing but couldn't help but admit that he looked fly in it once he tried it on. I didn't miss the anklet dangling above the sneakers he wore with his fit tonight.

Because Keanu was dressed in black, I decided to go with the black number that I'd picked up from one of the tiny shops along one of the strips we'd visited. The dress was made of real silk and hung dangerously low in the front. The back, too, was nearly fully exposed. Though it ran the length of my entire body, it still made me feel like I was wearing almost nothing. Before sliding it onto my body, I slathered lotion all over me. I didn't want to ruin the fabric with oil, so I skipped that step.

On my feet, I opted for a YSL pump that was black in color and as elegant as the dress I paired it with. The *Funny Bunny* polish on my toes and nails perfectly contrasted the black I was covered in. I completed my look with the AP that Luca had purchased along with a simple diamond tennis necklace that had been a recent gift from Laike.

I stood in front of the full-length mirror that was beside the bathroom and gave myself a once over. Utterly obsessed with my reflection, I decided against changing a single thing. *Flawless*. From head to toe.

Anxious to see Keanu again, I journeyed toward the deck where I was certain he was waiting for me. I slid the glass door back slightly and stepped out into the night breeze. The candle lit table that was only a few feet away was the first thing that caught my attention. Keanu's voice was the next.

"You look stunning," he said, causing me to snap my neck in the direction of his voice.

Dressed in all black with skin that blended easily with the night sky made it difficult to locate him. Closing my eyes, I tried gathering my thoughts and calming my drumming heart that kept pounding against my chest. When I reopened them, locating Keanu wasn't an issue. He'd simplified the task, wrapping his arms around me and kissing the top of my forehead.

"Hi," I greeted him.

"Hi."

"I'm starving," I admitted.

"You're gorgeous."

"Thank you, Keanu."

"Come on," he instructed as he took me by the hand, "let me feed you."

I wasn't sure how he'd managed the fireside dinner but watching the orange and red hues as I sat near was as beautiful as the view of the ocean. Paired, they were perfect. Keanu sat across from me, leaving me to wonder who would be serving our food.

As I opened my mouth to speak, a silver platter was

placed in front of me. Then, one was sat in front of Keanu. When the tops were removed, my stomach growled and mouth watered at the same time. I tuned, who I assumed was the chef, out as I marveled at the amazing presentation of the food that I had every intention of devouring. By the time he finished giving us the background story of the fish he'd chosen for us to feast on, I was already on my second bite. It was divine.

"Ummmmmm," I moaned with closed eyes and a mouth full of the flavorful dish.

"Enjoying it more than you do me?"

My eye popped open, searching for our company. Though his back was turned and he was headed back wherever he'd come from, he was still in earshot.

"Keanu!"

"I'm sure his woman sucks his dick, too, Lyric." He shrugged, digging into his food.

"Damn," he praised.

"Does it taste as good as my pussy?" I asked, feeling a bit vindicated.

"It doesn't. It's good but not that fucking good," he replied, putting more into his mouth.

I wished like hell I was the fish at the moment. I wanted Keanu to eat me just like that and moan while doing so. Just glaring from across the table made me incurably jealous.

"You didn't answer me."

"No. I'm not enjoying it more than I enjoy you."

"Good."

A comfortable silence fell between Keanu and I as we dug into our dinner. The proportions were large, but I was almost sure I'd finish almost the entire plate. The chef returned with a bottle of wine that had been produced locally and poured us both a glass. I was excited to try the new, dry red wine, but Keanu wasn't as enthused. He preferred something brown and something that would quickly elevate his state. However, he enjoyed the glass that had been poured for him. Paired with the weed he'd smoked, I was certain he'd get the buzz that he was in search of.

"Are you enjoying yourself?" Keanu broke the silence after he'd finished half his plate.

"I am."

"Are you enjoying me?"

"I am, and I hope to continue enjoying you long after we leave this island."

"Looks like this won't be the only island we visit, Lyric. To spend the type of time I want with you, it looks like we'll be boarding planes a lot over the next four weeks."

"I don't have any objections. Tell me when and tell me where, and I'll always be there."

"Will you?" His brow hiked when he asked the question.

"Yes, Keanu. What would make you feel any different?" I placed the wine glass down that I'd been sipping from. It was almost empty, again. The wine was delicious.

"I don't. It was just a question."

"Yes. I'll be there."

"What do you want, Lyric?"

"I don't understand the question."

"We've established what I want. What is it that you want?"

"I want you, Keanu, and whatever that entails."

"Done."

"I want your home to become mine. I've been considering a home higher in The Hills, but you're already there. Within the next few months, I'd love to transition. But I want to keep my home. Sometimes, I require space and sometimes, I'm sure you'll require space. That's where we'll take the space and time we need."

"Done."

"I want children, and I don't want to wait to have them. I've known you all my life. I wouldn't call it rushing things."

"You don't want me to yourself first?" He chuckled.

"Ever is four up on me. I have to try to start playing catch up, at least."

"You trying to have that many, Lyric?" He slouched in his seat and stared at me. His eyes were so demanding.

"Have you seen the way you cum, Keanu? I don't think you give me much of an option."

"I guess not, huh?"

"Not really. I mean, I'm not against birth control, either, but I'd like to cap it at two if we can. I'm not equipped to handle so many at once."

"Two is ideal," he agreed. "But what if there's more?"

"Then, I'll cross that bridge when I get to it. I'm sure my mom would love to have a squad of me and Luca's kids stomping through her center. Leave it up to him and Ever, and she'll never go out of business. The man wants a football team."

"And it seems as if Ever is willing to give it to him, too."

"She is. She's willing to give Luca anything that he wants. I love that for my brother. He chose the perfect mate."

"He did."

"I'd do the same for you," I admitted. "Whatever you want... if it's in my power, it's yours."

"There's not a doubt in my mind that you wouldn't. That's how I know I chose the perfect mate."

I could feel the slits in the corners of my mouth form as my smile did. My cheeks nearly reached my eyelids as I stretched my face beyond its limits. Keanu was just far too perfect, and I couldn't believe he was finally mine. Tears welled in my eyes. Finally, Ever's words made perfect sense. Happiness had a way of spilling from your eyes.

"You'd better not cry."

"Happy tears, Keanu. Happy tears," I told him as I

swiped them from my face. "I'm just so emotional these days."

"It's all good, baby girl. What else?"

"I want a new car, one that you've purchased. I want to feel good behind the wheel knowing my man copped it."

"Like you do behind the wheel of the vehicles your brothers be copping you?" he toyed.

"Even better. I'm going to feel even better than that."

"You know what you want?"

"No. Not yet. I'll know soon, though. I have my eyes on a few."

"Done, then. Whenever you decide, just let me know and it's yours."

"I only want to handle my family's accounts. Life was easier when that was the case. I also want to start a small financial firm for young, Black aspiring business-women. No matter what their credit score is, I want to offer them anywhere from two thousand to ten thou-sand dollars to get their business started. The loan amount will be based upon things like rental history. Interest rates will remain low and there will be a six to thirty-six month pay off period. I have to iron out the kinks, but I'd really like to do it."

"How can I help?"

"Invest. I'll need capital to help fund the first hundred loans that I accept, but after that, I should be fine. I plan to get my father involved."

"It's done."

"Anything else?"

"Your patience. It's commendable. I'm not perfect, Keanu. Just keep being patient with me, and I promise it will be worth it."

"I know," he replied with a nod.

"Question."

"Shoot for it," he encouraged.

"When you got the message I sent, what were you thinking? How were you feeling?"

"Like a nigga was on top of the world."

"You're exaggerating."

"I'm not. When I saw the name, I was a little thrown off. I'd been getting messages through Ever from Luca. Laike hadn't reached out other than through someone in the jam with me. But it was my birthday, so I was like... calm the fuck down nigga. She's just telling you happy birthday," he explained.

"I told you happy birthday on the phone that night."

"I know, but you have to understand that I had no idea you were sending me anything on the level that you did. I just wasn't expecting you to. But once I started reading it, I lost my shit. Internally, of course. One word kept appearing in the back of my head. One word, the entire time I read your message."

"What was that?"

I rested my fork on the side of my plate. I was officially finished eating. My stomach felt like it would bust at any second.

"Finally. It kept replaying over and over. I'm like, finally, she's ready for a nigga."

"So, what stopped you from writing even that?"

"I felt like it wasn't enough, not after the shit you'd sent me. I started typing some shit, but I quickly deleted it after realizing no words would accurately explain my feelings or enthusiasm hearing from you – and not on no brother, brother shit."

"It definitely wasn't."

Placing a hand to my lips, I tossed my head back as laughter erupted from my throat. The message I'd sent Keanu was the furthest from what he'd imagined, and I would've paid to see the thoughts as they ran across his head while reading it. Extremely nonchalant at times like Luca, I imagined his face was unchanging.

"Not at all. I feel like I'll never apologize enough for leaving you hanging the way that I did."

"It's okay, now."

"Not really," he responded with a shake of his head.

"But we're not going to go there tonight. Not at all on this trip. Let's just be thankful that that message got us here. For now, I'm satisfied with that."

"Me, too."

"I'm full," I admitted.

"That bitter ass juice you had me drinking got me

tired as fuck." He turned his nose up in the air, cracking me up inside.

"Yes. I forgot to mention just how sleepy wine actually makes you."

"Fine time to mention that shit. Feels like I just ran a marathon."

"If you want, I can clean up here while you go lay in bed," I offered.

"Nah. Clean up is included. You don't have to touch shit. I'd prefer you came inside with me. I know you just woke up but come keep a nigga company until I can't hold my eyes open any longer."

"Your wish is my command," I happily replied as I stood to my feet.

I watched as Keanu stood from his chair and stretched his long arms until his bones popped.

"Shit," he grunted. "Come 'er."

With an extended hand, he beckoned for me. Slowly, I made my way to him, not stopping until our hands joined. Together, we conquered the short distance into the room where Keanu pulled the curtains forward to give us even more privacy than we already had. Though there was no one close enough to see anything that we had going on, the chef's staff would be around to clean up what had been left behind.

"Get undressed and get in bed with me."

"I thought you said we're keeping our hands to ourselves."

"I'm not going to fuck you, Lyric. Not yet and not here. You'll know if I change my mind. I just want you to be comfortable beside me."

A little upset that he wasn't trying to stick his thing inside of my thing, I loosened my grip on him. As he'd requested, I removed the dress and shoes that I wore. I was left with nothing covering my treasured parts as I climbed in bed alongside Keanu.

"You're cold-blooded for that shit, baby girl," Keanu whispered as he pulled me close.

I rested my head on his chest as I replied, "You told me to get undressed."

He didn't respond. Silence quickly followed. The sound of the ocean, however, could still be heard in the distance. I could feel the change in Keanu's breathing as time escaped us. Though I closed my eyes, sleep was the furthest thing from my mind. I was simply attempting to capture a mental, physical, and emotional snapshot of the very moment.

Time with Keanu was precious, no matter how lengthy or short it might have been. Yet, this moment was above all the others. This moment injected me with serenity, consuming all parts of me that weren't settled to quickly settle them.

At the moment, nothing even mattered. Not a single thing. This moment was where I always wanted to be with him, mentally. When our worlds were rocky and emotions were crashing and burning, this would be my place of refuge. It's where I'd return each and every time to remind myself of what I knew was possible and on the other side of whatever madness we faced.

Long after his light snores began, I remained on his chest, basking in the ambiance. This was paradise. He was paradise, and I couldn't wait to spend the rest of my days with him.

When I could no longer stand the overwhelming emotions that accompanied the moment, I lifted from his chest reluctantly. I searched for my cell and found it next to the gold teeth that I loved Keanu in so much. They turned his sexy up so many notches.

Underneath the surface where I'd found our things, I opened the drawer and pulled out a matching bikini. Since we'd touched down, I hadn't thought twice about the jacuzzi but I was itching to get my feet wet, suddenly. We were surrounded by so much water, and I had yet to wear even one of the twelve bathing suits I had purchased or the three that I'd brought in my weekender bag.

I pulled the top over my head and tied the back. The panties slid on with ease, fitting my bottom perfectly. There was something about a simple swimsuit that always did the trick for me. The nude was a perfect match for my skin.

With my cell clutched in my hand, I stepped outside and closed the sliding door behind me. The Dior sandals protected my feet from the wooden planks beneath me as I made my way to the jacuzzi area. Once near enough, I slipped out of the sandals and into the warm water.

"Ummmmmmm."

It felt wonderful.

Sure not to get my fingers wet, I made myself comfortable. The view of the ocean's shore was stunning. I watched the water reflect the night sky, darkening quite a bit from this evening when we'd made it back to our villa. Nevertheless, it was still breathtaking. The nature sounds that I often played to get a good night's sleep was nothing in comparison to my reality at the moment.

I unlocked my cell and dialed up Ever. The phone rang three times before her voicemail picked up. It wasn't often that she didn't accept my calls, so I knew that it only meant she was being the busy bee that she was. Deciding to let her have her moment, I moved to the next best contact on my list. My mother's phone hardly rang before her voice appeared on the other end.

"I was just thinking of you, Lyric. I swear you read my mind sometimes, child."

"Good thoughts, I hope."

"Yes. Very good thoughts. Is everything alright?"

"Everything is perfect, Mom," I admitted, emotions running wild. The tears that fell from my eyes must've been the tenth thousandth ones I'd cried, but I couldn't help myself. Wiping my nose, I assured her once again, "It's perfect."

"What's the matter?" she asked, concern etched in every syllable she spoke.

"Mom, I'm in love. I can feel it in deep, deep in the crevices of me that I didn't even know existed. And I'm scared. I'm scared that maybe I've made the mistake of falling for someone who is forbidden for me and me for him."

"Oh, Lyric. Baby, you haven't made a mistake. Not at all. There's no one else in the world I'd rather see at your side than the person you've chosen. Ken is your equal."

At the sound of his name, my eyes bloomed and my heart galloped.

"How did you know?" I gasped.

"A mother just knows, Lyric. It's our job to know. I've paid close attention to you two for many, many years, even the years you ran from him when Luca was away. You were ashamed and couldn't face him. He looked for you every time he came by."

She was right. Mothers knew everything.

"Luca and Laike, they'll hate me for this." I groaned.

I wiped my eyes and leaned my head backward, looking upward at the sky. This was all so new to me. This feeling. But the relief that washed over me now that I'd told someone other than Ever was everything.

"They won't."

"Please don't tell them. Please don't tell anyone."

"I won't. Tell them when you're ready and don't let

anyone rush you into doing so, either. Not even Ken, although I know it must be a struggle for him."

"A major one. He hates it," I admitted. Even I hated it for him.

"It'll be worth it in the end, sweetie. Just don't wait too long. He deserves to love you loudly and boldly," my mom suggested. I took her words in stride, knowing she only wanted the best for me – for us both.

"I know. I just need a few weeks."

"Take your time, then. In the meantime, I need to get off this phone. Call me if you need me and know that my heart is full. I'm happy for you, Lyric."

"Thanks, Mom."

"I love you, baby."

"I love you, too."

TWELVE

keanu

I DIDN'T HAVE to pat the other side of the bed or open my eyes to know that she'd disappeared. Because the contentment that accompanied her presence had vanished, too. I wiped the sleep from my eyes and wobbled out of bed. Finally, the effects of the bitter ass juice she'd given me had worn off.

The villa I'd reserved for us had three rooms, a living room, kitchen, and everything else that came with a home. However, I knew that she hadn't drifted too far from the main suite. She hadn't the entire trip. Not even to explore the place. We were either out of the door, on the deck, or in bed. There wasn't much time for anything else, so checking the rest of the villa I knew would be pointless. Instead, I headed for the deck.

When I pushed back the window covers that I'd used to keep the chef and his crew from seeing inside, there she was. Her head rested on the back of the jacuzzi as her body and arms were submerged under water. Tranquility was written all over her beautiful face. The stillness that she was basking in, I wanted the pleasure of enjoying too. So, without interruption, I removed my briefs and stepped closer to the jacuzzi. Unfortunately, she heard me coming.

"Well... hi," Lyric spoke, softly.

My hard dick pierced the air in front of me, dangling over her head as I looked down at her.

"Hi."

I lowered my feet into the water one after another. The warmth was inviting and so was Lyric. Even though she was next to me, she felt so far away. I reached over and pulled her in my direction, not stopping until she was sitting on my lap.

Face to face. Nose to nose. Skin to skin. We sat in silence, listening as the jets on the large tub made the water bubble and pop. Lyric's hands wrapped around my upper shoulders as she watched me intently. If there was nothing else crystal clear in my world, the fact that she belonged to me for the rest of my years was. That alone made me excited just to see another day – especially knowing she'd be a part of it.

"Did you miss me?"

"Terribly," I confessed.

"You didn't sleep long."

"Because you didn't stay long."

Her eyes bounced around my face as we spoke to one another.

"Where do we go from here?" she asked before placing her lips on mine and then quickly removing them.

"Wherever love takes us."

The tiny fabric covering her body was driving me insane. I wanted it off and her uncovered as she was before I went to bed. I'd dreamt about sliding into her oasis while sleeping, and I was ready to bring that to fruition.

With the tip of my index finger, I curled it underneath one side of the fabric covering her breast and pulled backward. Her deep, dark pink nipple pebbled the second it was exposed to the night air. I repeated the movement and freed her right breast next. Her lips parted but before she could find the words to say, I placed the right tit in my mouth and then the left. I divided my time in between the two of them as Lyric began to grind on my lap.

"Keanuuu," she moaned. "No seeee... Oh my God."

"Fuck all that shit you talking," I told her as I lifted her from the water slightly.

I pulled one string and the entire bottom to her swimsuit fell from her waist. Her bald pussy stared me in the face and thought my mouth watered at the sight of it, I was dying to get inside of her. I lowered her back into the water, placing my dick at her center in the process. When I breached her entryway, I could feel her clawing away at the skin on my body.

"Baby," she cried out. "Keanu, wait."

"Nah. Ain't no waiting. Shut the fuck up and ride this dick."

No more words formed between us. Only movements. Lyric used the ledge, we'd both sat on that was built inside of the jacuzzi, for stability. With both feet perched on top of it and on the side of me, she obliged. Her thick, wide frame smacked against the water each time she lifted and lowered herself back onto me.

When I tried stretching my neck for the view behind her, imagining it was as wild as the movements she was making, I felt her hand on my chin. She forced me to straighten my neck and focus solely on her face. The sound of her ass slapping the water continued, driving me mad inside.

"Eyes on me," she demanded.

Unable to contain the beast within me, I grabbed Lyric by the neck, squeezing as I whispered in her ear,

"This pussy gone make me lay some shit down. Don't play with me or I'm going to be a big fucking problem."

Without releasing my hold on her, I gave her my eyes again as she'd requested. The smile that appeared on her lips held the same joy that I found in her orbs.

"I shoot well, too, Keanu. Stick my dick in anyone else and you'll both find out," she warned, not bothering to whisper.

Utterly obsessed with every fucking thing about her, I lifted her from the water with one hand around her neck and the other underneath her ass. We were still connected, still one, when I laid her on the wooden planks and thrusted into her without remorse.

"Cum on this dick," I instructed as spread her legs and thumbed her clit.

Once it was lubricated with her wetness, I slid it into her ass knowing that it would have her body convulsing in seconds.

"I want to feel you in there," she whimpered, looking straight up at me with those big, doey rounds.

Not quite comprehending or finding it hard to believe, rather, what she'd just requested, I asked, "What the fuck did you just say?"

"I want to feel you inside of me... *back there.*"

"That's not what you want," I warned, mostly because it was something that I was unsure of myself.

At thirty-seven, the request had been made several times by women I'd been involved with, but it was always one that I ignored. This time, though, I was strongly considering it and only because of the person it was coming from. If I was to experience such a forbidden act with anyone, it would be her.

"Yes. Please. Please, Keanu."

"It'll hurt," I informed her.

"I don't care. Stick it inside of there."

"Lyric, baby," I tried talking her out of it.

"Please," she begged, leaning forward and removing my heavily coated dick from her pussy.

Its slipperiness caused it to fall from her hand, but she quickly scooted upward and grabbed it again. Seeing as though she was determined, I didn't stop her when she placed the head of my dick at her asshole. Because I knew that there was no escaping her desires, my job quickly shifted to making the experience as pleasurable as possible for her. I focused on her lubricated clit in an attempt to trick her brain into ignoring the pain that I was about to cause her. As I thumbed her clit, back and forward, nearly bringing her to her peak, I slid into her ass, securing my spot and marking new territory.

"Fuckkkkkk. I'm cumming!" she screamed.

It was far too late for me. I'd already came.

The tightness of her ass milked my dick for everything it had, almost. Too invested to pull out or end things where they were, I leaned forward and placed my lips onto hers. Lyric's tongue parted my teeth and began a very slow, methodical dance with mine. Just like that, we stayed attached until I felt that she'd come down from her elevated state.

"Fuck me," she pleaded when I turned her loose.

There was nothing left to be said. I stuck my index and middle fingers as far into her pussy as it allowed, and worked them upward while stroking her asshole, simultaneously.

"Fuck," I grunted, trying to keep my composure.

She felt so good. Her pussy creamed, keeping me lubricated as I got acquainted with a new hole, one that I wouldn't visit often but would seemingly enjoy the time that I did spend inside of it.

And that was the motherfucking issue with Lyric. When that pussy of hers was involved, she could get whatever she wanted from me, out of me, and through me. I couldn't deny her. That's why I'd tried to keep my hands to myself this trip, but it wasn't possible. We were on such a beautiful island, and I wanted to make beautiful memories with my beautiful woman – looking at her beautiful face while I made her beautiful pussy spit up on my dick. Now, I was paying for it but the price was marvelous. It had me on the brink of my second nut.

"Shit, I'm 'bout to cum again," I announced as her pussy began to shower me with her feminine ejaculation.

lyric + kenu

IN A STEADY, constant motion, I rubbed the soft skin of Lyric's back while watching as our plane descended. Our time in Maldives had ended and it was back to reality for us both. The dark Channing sky met us with open arms. As the wheels of the plane pounded the ground with a thud, Lyric awakened from her sleep.

"Babe," she called out to me, eyes still closed.

"Yes, we've landed," I confirmed, already knowing what she was about to ask.

Her naked, flawless frame rose from the bed, quickly rushing toward the window that she lifted for proof. A sadness coated her round spheres when she returned around again. We shared sentiments.

"I don't want it to end," she sulked.

"Neither do I," I agreed.

"Spend the night?"

"We're not spending the night anymore, Lyric. My home is yours. Come when you want. I thought I made that clear?" I asked, pulling her closer to me.

"You have. I don't want to go home first. I want to stay with you," she whined, pursing those pretty lips of hers in the air.

"Then, you'll stay with me. I'll arrange for your car to be brought to my house and put into the garage until you're ready to go home. Let's get dressed because you're making my dick hard again. I'd rather get you home before I start thinking with my little head, again."

From one end of the plane to the other, I'd made love to Lyric. Slow. Addictive. Agonizingly good sex that I would have the pleasure of enjoying anytime and anywhere forever. That was enough to make my heart smile and my dick hard all over again.

We exited the plane, hand-in-hand, after getting dressed. The bags that we'd collected on the trip were instructed to be placed inside of Lyric's truck and brought to the house along with it. When we settled in my Jeep, reality hit us both, causing long, exasperated sighs to exit through our noses and mouths.

Even through dread, I placed the car in gear and began the journey home. Only a few seconds into our trip, I felt Lyric's palm brush against mine as she collapsed her fingers onto mine. I curved mine, fitting into the spaces between hers before raising the back of her hand to my lips and kissing it.

There was no music. The only rhythm heard was the one my heart made. That was enough for me. I was on too much of a high. Music would only dampen my mood.

When we finally arrived, it was Lyric who gained access to the house. Her keys were accessible whereas mine was still in the luggage that I'd carried on the plane, which was arriving soon. The key to my truck was left inside during our entire trip in case of an emergency. Hadn't it been, then it would've been Lyric's truck that we'd taken to my place because I wasn't digging through my bag to find mine.

For the first time in my life, when I walked through the door, the void that had secretly haunted me was filled. I was home, but so was she. And though she hadn't officially moved into her new dwelling, her presence still meant the world to me. The face-splitting smile that I wore as I wrapped my arms around her made her scrunch her face and frown up at me.

"Why are you smiling so hard?" she asked, patting my chest.

"Because it's happening," I shared. "Before tonight, each time I walked into my house to silence I felt like something was missing. After the letter, I realized it was you. Now that you're here and I'm not battling the silence, it feels fan-fucking-tastic."

"Yeah?" She smiled, too.

"Yeah."

"I'm happy that I've made your home a more comfortable place, then, Keanu."

"Our home," I corrected.

"Our," she repeated after me.

lyric + kenu

AS THE DAYS turned into weeks, the love I had for Lyric began to solidify. I looked forward to my nights with her. Though she required her space often, at least six of the seven nights a week, we were beside each other. I loved that shit.

Because with her, everything was so simple. She didn't require much of me other than me being myself. Her body heat kept me out of the streets and underneath her every chance I got. I turned in early almost every night just to make it back to her before she was too tired to interact with me for the night or dinner that she'd cooked got too cold.

Not only did she fill my stomach, but she filled my heart, too. With Valentine's Day slowly approaching, she even filled my home with red ribbons and hearts throughout it that I was adamantly against at first but grew to accept. This was what it was like having Lyric in my world. She spared no expense when it came to anything she was passionate about and love happened to be one of those things.

Love.

Family.

Finances.

That was her life. She was a numbers girl which was why I'd been changing the digits on her account daily so that she could begin the process to start her funding project. So that her account activity wasn't suspicious or flagged by the bank, she deposited small increments of nine thousand dollars that were subtracted from the three-hundred thousand dollar investment I'd made. It would get her first fifty to sixty clients out of the door with twenty-five hundred to ten thousand dollars in low-interest loans to get their businesses off the ground.

"Busy as usual, huh?" I heard Deidra say just as I hit submit on the order I was placing.

Every Sunday, like clockwork, I promised myself I'd send Lyric a hundred red roses. It was only my second time, but the amount of pussy she dropped in a nigga's lap after the first one had me ready to send her a hundred more every Wednesday.

Valentine's Day was approaching, and she'd made it clear that she was expecting the unexpected from me. I wasn't opposed. It was whatever when it came to her and she knew that shit. The hints she'd been dropping in the meantime, though, were helping me out a great deal. I appreciated every picture she showed me, every video she made me watch, every website she made me scroll with her, and every item she named as possible gifts.

If it was left up to me, I'd toss a ring on her finger and put a baby in her belly for Valentine's Day, but those would honestly be my gifts. I had to make sure she was covered, too. Besides, she still had a few weeks left to let her people know what was up with us. A ring would only reveal what they still didn't know.

"You know it," I responded, never looking up from my phone.

The confirmation screen appeared and though I'd read it just a week prior, I read it again. I wanted to make sure that I'd sent it to the correct address and the delivery would get to Lyric in a timely manner.

Her home. Mine.

My home. Hers.

We bounced around from house to house, mainly staying at mine but occasionally hers. Today, she was home for her weekly refresh. Her days were as busy as mine, but soon she'd only be spending an hour or two on accounts and then working on building her dream business. She'd already started implementing her exit strategy so that she could have the freedom to whatever the hell her heart desired.

Once I confirmed, I exited Safari and entered our text thread to pick up where we'd left off. Before I was able to respond to the last message she'd sent, Laike was calling my line.

"Laike, what's up, homie?" I answered.

"Sunday dinner, nigga?" he blurted.

From the noise of his background, I could tell he was somewhere handling business.

"I did not say call and ask that nigga. I told you to call and tell that nigga!" Luca yelled from a distance.

"Tell that nigga he's got three little ninjas. I'm not one of them. My pops dead."

"Nigga, you coming or what?"

"He ain't got another choice!" Luca interfered, again.

"And, if I don't?" I geared my question toward Luca.

"I'm shooting out the tires to that slow ass Trackhawk every time I see it. The folks at the tire shop going to know you personally."

"I never took well to threats," I quickly reminded him.

"I've never made any," Luca responded.

"I shoot back," shrugging, I replied.

"I shoot first."

"Liam. The nigga, Liam, made the request so be there. Luca's crib at seven."

"Why you niggas didn't lead with that?" I fumed.

"'Cause, that nigga ain't yo daddy," Liam howled. "Didn't you just say your pops dead?"

"Fuck you! And that big head ass nigga beside you," I told them as I ended the call.

Immediately, I dialed Lyric's cell. She picked up on the first ring.

"Hey," she crooned. Her silky voice caressed my heart. "Miss you much."

"Same," I admitted, watching my surroundings. "Same."

"What's the matter?"

"Sunday dinner," I shared.

"What about it?" she asked.

"Your father wants me to come."

THIRTEEN

lyric

SITTING across the table from Keanu wasn't exactly how I'd expected my Sunday night to end. As laughter filled the room, I found it hard to find humor in anything anyone was saying. In fact, I hardly heard anything other than the loud ringing in my ears as I stared off into the distance while everyone passed their plates around the table, instructing the person in front of their favorite dishes to load them up. My plate sat in front of me as I tried to comprehend exactly what was happening.

"Lyric," Ever whispered firmly in my ear as she squeezed my knee underneath the table.

"Huh?" I snapped my neck in her direction.

"Snap out of it, babe," she told me while grabbing the plate that was being handed to me.

"Salad?" she asked Laike.

"Yeah!" he yelled across the table.

Salad was my dish. I hadn't made it or brought it over but I was sitting in front of it.

"Thank you," I whispered in her direction.

The next plate headed in my direction. This time, I grabbed it and without asking, I piled the six-layer salad onto it. Still numb and out of touch with reality, I did the same for the next two that were passed along. It wasn't until everyone's plate was complete, that I realized I never put mine in the lineup. With it being left out of the rotation, there wasn't a single scrap on it.

"Lyric, you're not eating anything?" my father asked from across the table, seeing as though everyone was digging into their plates but me.

"Of course," I chuckled, nervously, "running my mouth and forgot all about my plate."

I lied. Though I hated it, to cover for my lapse it was necessary.

"Says she's trying to lose five pounds. I don't see why?" Ever interjected, "You're literally perfect but the salad is fire so I understand if that's all you want, still."

She was a lifesaver. As she patted my leg underneath the table, I rested my worries a bit. The pressure didn't seem so intense and my father's attachment to her words redirected his attention to a completely separate topic.

"Five pounds?" He sniggered. "You're definitely your mother's child. Five pounds where, Lyric?"

"From that head of hers," Laike interrupted.

With a shake of my head, I decided against responding to either of them. I didn't have the words, anyway. Luca's eyes caught my attention instead. They pierced right through me, concern scribbled in the round, brown circles. Lifting a thumb, I assured him that I was fine. With a nod, he accepted my response to his non-verbal communication before digging into his plate.

My phone vibrated between my legs, scaring me half to death as I piled the salad onto my plate. Though there was a rule prohibiting phones from the table, I always kept mine near. Once I was satisfied with my proportion of salad, I unlocked my cell with my passcode being that I couldn't lift it to my face for facial recognition. I'd be caught red-handed.

The black heart that rested beside the word Babe hiked my heart rate. The vessel drummed against my chest as I struggled to release the stream of air necessary for the continuance of life.

Tighten up.

My eyes found his a half-second after reading the simple instruction. With a nod, I agreed. The gray bubble formed as his eyes fell from mine and down toward his cell. I waited with bated breath as he began typing again.

Tonight is the perfect night, he suggested.

Beads of sweat formed underneath the layers of clothing I wore. I could feel the moistness of my skin as I perspired, my pores opening and allowing sweat to surface.

Two weeks, I responded, swiftly.

The last thing I wanted was Keanu getting any ideas. I at least had that left. He'd given me the time, and I wanted to reserve every second of it.

Two weeks, he replied.

Sighing in relief, I finally picked up my fork and dug into my salad. From across the table, his lips turned upward into a smile – one that hardly concealed the disappointment that radiated from his bones. And, just a bit more, I shrunk at the thought letting him down again. Before I was able to get too caught up in my feelings, I heard the screeching of Ever's chair as she slid back and stood.

"Where are you going?" Luca asked, standing, too.

The pair was in sync, so much so that it was hilarious. I wasn't even sure if they noticed, but they'd truly become one. My brother was head over heels for the dirty blonde bombshell and I couldn't blame him. Hell,

I was in love with her too and had been for the last decade. She was addictive, her and that angelic spirit of hers. One couldn't help but grow attached.

"Remember that thing," she said, lowly.

Nodding, Luca seemed to have quickly been reminded of whatever she was referring to. He tossed his dinner napkin on the table and followed behind her. The two disappeared around the corner in seconds, leaving my mother with a smile on her face and my father shaking his head.

"He just can't stay off the poor girl. Her little body won't ever catch a break." My father huffed.

"Did you forget that we have three children, all two years apart? Meaning, that there was only about a year in between all three of my pregnancies? 34. 36. 38."

"I haven't forgotten. I made them," he sassed.

"Then, act like you know," my mother responded, "and get ready to see her with a few more swollen bellies because your son made it clear from a very early age that he wanted a family twice our size."

"Yeah. I remember that, too."

"Him and Lyric are our only hope, anyway."

"Y'all not going to start talking about me like I'm not at the table," Laike interjected, munching on the stuffed salmon that was almost completely gone.

"Well, it's true."

"For all of y'all's information, my time is coming, too. All these kids and all this love got me feeling a way.

Even Lyric done settled for a lame. So, maybe I'm y'all's only hope."

Everyone at the table burst into laughter. It seemed as if Laike had consumed too many of Luca's bar contents. Keanu's face was unchanging. Hearing Laike refer to Collin wasn't exactly funny to him, especially not when it was actually him whom I'd settled with.

"This nigga," he spoked, shaking his head.

"Oh, son, you're right behind him. I ain't getting shit out of you, either. Birds of a feather flock together," my father tittered.

"I'm well on my way, old man," Keanu stated as a matter of fact.

My mother's eyes found mine quickly. I closed mine, immediately, praying to God that Keanu didn't continue. He, too, had been drinking whatever Luca was feeding their bellies before we all sat down to eat.

"I can speak for this nigga, but as for me... I think it's about time to retire and get me a little forever thang," Laike blurted.

"I'd sure like to see that," a familiar voice spoke from behind me.

I didn't have to turn around to see who had entered the dining hall. The contortion of Laike's face as he swallowed the lump in his throat told me everything I needed to know." Gnawing on the inside of my jaw until I drew blood, I waited for our new guest to round the table. Now, the seat between my mother and I being empty made more sense. It was the one that was directly across from my brother.

"Baisleigh," my mother cheered, "I wasn't expecting to see you, tonight."

Family dinners were private events, but according to history, Baisleigh would always be part of our family. She and Laike shared a long, difficult past that could've been as beautiful as Ever and Luca's but he'd chosen to break her heart instead of nourishing the love she had for him. And she'd stuck around for his antics. But to her credit, after years of disappointment, she walked away without looking back again.

"Ever insisted I come."

"Yes, because someone planned to be stuck on the couch on such a special day."

"If we're being fair, my couch is very, very comfortable."

The black one-piece that Baisleigh exposed when she removed her coat was sickening and so were the curves underneath it. I cringed, watching as my brother nearly foamed at the mouth. His eyes never left her frame, watching as she turned and handed her coat to Luca.

"Liam, Lyric, Ken," she spoke to everyone at once. "Where are the babies?"

"Upstairs with San," Ever informed her as she lowered herself into her seat, again. Baisleigh took the seat next to me.

"Okay, body," I whispered as I leaned over.

"Too much?" she asked.

"Just enough." I sniggered.

"Now, what's this about you retiring? Is hell close to freezing?" Baisleigh chuckled. "Or is Ashton Kutcher casting for Punk'd?"

Scooting his chair back slightly, Laike wiped his face with his dinner napkin and leaned back in his chair. His entire demeanor changed whenever she was in the equation. As much as he claimed to be past that part of his story, I knew that Baisleigh's escape was still a thorn in his side. Since her, he hadn't slowed down long enough to even see what the girls he laid down with really even looked like.

When she was near, Laike got his act together. He actually made sense. And, for the life of me, I couldn't understand why he hadn't rekindled the flame between them. Though it was low, the fire was still there. I could see it dancing in both of their orbs.

"Happy birthday, Baisleigh," calmly, he said, eyes fixated on her.

"Thank you, Laike."

"Oh God, it's your birthday!" My mother scrambled.

"Which is why Ever spent all evening making this damn cake," Luca complained, appearing with a colorful cake that resembled Baisleigh's House. Gold candles protruded as sparkles crackled and popped.

"Of course you did this," Baisleigh said, emotions

quickly overwhelming her. "Really, Ever?" She fanned her glossy eyes.

"You deserve to be celebrated," Ever told her.

As beautiful as the cake was, it was hard to keep my eyes off it and on Laike. The heaviness ingrained in his features and body language had me in a chokehold. Cumbersome Laike didn't appear often and when he did, I felt like it was my personal duty to relieve him of whatever stress resting within him.

"Thank you so much."

"Luca and I got you something we thought you could use in the near future," Ever explained.

"What?"

Ever dangled a set of keys between Baisleigh and I. "We found a truck for sale that used to be a mobile restaurant. The owner retired and had no use for it. It's practically brand new. We were thinking that you could be amongst the many food trucks the city needs."

"Get out of here! I've been thinking about this for so long. I just didn't have the energy to put into finding a truck."

"Now you have one," Luca said.

"Oh my God. Thank you guys so much," Baisleigh chanted, standing up and wrapping her arms around Ever's neck and then standing in front of Luca, who was still holding her cake.

"Make a wish, birthday girl," I encouraged.

Closing her eyes for a split second, Baisleigh made a wish before blowing out her candles. She returned to her seat and Luca placed the cake out of the way on one of the many counters in his kitchen.

"Where's my gift, Laike?" she asked as soon as she sat down comfortably. One thing about Baisleigh, she didn't let up when it came to my brother. She made him own up to his shit and keep his word.

"In my car." He chuckled, probably thinking the same thing that I was.

"You got me one for real? Seriously?"

"Don't I each year?"

"I don't consider money a gift. There's no thought put into that."

"Well, good thing I didn't get you money this year," with a shrug, he told her.

"Ok, so go get it," she instructed.

"Come with me," he insisted.

Without hesitation, Baisleigh scooted her chair back and stood again. Laike followed suit, tossing his dinner napkin on the table and leading her out of the room. While everyone watched them exit, my eyes found Keanu's again. Although he was only a few feet away from me, I still felt like I missed him dearly. I couldn't wait for the moment we were alone, again.

"She's over that nigga and he doesn't even realize it." My father grunted, "Hmph."

"Oh, I think he is well aware. I'm happy she has put all of that behind her," my mother followed up with.

"I think there's still something there," I opposed.

"A little," Ever agreed, "but, definitely something."

"If he got his shit together and stayed on her long enough, she'd finally give that nigga another chance. But he ain't going to do that. It's too much like right." Luca shrugged.

"When it's all said and done, he's going to get her," Keanu finally spoke.

Everyone had their own opinions about the two that had exited and returned ten minutes later. When Baisleigh sat back down, she was not empty-handed. The iciness of her wrist caused chill bumps to rise on my skin due to the sudden change in the temperature.

"Ok, money," I joked.

"Isn't it lovely?" She held her wrist in the air, twirling it so the diamonds could hit the light.

The AP that Laike had blessed her wrist with resembled mine. So did the rope around her neck. Laike had dropped a bag on Baisleigh for her birthday, and I wasn't mad about it.

"It is."

"Reparations," she laughed, "reparations."

"I know that's right," I agreed. "I know you said you don't consider money a gift, but it's about all I've got on me right now. Maybe this can help get your truck started with renovations."

I stood, walked over to the counter that my purse was sitting on and removed the nine thousand dollars that Keanu had given me before he left this morning. It was supposed to go into my bank account, but I had other plans. I'd replaced the money, but for now, it was Baisleigh's.

"That's nine."

I handed her the large stack of money before taking the seat beside her.

"I'll transfer that back into your account," Laike suggested.

"I think you've spent enough," I reminded him, pointing at Baisleigh's wrist.

"Not really." Laike shrugged.

"Okay, big money. You know the routing and account number, then," I replied.

"I do."

Conversation continued as silverware collided with the glass plates over and over. When everyone finished their helpings, Baisleigh's cake was served as dessert and the celebration moved from the dining hall to the screened portioned of the gazebo that was heavily insulated for Channing winters and finished off with a long fireplace that was better than controlled heat.

Keanu, Luca, Laike, and my father busied themselves with a game of Spades while the ladies settled on the oversized sofa that could fit up to eight. Conversation pieces ranged from Ever's birth plan to Baisleigh's plans for the truck that Luca would have delivered to her home the following day.

"I'm going to empty my bladder and refill my cup," I announced, standing from my seat and stretching my limbs. "Anybody need anything from the kitchen?"

"No."

"I'm good. I want next at this table," Baisleigh admitted.

"I'm fine," Ever confirmed.

I left the crew outside and made my way into the house. Out of sheer habit, I checked my phone for notifications but there were none. Not even random messages from Collin who was still trying to figure out why I'd broken up with him over dinner the night that I left Channing for Maldives with Keanu.

Every few days, he'd send a random text that I ultimately ignored. After responding to the first he'd sent, I figured there wasn't a point of responding to the rest. I'd made it clear that our relationship was strictly business from the moment I left the restaurant that night and to use my business line if he needed me.

As I made my way through Luca's home, the sweetness of the freshly cut cake served as the prominent fragrance. I imagined how pleasantly surprise Baisleigh must've really been to know that Ever had put in the effort to make her day special. Baisleigh's family were always celebrating someone's special day, so it was appalling that she wasn't somewhere partying with them.

However, I understood her completely when she mentioned it being a year of peace and quiet for her. I was applying the same sentiments to my life. It had always been that way, but lately my life had seemed a bit unpredictable, especially with my accounting clients involved in my day-to-day. So, getting back to my quiet and calm was high up on my priority list.

I closed the door behind me as my bladder began its foolishness. It was as if as soon as I was close to the bathroom, suddenly I couldn't hold my urine. I wasn't sure if your body knew when you were close to the toilet or the head started to play games. Either way, the sudden urge was irritating, making me bounce around as I tried to unbuckle my belt and get my pants down.

"Ahhhhhhhhh."

As I emptied my bladder. I closed my eyes and savored the feeling. It was unmatched. Every liquid I'd consumed in the last few hours since being at Luca's was released.

I quickly wiped myself with the thick tissue I'd rolled on my hand. The pink strip that appeared on the white cotton warned me that my time was near. Within the next day or two, my period would bring on the pain that I wasn't quite ready for. Nevertheless, I was thankful for evidence of its presence.

After cleaning my hands, I dried them with the guest towels that Ever preferred over paper towels. Somehow the smell of them during her pregnancy with Lucas made it hard to keep her food down. Even at the sight of them, she'd turn green in the face.

I opened the door of the bathroom, expecting to race back to the backyard but was stopped in my tracks by a hard chest and familiar scent. Keanu pushed forward, forcing me back into the bathroom and locking the door behind us. Before I could begin to protest, his lips were on mine and his hands were tugging at my belt buckle.

"Keanu," I rushed out once he turned my lips and tongue loose.

"I don't give a fuck, Lyric," he whispered.

I wasn't sure how he'd managed to get my belt unbuckled, but I felt my pants at my knees. He left my thong up on my waist but pulled it to the side. Fucking me with my underwear on was a fetish of his that I'd recognized. For that reason in particular, I'd spent a fortune on new, sexier panties than I already owned. My collection was top tier, now. It hadn't been mediocre before, but period panties and bloomers I wore on lazy nights were no longer in the lineup. Even the ones I'd purchased for those menstruating days were seamless, soft, and appealing.

"My period is coming," I warned.

"Good, then I'll either knock that motherfucker on down or keep running red lights."

He pulled the thin band of my thong to the side and palmed my ass. His large hands caressed my cheeks just before he lifted his right hand and brought it down on my right cheek. Hard and without remorse, he slapped it, simultaneously penetrating me.

"Keeeeaaaaaaannnnuuu," I moaned as he entered me without warning.

"Fuck, this shit is ridiculous," he complained.

I could feel my wetness lubricate his rod as he drove it into me over and over again. The ponytail I wore was easily wrapped around his left hand as he held my waist with his right. Forcing my eyes on his as we stared at each other through the mirror, Keanu never missed a beat.

"You see this shit?" he asked.

"Yeeeesss," I moaned, forgetting that we were far from home and playing a dangerous, dangerous game.

"You look so fucking good." He grunted, slapping my right cheek, again.

We were perfect. I couldn't close my eyes if I wanted to. The sight of us, together, in utter bliss was too addictive. I loved the way he stared back at me, but his attention wavered every few seconds as his eyes fell from the mirror to my ass. I could feel it as it jiggled with every stroke he administered. The sound of our wet skin smacking against each other and our labored breathing were the only things that could be heard throughout the bathroom.

And for once, just once, I didn't care who could hear us or who'd be privy to our secret if they caught us as we exited the bathroom. For once, nothing mattered. Nothing but Keanu and me. And, for once, it felt good not to give a damn about nothing or no one but myself and my desires.

"I'm about to bust all in this pussy," he warned me.

This time, I didn't have to beg. He knew exactly

what I wanted, and he was going to give it to me, *all of it*. My climax crushed every nerve in my body in anticipation of his semen, causing my knees to buckle beneath him.

"Oh fuck. Oh fuck!"

"Cum on this dick, Lyric," he encouraged as my sliminess coated his shaft.

Keanu made it in second place. But for the first time since we'd been intimate, a second or third round wasn't in his plans. His arms stiffened as his veins protruded. Our eyes locked on one another's through the mirror.

"Damn, baby girl," he whispered, closing his eyes.

We both remained still, basking in the after-sex glow. Seconds passed before we came to our senses. Still, we took our precious time readjusting our clothing and preparing for our departure.

Addicted to our scent and the feeling of his semen slowly oozing out of me, I didn't bother scrubbing him from my body. Neither did Keanu. He wore my fragrance like his favorite cologne. We stood at the sink and washed our hands.

"I'll go first," he said to me, hand already on the door handle.

Before opening it, he kissed my lips. Twice. Then, my forehead. Then, my lips, he revisited.

"Wait," I called out to him right after he'd turned around.

"What's up?"

"I love you."

The corners of his lips curved upward into a dimpled smile. "'Til death."

He disappeared behind the door, making sure to close it after himself. I counted down from ten, slowly, and then pulled the door open to exit. The unexpected frame on the other side made my chest ache and my head hurt instantly.

"Ummmm. Hmmmmm."

Hearing Ever's voice put me at ease as quickly as it had gotten me worked up. The sweat that popped up on my forehead dried within seconds.

"You scared me."

"You should be scared," Ever insisted. "If I noticed you two missing, then it's possible that I'm not the only one. You're walking on thin ice, mommas."

"I came to use the bathroom. It was him who came in behind me."

"Have you seen yourself in this outfit? I'd come behind you, too." She chuckled.

"You think anyone noticed?"

"No. Right after Keanu left, I realized what was happening. I told everyone I was about to drag you upstairs with me to put the girls to bed so that's where they think you are."

"Okay, well, then that's where I'm headed."

"Not smelling like caged sex and semen, you're not," Ever stated as a matter of fact, unfolding her arms from on top of her big belly.

"But, I always help you put them to bed. Don't do me like that." I laughed, amused at her description of how I smelled.

"No ma'am. Not tonight. You can tell them good-night but stay at the door. You need a bath."

"Are you really serious right now?"

"Yes. I'm really serious right now," Ever confirmed. "Now, are you coming or not?"

"Already did," I toyed with her.

"You know what, that's okay. Gone on back outside. This will only take me a minute. San has already done the hard parts."

"Nooooo. I'm coming with you," I whined.

"No, you're not."

Before I was able to get out another word, Ever turned and headed upstairs. Trying to put more time and distance between Keanu and I, I waited in the hallway a little longer. When I finally counted down from sixty, I began making my way back toward everyone else.

My presence didn't seem to be missed and neither did Keanu's. When we returned, Baisleigh was at the table playing Spades. She'd replaced Keanu and the fellows didn't seem too happy about it either, especially since the girl knew how to work her hand.

I fell into a comfortable silence, my eyes meeting Keanu's every few seconds. He sat off to the side, alone, as he always did. His hands were in his pockets while he watched cards being slammed on the table.

Though he looked absolutely stunning in the black denim and hoodie that he wore, the cumbersome look on his face that reappeared for a brief second every few minutes didn't go unnoticed. I'd seen it flash across his features three times too many before I unlocked my cell and opened our barely utilized text thread.

Let's go home, I messaged him.

From a distance, I watched as his head dropped and he opened the message I'd just sent him. Keanu looked up at me, instantly. He didn't have to respond through text for me to gather his thoughts. In fact, I observed him shut his phone down, stuff it in his pocket, and reach for the sky as he stretched. Then, those words I was waiting for came out of his mouth.

"I'm about to head out, family." He groaned, body still twisting as he stretched.

He'd released a load of cum inside of me just minutes prior. Sleep would come easy for us both once we were settled. A shower and sounds from the nature station would be all we needed for a good night's rest.

"I'm right behind you. Hit me up tomorrow about that!" Laike yelled over the shit talking Spades consisted of.

"Bet."

"See you around," Luca told him, never taking his eyes off the table. He was focused.

Keanu erased the space between us before leaning over and wrapping his arms around me. Time stopped. The world paused. Everything halted. In a room full of people that meant the most to me, all I saw was us. All I felt was us. All I knew was us.

His woodsy cologne with amber undertones was a treat and so was his broad shoulders that I rubbed up and down. I could feel his skin on the side of my face and hungrily, I wanted to taste the skin of it to familiarize myself. His frame towered over me, making me feel like a damsel in distress. My only request was that he – and only he – be my savior.

When he pulled away from me, a void was immediately felt and the world continued as it was. I stared on as his body moved down the line to hug my mother and then Ever who had seemingly appeared while I was in his trance. She hadn't wanted to touch me, but gladly allowed Keanu to wrap his hands around her as she smiled.

Fraud, I thought.

"I wouldn't know how to act if that was all mine. That's a whole bunch of man, baby. I don't blame you for whatever trouble you're going to get into with that."

My mother leaned over slightly and whispered so that only Ever and I could hear her. I assumed she already knew that Ever wasn't blind to the facts. She was my best friend. There was nothing I didn't tell her.

She held my greatest secrets and though she was married to my brother, they remained between us – even if that meant confrontation in her marriage when the truth was revealed. She'd made it very clear that she was a friend before she was a wife and that made my heart explode. My girl was the best ever. Not everyone still valued or prioritized their friendships when they got married or into a serious relationship.

Not Ever.

She was different. So was I. I always felt like friendships were more important than relationships. Because when those relationships were over, it was usually your friend who's shoulder was there for you to cry on. Of course not every friendship was necessary to prioritize, but the ones like Ever and I were blessed enough to have, they were worth it. That's why we both put ours near the top of our list.

"Only good trouble." I sniggered, placing a hand on her thigh.

"I know. That's the best kind... the fun kind."

"Don't I know," Ever added, rubbing her belly. "I'm five troubles in."

Before we knew it, we were all hunched over in tears laughing. She knew trouble all too well. By the time it was all said and done, they'd be best buds because Luca was going to keep getting her into trouble if she let him. I knew my friend. She would.

At the thirty-minute mark, my leg was bouncing up and down while I rotated my cell between my sweaty palms. For the last twenty-nine minutes, I'd been ready to leave Luca's home but without drawing suspicion. Keanu had just left.

"Ok, I think my time has come," I announced as I stood to my feet.

"You leaving?" Luca asked, turning all the way around in his seat.

"Yes. You guys have been letting San do my job on Sunday nights when we're having dinner so now there's no use for me here." I sighed, forging my sadness.

"I'll relieve her early on Sundays if it's bothering you but somehow, I think you're lying."

"She is," Ever interjected.

"Figured."

"Pops, y'all ready to roll?"

"Yeah," my dad replied, laying his hand on the table. They'd just started a new game but hadn't began playing yet.

"It's about time for me to get in bed, too. I have to open in the morning." Baisleigh yawned.

"I'll walk you out," Laike quickly insisted.

"Or I could just walk out with everyone else," she suggested with a shrug.

"I'm part of everyone else, B, so I'll walk you out," Laike reiterated, obviously working Baisleigh's nerves.

As much as I wanted to laugh, I didn't. According to Laike and Baisleigh, they were past each other. But I didn't know a man on earth that was casually purchasing a seventy thousand dollar watch for an ex that he hadn't touched in years. It didn't matter how much either of them tried to bury their past, it was evident that their feelings for one another had the ability to withstand the test of time. Even if they never explored them, they weren't easily hidden. Even a blind man could see right through them.

We piled into our car, everyone on their way to their respectable dwellings. My mother and father were the last to leave, Baisleigh being the first with Laike and I behind her. When I pulled to the end of Luca's street, I contemplated making the left turn instead of the right one that would lead me to Keanu's place. With my father at the wheel behind me, I was certain he was paying close attention to every move I made. With good faith that my mom would keep him off my trail, I made the right turn with shaking hands and raised bumps on my skin.

Six minutes later, I pulled into Keanu's driveway with a galloping heart of glee. Aside from dinner, I hadn't seen him since the early morning. Missing him was an understatement, and being underneath him wasn't good enough. I wanted to be in his skin. But, first, I needed to pull my car into his garage just in case one of my brothers decided to come by. I had no intention of going anywhere for at least the next forty-eight hours, so it would be there for a while.

My car filled the second stall of the four car garage. Keanu's old Camaro that he'd given Kale was in the first. I smiled as I exited my truck, remembering the day that Keanu had gotten that car. I thought that he was the sexiest thing on earth behind the wheel.

"Still is," I whispered, shutting the door behind me.

I entered Keanu's home, which was now considered our shared living space, through the garage. It was quickly becoming my only entrance being that I needed my car there for concealment. There had been a few times I'd been bold enough to leave my car in the driveway and come through the front door, but I always knew that Keanu would move it for me, eventually.

"Babe?" I called out through the house the second my feet hit the floor.

"Ba—" I cut off after noticing the familiar tone in the background.

Too busy making sure that I locked the door behind me, I hadn't realized there was music playing in the distance. There was no way Keanu would hear me. He was famous for blasting his beats so loud that the music felt more like it was in his head than coming through his eardrums.

I stepped deeper into his kitchen, where the garage entrance was, immediately irritated with whatever I'd stepped in on the way inside. I could feel the imbalance as I took a step, alerting me that something was underneath my shoe. I leaned over and rested my weight on the wall as I pulled a red petal from my shoe. I held it closer to my face to examine it a bit more before concluding that it was indeed from a red rose.

I could hear my curls as they slid across the back of my coat when I turned my head. The display of red rose petals was only a few steps away from the door which I was still posted by. I took a few more steps, rounding the kitchen island and then the kitchen exit before the full bed of petals began to lead me up the stairs.

"Keanu." I smiled. "What do you have up your sleeve?"

My mouth felt like it would split in two at any second. I felt like one of the girls in the fairytales that had impossible things happen to them on their quest for love. Keanu wasn't exactly over the top yet because we were still working on publicizing our thing, but I had a feeling he'd do the impossible the minute we came clean about our dealings. Lavish trips, surprises, shopping sprees, private dinners, private flights, private yachts, extravagant celebrations, and more. He was that guy. Though I'd never seen that side of him, for me, I knew what was possible.

When the first set of roses ended, I stood in front of the bed of the master suite. On top of it, there was a lace teddy and a pair of boots that I was certain stopped somewhere on my thighs. They were both black in color and accompanied by a black blindfold.

"I guess it's not bedtime," I whispered, following the second trail where the first trail of roses left off.

When I entered the enormous bathroom, there stood Keanu next to the tub of running water. His pearly white teeth sparkled behind his smile. I couldn't help but wonder why looking so fucking good hadn't been made illegal because it was a damn shame.

"What are you doing, baby? What's all this for?"

"For you," he answered, never batting an eye and looking me square in mine.

He stepped to the side and it wasn't until then that I noticed the display behind his shirtless frame. Crumbled petals lined a huge sign that sat on an easel. As my eyes glossed over, it became harder to make out the words. But, eventually, I did.

Be My Lady? It read.

Turning toward Keanu, again, but this time with a tear-stained face, I nodded my head.

"I'm already your lady! Aren't I?"

I hated the validation I sought so often. It almost made me cringe after certain questions were asked or certain responses were anticipated. But as much as I disliked what I'd always thought of as a flaw, it was a part of me. The fact that the people I love dearly recognized it from the time I was a little girl and validated me every step of the way, I didn't seek it from outsiders. They didn't mean well, so their cents would never make sense in my world.

"Yeah. I just felt like you deserved to be asked. You know, for memory sake? Shit, for you to plan money-guzzling anniversaries and shit in the future. You know, a day that actually means something for us both."

"Yeah?" I nodded, wiping the corners of my eyes.

"Yeah, baby."

"I think you just wanted to mark an anniversary so

you can have an excuse to spend money, not me," I corrected.

"Aight, you got me. But, still. You deserved this too," he told me. "Crybaby."

He stretched his arms. Still fully clothed from head to toe, I ran into them. It wasn't until I heard him wince that I realized I might've been a bit too excited. As quickly as I'd collided with his chest, I backed away. It was then when I noticed the clear patch over the left side of his chest.

"Oh God. What happened? Are you okay?"

Keanu nodded. "I'm okay, baby."

"Then why... what happened?"

"I got a new tattoo," he explained.

"Today?"

"Yeah, to kill time before dinner."

"I had no idea."

I made my way to the tub and turned the knob. The water was full and near overflowing. So lost in each other, we weren't paying attention to it.

"You want to see it?"

Keanu moved closer. When I stood upright, again, he was already in my face.

"Uh, sure."

Slowly, he peeled back the clear wrapping that actually made it pretty hard to see what was underneath. Keanu's skin was so dark and blended so well with ink that it was sometimes hard to tell that he even had so much ink on his body. It was only in the beaming sunlight and when we were cuddled in bed that I was reminded.

Once the wrapper was off completely, he moved underneath the light and waved me over to join him. I stood on the tips of my toes to get a closer look and the moment it was clear to me what was written on his chest, my eyes bloomed from their sockets.

"Keanu!" I fanned my face, stepping away from him as I tried lowering my body's temperature. The coat was the first thing to come off as I walked toward the bedroom. I needed to put some space between us because he was simply too good to be true. He was too good to be mine. He followed me into the closet where I hung my coat and turned to meet his eyes, again.

"You like it?"

"I love it," I admitted, "I just... I don't know what to say."

"You don't have to say nothing. As long as you like it, I'm good."

"I love it."

I traced the letters of my name on Keanu's chest. Softly and slowly, I followed the cursive writing that led to the small red heart that was just beneath the last letter.

"This doesn't mean I have to get your name next, do it?" I asked, chuckling in the process.

"Nah. This is something I wanted to do for me."

"Good because, I—" I began.

"Hate needles," Keanu finished my sentence. "I know, baby girl."

"You remember everything."

"When it comes to you, I do."

"The teddy and the boots on the bed? You have some explaining to do."

"I'm not explaining shit. You know what time it is. You must've missed the cuffs? I'm about to pin your ass down and suck on that pussy until you're delirious. Then, I'm going to fuck you like the slut you wish to be fucked like before I tuck you into bed," he briefed me while wrapping his hand around my neck and leaning down for a kiss.

"Maybe needles aren't all that bad, huh?"

keanu

STIRRING awake as the sun touched my skin, I came to the conclusion that there was almost no better feeling than waking up with Lyric's limbs entangled in mine. *Almost*. It nearly topped the euphoria I felt at the moment, but this was unmatched.

I lifted the covers and located my woman immediately. She was never hard to find when at home with me because she was always in one of four places. On my dick, sucking my dick, beside me, or in the kitchen. They were her favorite spots. Occasionally, I'd find her by the television, but she didn't watch much of it.

Lyric's eyes found mine, but she never lost her stride. Under her command, my softness quickly hardened, and she was able to work with a fully erect dick. Her insatiable appetite for morning meat was always the perfect way to be awakened from my sleep.

"Good morning," I spoke, the rasp in my voice causing me to clear my throat immediately after.

"Good morning," she replied, only removing my dick from her mouth for a second to speak clearly.

Her pouty lips stretched to accommodate me. With both her small hands, she tended to the lower end and saved the top portion for her mouth. Thick, bubbly saliva lubricated me, all produced from within her jaws.

"Sit on him," I insisted, desperate to feel her warmth.

When I'd made it home last night, she was already asleep. Too exhausted from the day's activities, I slid into bed behind her after my shower. Within minutes, I was in a deep slumber.

Lyric wasted no time wiping her face and removing one of my t-shirts from her body. She was the sexiest in them. I found myself buying extras just so she could have an unlimited supply. Finding her in my bed most nights with one of them covering majority of her privates with a chunk of ass and pussy peeking out the bottom had quickly become one of my favorite discoveries.

Her perfectly contoured frame lifted as she reached beneath and grabbed ahold of my dick with her right hand. Lyric placed it at her entryway before sliding down until I'd hit rock bottom. We both released content sighs.

Her hands rested on my shoulders once she was situated in her new position. Mine cupped one of her breasts while the other cupped as much of her ass cheek as I could. Up and down she glided on my dick, slowly and addictively, causing me to close my eyes and focus on something other than her flawless body and unbelievably good pussy.

Her wetness consumed me. The sound of her sliminess was the only thing I heard in the air as she fucked me like only she could. When she leaned forward and began to whisper in my ear, I thought that I'd never recover from the load that I let off in her.

"Cum inside of me," she demanded. Within seconds, her wish was granted.

lyric + kern

"HAPPY VALENTINE'S DAY," I whispered in Lyric's ear as I cleaned her breasts, neck, and chest from behind.

I'd already scrubbed down before she'd decided to join me in the shower. I was happy she had because I was starting to miss her while alone with the water.

"Happy Valentine's Day."

"If you've made any plans for the day, cancel them. You're rolling with me."

"Other than dropping gifts off to my nieces, I don't," she explained.

"We'll have to move some shit around to make that happen. Your car is at your crib."

"Not if we take it to their school," Lyric enlightened me.

"Your mom's spot?" I sucked the skin of my teeth and shook my head. "Today the day you broadcast our shit, yeah?"

Even the thought brought a smile to my lips, I had so many plans for us and so much in store for Lyric. All I needed was for her to come clean with her people. Once she did, it would open the flood gates that I never intended to close – ever.

"No."

Her response stung a bit, though I wasn't expecting anything different.

"Pulling up there, what other choice do you have?"

"My mother knows," Lyric revealed. Now facing me, she placed her arms on my shoulders and waited for whatever was next to come out of my mouth.

"What you mean?" with furrowed brows and lowered eyes, I inquired.

"She knows," she elaborated. "She knows about us, already."

"When did you tell her?"

"I called to tell her while we were in Maldives but she beat me to the punch. She just knew. Somehow, she just knew."

Instead of picking at the silence that met the end of Lyric's sentence, I let it be. There were several thoughts running through my head, but it wasn't the time or day to reveal them. I would in time, but for the moment I simply wanted to enjoy Lyric's company and prepare her for the eventful day we had ahead of us.

Our shower ended, and we both stood on the plush bathmat drying every inch of our bodies before stepping on the tiled floor. Lyric made sure we both had bath slides, but neither of us had remembered to bring them back into the bathroom where they belonged prior to our shower. However, the fluffy drying mat that she'd added to the floor was perfect for the task at hand.

Lyric's small feet trekked behind me, attempting to keep up as I made my way into the closet. We were still utterly content without any words being spoken. As soon as she walked in the closet and found the white Chanel bag hanging from the second hook on the side she'd been storing her clothing, she could no longer keep quiet.

"For meeee?"

She turned around, placing her hands on her chest.

Easily the prettiest I'd ever seen in my years, Lyric's entire face formed a smile. From the top of her forehead to her chin, gratitude was evident.

"For you," I assured her.

As I pulled a pair of underwear on, she removed the bag from the hook and sat it on the floor. Still wrapped in her towel, Lyric removed the large black box from inside the white bag. She carefully untied the bow and began the process of extracting the contents of the box. I was convinced that most of the money spent on the bags went toward the packaging.

When she finally reached the large gray Caviar Quilted bag that had set me back almost five figures, her hands brushed over the bag as if it was pure gold. She lifted the bag from the box, leaving the dust bag inside, and examined every inch of it. She, then, opened it and began to examine the inside.

"It's authentic. Don't insult me," I humored, pulling a white shirt over my head.

"Never hurts to be sure," she replied, then finally stood to her feet.

On the tips of her toes, she leaned forward and rested her lips on mine.

"Thanks, babe. I love it. I needed this bag to match my gray fits. This is so perfect."

"Get dressed so we can get our day started. Dress comfortably."

Deepening our connection, I parted Lyric's lips with my tongue. She received me well, sucking on my shit before setting it free to roam her between her jaws. My hands, with minds of their own, found her ass cheeks beneath the towel that was wrapped around her body and squeezed them both.

The softness was still something I was getting used to. Lyric's skin was like butter. She took such good care of every inch of her body that it easily set her apart from any other woman I'd ever encountered.

When I finally pulled back, I slapped her cheeks and sent her back to the other side of the closet. It had always been empty. I imagined I was saving it for her, even if not intentionally. With my closet being the size of a full, spacious bedroom, our things would easily fit if kept organized.

If space ever became a problem for Lyric, I'd already chosen the bedroom that I'd gut to make her dream closet and glam room. The ones at her place were sweet, but I knew I could top them. Well, Laike could. He was the fucking architect.

"Ummmm," Lyric moaned before tearing herself away from me.

I quickly pulled on the red Nike sweatsuit that I'd purchased especially for Valentine's Day and headed downstairs where I'd left my timepiece and chains. While Lyric prepared for the day, I decided to hang out on the first level.

Football season had ended but the highlights were still rolling. I powered on the television to hear the analyst talk shit about players that they couldn't go up against on their best days. I'd always thought it was hilarious for a bunch of niggas who'd never been in the field to pick apart every aspect of a game they'd probably never played or played as a kid but never on a professional level unless they were simply a guest of the show.

As the bickering went on in the background, I grabbed a fresh bottle of water to hydrate. Luca, Laike, and I had stayed out way past our bedtimes kicking shit at Oat + Olive. We ended the night at the strip club, helping one of their loyal employees celebrate his thirtieth birthday. By the time I made it in, all I could do was shower to wash the scent of cheap perfume and body spray off my skin before climbing in bed behind Lyric.

Almost an hour passed before I heard her footsteps behind me. I turned around to see Lyric dressed in a pair of black leggings with the ugliest boots I'd ever seen in my life on her feet. She was obsessed with them, but I hated to see them coming. Sharks are what she referred to them as. I was still trying to figure out what was so special about them. Nevertheless, she was stunning in a black, fitted top to match. It came all the way up her shoulders and stopped right underneath her chin.

"I'm ready," she announced.

Without hesitation, I powered off the television and placed the remote on the table. The things were so easily lost and a headache to locate. To avoid those problems as much as possible, I tried making sure that I laid it in the same spot whenever I was finished using it.

"Let's ride."

I insisted that Lyric lead the way as I followed. She hesitated briefly before continuing out of the door. When we finally reached the driveway, she immediately turned around toward me with a hand on her hip.

"Keanu," she said with trembling lips, "Baby, what is this?"

She looked from me and then to the Bentley truck in the driveway that was wrapped in a tan bow. Then, her eyes were on me again. Seeing Lyric so conflicted as to what to say or what to do because she was so full of gratitude brought me sheer joy. I watched as she crumbled a little more before finally responding.

"Wasn't that at the top of your list?" I asked, reminding her of the three vehicles she'd shown me after we returned from our trip.

"Yes, but I wasn't expecting you to actually get it."

"Well now you know... When it comes to your nigga, baby, expect the unexpected, aight?"

Nodding, Lyric ran toward me. She'd unknowingly put a little distance between us as I stayed behind to get a full view of her reaction to seeing her dream car sitting in my yard.

"Thank you so much, baby!" she screamed as she jumped into my arms and wrapped her arms around my neck. She squeezed tightly.

"You're welcome, love," I replied, hugging her even tighter.

From side to side, I rocked Lyric until I felt her grip loosen. There was no doubt about it. I wanted to make her the happiest girl in the world, and I was well on my way. Love, patience, affection, validation, and material possessions were the way to Lyric's heart. I'd learned her awfully quick and would do everything in my power to make sure I gave them all to her, continuously.

She slid down my legs, and we stood face-to-face. The big smile that was painted on her face was accompanied by glossy eyes. Lyric shook her head, adamant about whatever was on her mind.

"What?" I asked.

"I'm not going to cry," she boasted.

"Well, that's a fucking first," I chuckled, "come on. Let's check you out and see what you're working with."

By the hand, I led Lyric to her truck. I handed her the fob that was in my pocket and let her do the honors. She unlocked the doors and opened the driver's door of her new, black Bentley truck. Lyric squealed as she hopped in the seat and began running her hand across the steering wheel.

"I can't believe you, Keanu. How can I ever top this?"

"You don't have to. I'd rather you spend your days topping me than trying to top the gifts I give you," I revealed.

My dick hardened at the thought of her lips wrapped around me. She was gifted, very, when it came to sucking the cum right out of my shit. And though we'd gotten lost in one another over an hour ago, staring at her in her new truck had me ready to take another dive.

"Then, I guess I should start now," she purred, tilting her head as she gazed back at me.

Without hesitation, Lyric fell to her knees. She didn't give a damn if she scuffed them in the process. Her craving for my girth inside of her jaws was unbearable and wouldn't be contained until she had it there. She was a menace when it came to intimacy and me. I loved that about her. Pulling every particle of saliva that she could muster, she spat on my hard dick before gripping it tightly.

"Shit," I groaned, flinching as her spit lubricated my dick.

Although she couldn't get her hand around it entirely, her nails connected where her fingers wouldn't. Her fingers easily glided up and down my missile by way of the saliva she'd lubricated it with. Lyric found my partially closed rounds, hers taunting me from below. She was well aware that shit drove me crazy but she did it anyway, every fucking time.

Lyric drenched her left hand in the pool she'd made on my dick. Lowering it until she felt my balls, she began to massage them. Her eyes never faltered as she opened wide and accepted me into her mouth.

She didn't ease into it. Never did. She wanted the whole thing and she wanted it immediately, too. She consumed every inch of me that was possible. It wasn't until my head poked the back of her throat, igniting her gag reflex that Lyric pulled me from her mouth completely and allowed the slime her move had summoned to trail from my head and eventually fall onto her chest. Still, she looked me in the eyes, unfazed by nearly killing herself in an attempt to consume me at once. I slapped the side of her cheek and gave her the praise she was begging for with those big, brown, doe eyes.

"Good fucking girl, baby. Good girl."

"Ummmm," Lyric savored the taste of me, humming on my dick as if it was her favorite candy bar.

"Fuck!" I grunted, feeling my nut rise.

Staring into my eyes and massaging my balls, Lyric worked every muscle in her neck. Lethal. Baby girl played no fucking games.

"Open wide. Let me see that fucking tongue," I demanded, pulling my dick from her mouth.

When she obliged, I began stroking myself long and slowly. My nut began to seep from me and onto her tongue as the rest of me stiffened. Before I could even stop cumming, Lyric's lips were wrapped around me again.

She sucked my soul through the tiny hole in the head of my dick. I was already trying to come up with a way to pay her ass back. I hated when she sucked me dry. Before Lyric was able to even finish her helping of my cum, I pulled her from the ground and forced her into the driver's seat.

I parted her legs, too impatient to pull down her clothes, I ripped through layer after layer until her baldness stared back at me. What a beautiful fucking sight. The wind hit her hot ass pussy, cooling it down upon contact. I leaned into her ride and placed a hand around her neck. I lifted her slightly before licking her lips. She did the same, locking me in place as she assaulted my mouth.

"I love you," she moaned into my mouth.

"'Til death," I responded, pulling away from her.

I wanted her pussy on my lips, and I wasn't talking about later. That shit had to happen now.

Still impressed with its thickness and overall plumpness, I licked my lips in admiration. She was a blessed girl. I used my hands to push her legs over after parting them completely, opening her up and exposing her to more of the crisp air.

Her pearl greeted me with a glisten. Glossed with her arousal, it displayed her true desires. She needed everything I was about to give her – and with pleasure. Just like the rest of her, it looked pretty fucking healthy, too, and palatable, prompting me to extend my tongue past my lips and onto her pink flesh.

"Ahhhhh." Lyric imploded.

"Open them fucking legs... *wider*," I demanded.

With eight thousand nerves on the tiny bulb, I

desperately wanted to tap them all, internally and externally. But, for now, I focused on the exterior of the sensitive nub, caressing it ever so gently as Lyric squirmed beneath me.

"Oh my God, Keaaaaaanu," she cried. "Right there."

"Right here?" I teased, applying pressure to the spot she'd deemed as most pleasurable.

"Ummmm hmmmm," Lyric barely responded, verbally, but nodded her up and down to confirm.

Before I was able to respond with the words that were at the tip of my tongue, the sound of tires hitting the pavement of my driveway startled me. I looked up to find Laike's whip pulling into my driveway. Attempting to remain calm, I removed myself from Lyric's personal space and forced her deeper into the truck.

"Laike," I forced out, blood boiling and adrenaline pumping.

Lyric quickly realized what I was saying to her. She straightened herself up and quickly climbed into the back of the truck as I shut the door. Before doing so, I grabbed the key fob that she'd left on the seat.

Laike had already parked and hopped out of his vehicle by the time I was headed in his direction. With the smell of Lyric's flesh still on my lips, I greeted her brother.

"Fuck is you doing over here?"

"Shit, you ain't got a bitch and neither do I. I

assumed we could spend the day together like the lovers we are," Laike joked, wrapping his arm around me.

"Speak for yourself, nigga," I told him, pulling away so that Lyric's aroma wouldn't alarm him.

A long and loudly, Laike whistled as he admired the Bentley truck in my driveway.

"Big shit, huh?" he asked. We stood behind the truck, both silent for a brief moment. I wanted to keep him right where he was because if he was to see the bow on the front then he'd know it wasn't for me. It was a gift to someone else. That someone happened to be his sister.

"Something like that. Nigga, I know you planned on laying up with me all day and shit, but I've got moves to make. So hop your sad ass back in your ride and go find you a nice young lady to take to dinner or something. Shit, hit up Baisleigh."

"Baisleigh ain't fucking with me, and I'm not about to disrupt that girl's world with my bullshit. That's dead," he exaggerated.

"You sound like a sad fucking song," I chuckled, "because we both know you want that old thang back and so does she. Whenever you both stop being stubborn, beautiful things can happen, man. I'm here for it."

"You sounding like a therapist or some shit. That's my fucking que to leave. If you're free tonight..." he yelled as he headed for his car. Instead of finishing his sentence, he placed an imaginary phone to his ear.

With a shake of my head, I waved him off and headed for the house. Once he was out of the driveway and burning rubber down the street, I turned around. Anger surged through me as I unlocked the door to Lyric's new truck.

"Get out!" I yelled, gnawing on my bottom lip in frustration. "Get the fuck out, Lyric."

"What is your problem?" She grimaced, climbing out of the backseat.

"You. You're my fucking problem!" I admitted.

"How am I your problem, Keanu?"

"Because you want to keep secrets and shit, putting me in fucked-up situations! That was your brother, Lyric! Your fucking brother! He pulled up while my face was planted in your pussy. That shit could've went all wrong. Do you not understand how much of a dangerous game you're playing? Hmmm?"

"Keanu, it's not that serious." She stood a few feet away from me, far too calm for my liking.

"It is that fucking serious, but you're too fucking immature to figure it the fuck out. I'm not your secret to keep, Lyric. If that's what the fuck I was on, then I'd go be somebody's side nigga!"

"Why are you yelling? Calm down!" she fussed, pissing me off even more.

"Calm down," I sniggered, "calm down. She told me to calm the fuck down."

With my hand on my hip, I paced a small portion of the driveway, shaking my head and trying my hardest not to snap.

"Why am I yelling? Why am I yelling? Maybe because I just had a full conversation with my fucking nigga with his sister's pussy on my breath!"

"Two more weeks, Keanu. That's all I ask for."

"Fuck that. Today! Today is the day."

I dug into my pocket and retrieved my cell. After accessing my contacts, I typed in Luca's name. He was the first one I'd start with and then add Laike to the call.

"Do not do that, Keanu," Lyric warned.

"Or what? Or what, Lyric? If I do, what? What the fuck can happen besides them being in their feelings for a few days and then getting over it? Huh? And, who's to say they will even be in their feelings? Hmm. What you don't understand is you're not a kid anymore. You're a grown ass woman with a grown ass pussy that I love to suck and fuck and don't give a damn what nobody thinks about it. Open your fucking eyes and stop being so green! You're fucking this experience up for us both! I can't even be that nigga for you because you'd rather be a secret. You know what, Lyric. Fuck this. Fuck this and to be quite frankly, fuck you."

"Keanu," she softened, tears forming in her pretty eyes.

I couldn't even look at her for long because I knew

the words I'd say next would break both of our hearts, but they needed to be said. I was tired. Tired of hiding and tired of waiting. She deserved better than that and if I couldn't give it to her then there was no need for me to be around.

"This ain't going to work, Lyric. Me and you, that shit dead. When you grow the fuck up and are ready to step to a real nigga, you know my number. You can keep the truck and whatever the fuck else. I'm good on you, baby girl."

I extended my arm to hand her the key fob, but she refused to accept it. Tears fell down her cheeks that she wiped over and over. With shaking hands, she unlocked her phone and began pressing buttons.

"Here," I offered her the keys.

"I don't want the fucking truck, Keanu. I can find my own way home. I'll send back the eighteen thousand dollars you've given me so far for my business. Anything of mine that you find in your home, toss it. I don't want that shit, either."

I watched as Lyric made her way to the end of my driveway. With her head hanging, she stood near the mailbox, leaning against it for support. As I gazed from afar, I shoved my hands into my pockets, trying my hardest not to call out to her or run after her. My right hand grazed the ring that was deep in my pocket.

It was the one I'd been working on the customization for since the week I'd been released from prison. It wasn't until two days ago that I got the call that it was ready. It was perfect, too. I knew that Lyric would love it and that's why I wanted to put it on her finger for Valentine's Day.

But the thought of me not asking her family for her hand in marriage and her risking losing it because she had to take it off so often, being that her family was clueless, kept me from sliding it on her finger when she finally came downstairs after getting dressed.

For six minutes, I stood by my door waiting with Lyric. And every second of that six minutes, I wanted to stop her from leaving and usher her back into my home, but I couldn't. If it meant more secrecy and more suppression, then I didn't want it. I didn't deserve that. Neither did she.

lyric

"SHIT, LYRIC," I chastised as I tossed my legs over the bed and stood to my feet.

It felt as if my world had been flipped upside down once I was upright. My plan to speed walk to the bathroom was quickly put to rest the minute I began seeing small, invisible capsules of space floating in the air. Lowering myself back onto the bed and closing my eyes to stop my world from spinning was my only option.

Wait. Wait. Wait, I thought, trying to make sense of the fuzziness of my head.

Once the aching subsided and I felt as if I'd gotten my bearings together somewhat, I reopened my eyes and stood tall. This time, there weren't any little speckles of nothingness fluttering through the air. I made it to the bathroom connected to my bedroom unharmed.

When I arrived, my desire to feel the coolness of the floor against my skin overruled any other thoughts circling around my head. Slowly, I lowered my body an inch at a time until I made contact with the floor. The cold tiles against the skin of my arm was nearly painful at first, but the pain quickly transformed into relief as I continued to descend.

"Ahhhhhh," sighing, I wrapped my arms around my body.

Oh, Em. For two days straight, I'd nursed my niece back to perfect health after she'd caught a virus from one of her friends at school. To avoid spreading it throughout the household, I agreed to keep an eye on her. Our biggest concern was Ever's health. No one wanted to chance her stressing the baby if Emorey happened to share her virus with the rest of them. I sacrificed myself for my little human, and I was about to pay for it.

For the last hour, I'd laid awake in bed feeling as if

a truck had been dumped onto my body. The achiness was agonizing coupled with nauseousness, and I was pretty darn close to making an emergency call to one of my family members.

Oh God. It felt as if my insides were attempting to escape through my nose and mouth. Quickly, I sat up on the floor and leaned my head over the toilet, clinging to the seat with my hands. Everything I'd consumed for the last twenty-four hours tried to evacuate my body at once.

My stomach caved and my throat burned while I continued heaving, each time filling the toilet bowl with more contents of my stomach. I wasn't sure how Emorey had managed to stay up in spirits while going through the same, but baby girl was a rider. As for me, I wanted to call crying to my mother.

"Shit!" I yelled, spitting out what I expected to be the last of my session.

My nose watered, running down my lips and slightly into my mouth. I wiped it all with the end of my shirt. The taste of puke in my mouth was repulsive enough to have me leaning over the toilet again. This time, the gagging produced nothing. My stomach was completely empty.

I flushed the toilet to get rid of the smell as much as possible. That alone was making me feel as if I needed to puke again. When I was finally able to stand to my feet, I realized just how much better I felt. I wasn't one hundred percent, but I was so much better than I was when I walked into the bathroom.

I turned the handle for cold water, then proceeded to rinse my hands and then my mouth. Once I'd spit out a few handfuls of water, I grabbed my toothbrush and squeezed toothpaste onto it. The second it touched my tongue, my doorbell sounded.

There was only one person who hadn't been scanned into my system yet. Assuming it was him that had shown up to my house unannounced and uninvited, I took my precious time finishing up in the bathroom. Then, I took the stairs that led to the first level in order to reach my front door. When I heard little voices on the other side, my heart danced in my chest.

"Why didn't you just come in?" I asked Luca when I opened the door.

"Trying to respect your space. You're in a relationship and shit. I don't want to walk in on some shit I'll regret seeing the rest of my life. Especially not with the girls."

My family, most of them, was still convinced that Collin was in my life. Though it had been Keanu that was occupying my time, I allowed them to think whatever it was they wanted to.

"I'm alone, Luca."

"Ever's in labor," he rushed out. Though calm, I could tell that he was excited to meet his new addition.

"Ever's in labor?" I asked the rhetorical question. "Oh my God. For how long?"

"For like the last four hours. Her water broke about forty-five minutes ago. We're not sure when this nigga coming. I need you to handle the girls for me this morning."

They all stood next to him with smiling faces, even Elle. She was usually in Luca's arms, but his hands were full.

"Of course! Did you bring baby girl some boobie milk from breakfast?"

Elle only consumed her mother's breast milk as her beverage of choice if it wasn't water she was drinking. In the last few weeks, Ever had been training her to drink out of a cup so that she could give her boobs a bit of a break before the baby came. I assumed she had a feeling he was on the way although he wasn't due for another week or so.

"Yeah. I put it on ice. She just let her nurse right before her water broke. Elle should be good. You can give her some water and send the milk to school with her."

"Sounds like a plan."

"You good? You look like shit," Luca stated the obvious.

"I am now."

Nodding, I took the girls' bags from his hand and ushered them all into the house. "Come on, gang."

"Mommy is having a baby, TT! He name is Lucas," Emorey cheered after she'd made it inside the house.

"I know, Em. Isn't that exciting?"

"Yes. Now daddy isn't the only boy. We will have two," she explained.

"Yes. That's right, baby."

"Take them to school early. Moms can drop Essence off at her school. You look like you could use some rest." Luca's handsome face was riddled with concern.

"I can drop her off. It's fine. I'll take them when I drop her off. I think Emorey gave me whatever virus she had. But after some ginger ale and crackers, I'm feeling a lot better."

"Alright. I don't know how long this shit about to take with my lil' nigga. Hopefully, he decides to come on up out of there and not give her too many issues. If you need me, call me."

"I won't do such a thing. You have bigger concerns than me and this little stomach bug. I'll be fine." I waved him off.

"Shit, you must not have walked past a mirror on your way down," Luca chuckled, "it ain't looking too good, baby."

"Shut up!" I hit him with one of the bags in my hand.

"I'm just saying. If you don't want to hit me up then hit up Laike or Ken. Both of them niggas up and alert, waiting on Lucas to touch down. I can have one of them shoot over here with some medicine if you'd like."

Simply hearing his name was triggering for me. I

could feel the lump swell in my throat as I said a few final words.

"Luca, go home to your wife. I'm fine. Call me when the baby gets here, and I'll try to come by."

"Not if you're sick," he emphasized.

"I'm not sick. I promise. Not really, anyway. Okay. Well, at least I can stand by the door and see him. Hell, see Ever. I can't just not be there. It would crush me."

"Aight. I'll call you but if you're still feeling like shit then don't come our way."

"I won't. I promise."

Ken. It had been three and a half weeks since I'd heard anything from him. I'd mailed him the check for eighteen thousand dollars as promised, but the money had yet to be drafted from my account. I checked it daily to be sure.

As I closed the door behind Luca, Keanu's handsome face flashed before my eyes. I could still taste his skin on my tongue from the last time I'd feasted. Even the thought of the way I missed his powerful, unmatched stroke made my center throb. And his presence, I was miserable without it the first week of our split.

However, he'd made it clear that with me wasn't where he wanted to be. He was too invested in the fact that I wasn't ready to expose our truth. He'd given me a month but that month hadn't passed at the time of our disagreement. His obsession with their blessing drove me up the wall, only proving my point for waiting to begin with. We hadn't even lasted a month.

The possibility of separation was always in the deck of cards. Not only with Keanu, but with anyone which was why I held out on involving my family until I knew things were solid. Of course I understood that Keanu was solid, but our relationship was an entirely different thing.

Not once since we'd broken up had he called or texted me. Neither had I seen him. I'd purposely locked myself inside and buried myself in work to keep my mind off him. After week one, it got a little easier and missing him was a little less agonizing.

He was stubborn – as stubborn as they came. I knew that before getting involved, which was why I wasn't surprised that I hadn't seen him around or heard from him. And, me, I was too prideful. The thought of reaching out to him the first week made me cringe. So, I took my loss like a champ and decided to keep pushing.

Collin had texted me a few times in the past few weeks, but not even he was on my radar. To be quite honest, I simply wanted to be left alone. Lately, I'd been a bit more irritable than usual and preferred peace and quiet over company or human interaction. Sleep had become my refuge. I could nap all day and it would be the perfect day for me.

"Come on, girls. Let's get some breakfast going."

I ushered everyone into the kitchen and began pulling out contents of the fridge and cabinets.

"Mommy made us fruit!" Emorey shouted, bouncing up and down at her seat on the table.

"Yeah? When?"

"Before we left," Essence intervened.

"Of course she did," I whispered to myself.

Ever was the definition of a real life heroine. She was unstoppable. In full blown labor with her sac busted, she was passing out bowls of freshly cut fruit to the children and breastfeeding the tiniest one who was approaching two.

"Well, are you girls hungry?"

"Mimi feeding me at school," Emorey chimed in.

"I'd like a glass of milk," Essence told me.

"And what about you, Elle?"

I leaned down and scooped up the baby of the bunch. She snuggled in my arms, obviously still sleepy. The clock hadn't even struck seven so I imagined they'd been up since about five thirty or six.

"Night night." She yawned.

Though her vocabulary was limited, she knew how to say the most important things. Milk, boob, play, night, tub, stuffy, mommy, daddy, Em, Es, and TT were amongst the few words she recited with ease.

"You sleepy, Elle? Awwww. TT's baby."

I cradled her head in my palm and lowered it until she was laying on my shoulder. Caring for my nieces came so naturally to me. It was like second nature though I didn't have children. The thought of one day having my own to care for often arose while they were around. The day that I became a mother would easily be the happiest day of my life. At my age, I was hoping it came sooner rather than later.

With Elle in one hand, I restocked everything I'd removed from the cabinets and fridge. My plans to make Minnie Mouse pancakes were quickly abandoned. Emorey wanted to wait until she got to school for her Mimi to feed her, and Essence only requested a glass of milk. Elle had already nursed and eaten fruit, so I was sure she'd be alright until she got with her Mimi as well.

I decided to hang out in the living room with the girls until my phone alarm warned me that it was seven-fifteen. Essence needed to be in class within a few minutes, and I had to make sure she was accounted for. Elle was sound asleep on the couch where I'd laid her. While she rested, I sprinted up the stairs, suddenly full of energy that I couldn't find or muster just an hour before when I was bent over the toilet. I pulled on some decent attire and marched back down the stairs to round up the girls.

I dragged the spare car seats in my downstairs closet with me to the door and left Elle on the couch while I stuffed them into my truck. Emorey loved the brown seat, so that's the one she hopped into once I'd strapped it in. Essence sat in the booster seat between the larger car seats. When I finally brought Elle out, I laid her in the tan seat that was reversible. She was able to lay down comfortably instead of sitting up with her neck dangling the entire ride. Although it was a short one, I didn't want my baby to be uncomfortable.

lyric + kerui

WITH ESSENCE DROPPED OFF, my final drop-off was at Eisenberg Smiles. Both Emorey and Elle attended. Both girls loved their school. Not only because it was a great place to be but because their Mimi spoiled them rotten and preferred them in her care than anyone else's at the center. She'd extended her office to accommodate her grandchildren and taught them just as much as the teachers in the classroom did. The only time she allowed them to go to class was days that she was either swamped with work or had to take time away from the office. Neither was often.

I pulled into the parking lot and up to the spot that was labeled for mothers with three or more children. Ever's name was specified on the first, brushed onto the cement as if she was a queen of some sort. Secretly, I was hating and couldn't wait to have a personal spot in the parking lot someday. For now, I planned to steal Ever's every chance I got.

"You ready, Em?" I called out, staring in the rearview mirror.

"Yes. I'm ready!" she cheered, sipping from the water in her cup she'd brought with her.

"Alright, then. Let's go."

I slid out of my wagon and walked around to let Emorey out. The energy I'd somehow discovered before leaving home was slowly inching away from me. And though I hadn't eaten anything yet, I felt like I needed to plant my face in the closest toilet. I wasn't sure what my gagging would produce being that my stomach was empty, but I'd have to wait and see.

Once Emorey's feet were on the ground, I walked around to Elle's side and unbuckled her. She was still sound asleep. Waking her was cringe-worthy, but I needed her to walk. Holding her simply wasn't an option for me at the moment.

"Noooo," Elle cried, waving her arms as I removed her from her seat.

"I know, TT, but we have to wake up for a little bit. You can go night night with Mimi."

"Mimi?" Elle immediately perked up. Her eyes swelled and the tantrum stopped before it had completely begun. Mimi was always the magic word – and Daddy, of course.

"Yes. Mimi is waiting for you inside. You want to walk in like a big girl for TT?"

"I walk, TT."

"Yes, baby. Walk alongside Emorey. Take her hand," I instructed Elle as I placed her on the ground next to Emorey.

The two grabbed hands and began their walk toward the door. I locked up my truck and followed behind them. At the moment, I didn't care to see Mimi and anyone else. My only concern was reaching the restroom before I ruined the halls of my mother's daycare center.

When we entered the building, the first face we saw was my mother's. She was on her way to her office with donuts in her hand. She quickly sat them down and headed our way when she noticed us coming through the door.

Both girls took off in her direction, and I made my way to the restroom. If I opened my mouth to say anything, I knew that it wouldn't end well. So, I didn't. I entered the restroom for visitors that was right after my mother's office, but on the opposite side. It was a single-stall restroom, which made my journey to the toilet so much easier. Crouched in front of it, I began emptying my stomach of whatever was left. There wasn't much, but enough to keep me heaving for a full five minutes.

I felt like my world was ending as my feet numbed and legs began to ache from the position I was in. Sweat beads formed across my forehead, and my body felt exceptionally warm. Though I didn't have a fever, I felt like my body was burning up on the inside.

"This can't be life," I moaned, finally able to lift myself up.

Feeling the weight of the world on my shoulders, I

rinsed off at the sink. As I stared back at my reflection in the mirror, I was beginning to think that whatever was going on with me might've been more than a stomach bug. I'd watched my best friend struggle through the beginning of two pregnancies and the symptoms were identical. Her body was trying to get acquainted with its new addition which led to morning sickness, fatigue, fever, and a list of other things. I pulled the door of the restroom open with heavy thoughts and an even heavier heart.

"I see you done went and got yourself into some trouble," my mother said as I exited.

I wasn't expecting to see her on the other side of the door. I'd thought she was busy with the girls but there she stood. With her arms folded at her chest and furrowed brows, she stared at me. I imagined I looked like a total mess. It felt like it.

"I see you're following me and assuming things that just aren't accurate." I yawned, exhaustion hitting me hard at once.

"Lyric, answer this one question for me," she insisted.

"I'm listening, Mom."

"When was the last time you saw red, red blood? Ya know, had your period."

"Emorey was sick a few days ago, Mom. Have we forgotten? I kept her. Nearly half her class was out with the same stomach bug. She passed it along and now I'm not sure if I'm coming or going."

"Um, hmmm."

"Mom, I haven't gotten into trouble. Not yet. Besides, I haven't seen Keanu since Valentine's Day. That was four weeks ago," I explained to her.

"And why not?"

"His obsession with my brother's knowing our status caused him to blow up on me. He gave me a month to tell Luca and Laike, then got upset because I wouldn't tell them sooner. I'm not sure what his deal is and neither am I trying to find out. Maybe it's best that he be with someone who he doesn't have to conceal his adoration for. I wasn't asking him to wait a lifetime. Just a little while to make sure that we were perfect for each other. Valentine's Day only proved that we weren't."

"Lyric, you two have a lot to learn, baby. This isn't the end of the road. Trust me. You two have at least eighteen more years of each other's bullshit. Trust me when I tell you that it ain't the type of bug you think it is crawling around your stomach," my mother preached. "So prepare to make amends, and I'm going to start preparing for the new member of the Eisenberg crew."

"Mom, you're being dramatic." I huffed.

"I've had three, Lyric. I can practically smell the motherly scent we all possess coming from your pores."

"Uh. Maybe because I've been playing momma bear for the last two hours since Luca showed up with the girls," I reminded her.

"This has nothing to do with the girls."

"I'm not sure what you want me to say."

Folding my arms, I rested my head on the wall behind me. I felt like my world was spiraling out of control. Instead of crying on my mother's shoulder like I truly wanted to, I maintained my pride and waited for whatever was next to come from her mouth.

"It's not about what I want you to say. You don't have to say anything. It's what I want you to do and that's schedule an appointment with your physician. But, before you do that, I want you to go home and get some rest. Don't even think about opening your laptop. Go home and get some rest. And, when you wake up, I want you to consider how you're going to approach your brothers and father with this because playtime is over. It's time to put your big girl panties on," my mother expressed before leaving me standing in the hallway with my heart on my sleeves.

I could feel the tears hit my cheeks as I exited her building. My trip to the car felt unnecessarily long and even more tiring than the trip I'd made going into the daycare. And the second I settled in, the levees broke.

My chest sank and then rose again, sank and then rose again. I could feel my shoulders as they shook uncontrollably, with each whimper. The tears fell freely in the palms of my hands where I rested my head. Life for me was happening and it was happening whether I wanted to participate or not.

To make matters worse, the one person in the

world I wanted to call wasn't available. She was busy preparing for another monumental event that would expand their family and be remembered for years and years to come. As much as I loved my solitude, right now I wanted my best friend. I needed her, but my crisis wasn't her emergency and knowing that, I tried my hardest to pull myself together. It was better said than done because the tears just kept coming.

Saltiness seeped into my mouth, settling on my tongue as I wept. The emotions I'd bottled up for the last nearly four weeks came crashing down on me at once. Every part of my frame shook from the heart-shattering tears that fell from my eyes.

It wasn't supposed to happen like this. The thought resurfaced over and over while I spent a full twenty minutes in my truck trying to pull it together. My eyes revisited the door of my mother's building to make sure that she hadn't decided to come outside. The last thing I needed was her standing over me, telling me what I already knew to be true. It would only be salt on the wounds that were already there.

When the tears stopped long enough for me to see clearly, I started my engine and pulled out of the parking lot. My stomach growled, but I was too afraid to eat anything. The way I'd been hunched over the toilet all morning, food was the last thing on my agenda. Even the thought of it was revolting. So, instead of stopping for food, I made the short drive home. Settling for water and rest was more of my speed. Anything else would take too much effort and be far too great of a risk.

Lyric + Kenn

I AWAKENED from my slumber with an appetite and swollen eyes from the crying that continued until I was sound asleep, cuddled with the blankets that caught the tears my tissue didn't. Although my head was pounding from starvation, I felt so much better than I did when I'd gone to sleep.

5:22p. I'd slept the entire day away. As well rested as I was, it was worth it. Seeing as though I only had a few minutes to pick the girls up before my mom's center closed, I decided to grab them and then something to eat for us all.

Notifications filled the screen of my cell. Some from Luca and one from Ever. Laike had called, and I had a few numbers I didn't recognize. There was also one from my mother letting me know that she'd drop the girls off around 5:30p. Before I was able to respond to the message she'd sent me, her name appeared on the screen.

"Yes?" I answered, voice still raspy from the lengthy nap I'd taken.

"Hey," she greeted, "Open the gate. The girls and I are pulling in."

"Okay," I responded before ending the call.

I opened the app that controlled my gate and opened it for my mother. Her bringing the girls to me was a pleasant surprise, but one that I was pretty darn satisfied with. She'd saved me some time and effort. Hadn't Ever specifically requested silence in her birth plan, the girls would've been home with San. In an attempt to grant every request on her short birthing plan, keeping the children out of the house was top priority. As I waited for my mother and nieces to burst through my door, the messages I'd received from Luca contradicted everything we'd discussed about their care.

He's here. Ever is already missing the girls. We'll give her a few more hours with Lucas and then once the girls are from school, you can bring them.

Look at this little nigga, Lyric. Blonde ass hair and these big ass blue eyes. Who done gave me a fucking white baby?

The attached image made my ovaries ache. With large, full jaws, a head full of blonde hair, and the biggest blue eyes I'd ever seen on a baby, he was everything I'd imagined he'd be. He reminded me of his sister, Elle, when she was born, but with fatter cheeks and even larger eyes. But their resemblance was still stunning.

"Oh my God!" I cooed.

"Oh my God, what and why are you sounding like

that?" My mother's voice startled me. I hadn't even realized she'd come in.

"Hi, TT," Emorey greeted me, first.

"Hi, Em. Essence. Elle."

"Hey, TT," Essence responded, still standing near her Mimi. Those two were partners in crime as well. Essence could get whatever she wanted from her Mimi, including the Louis Vuitton mini that she wore on her arm.

"Uh, that's new," I acknowledged the bag she was holding onto for dear life.

"Ummm. Hmmm. Being the oldest of four and helping take care of your siblings has its rewards. We picked up one after school for her," my mother chimed in.

"Okay, then. Essence is officially one of the girls, now. Turn around for TT. Let me see what you're working with," I cheered, mustering all the energy I possessed.

Too shy, Essence stepped behind my mom so that she was out of plain view. Not bothering to bring her out of hiding, I focused more on the task at hand. I had to get them to their mother and father in one piece.

"Alright, girls. We're going to head to your house in a few minutes. Let auntie get herself together. I just got up from a long, much-needed nap," I explained. "Elle, baby girl, do you miss Mommy?"

"Mommy?" Elle perked up, immediately. She was

still snug in my mother's arms, but it was obvious she, too, was ready to see Ever.

"Yes. Mommy had the baby. She's ready to see you guys."

"Are you sure you're up for it? I can drop them off. I would've if I'd known Luca and Ever were ready for them."

"I'm fine. I need to get out of here or else I'll go crazy."

"Your eyes are swollen, baby. I don't think your brother should see you like this."

"It's fine. I'm emotional. My friend just had a baby. I've cried at the birth of all three of these. This is nothing new to Luca."

Shrugging, I stood to my feet and stretched long and hard.

"Alright. Your dad and I have dinner plans at seven. If you need me, call my cell."

"Go enjoy yourselves. I'll be fine."

"I'm going to call your brother before I leave out tonight. I imagine I could pick the girls up for school in the morning and see Lucas. I bet I've seen him before — in one of these three girls." She tittered.

"You have... in that one."

With my index finger, I pointed to the one in her arms. Lucas was her twin, only with blue eyes. The two of them were the perfect combination of Ever and Luca, but Ever's genes just didn't play fair. All of her children were nearly identical to her. She had super genes. This, I was convinced of.

"You want to see his picture?"

"No. It'll ruin my first encounter. Your dad and I will get over there in the morning. I'll let them have the day for themselves. I know Ever is tired." Sighing, she kissed Elle on her cheek.

Elle was reluctant to climb from her arms when she kneeled. With outstretched arms, she welcomed the girls inside for a hug.

"I'm going to get out of here. You and I should plan dinner next week or maybe a staycation next week-end," she suggested.

"Dinner sounds doable," I agreed.

"Good. We'll chat about it later. Girls, be good and give your brother plenty of kisses for me."

My mother was out of the door less than a minute later. I rounded the girls up as I considered what I'd be wearing for the evening. With the way that I was feel-ing, I knew that it would be something simple.

As I walked inside of my closet, the light automati-cally illuminated the space. I grabbed a pair of matching basics. It was March and the weather was nice out, but there was still a chill that required an insulated top, jacket, or coat.

I pulled the ivory top over my head, barely able to get the fabric over my boobs before the bottom of it rested at my waistline. The pants were the same color and material making it hard to get them over my curves, but I managed. I topped it off with a cropped jacket of a slightly darker shade, Yeezy boots, and a ball cap because my hair wasn't exactly presentable. It had been through hell right along with me this morning.

The girls and I loaded up in my truck and headed for their house. It wasn't until I pulled into Luca's driveway that I realized I hadn't stopped for food. My stomach protested as I shut off my engine. Laike's car was also inside of Luca's gate, letting me know that he was inside sharing precious moments with our nephew. Jealousy budded inside me at the thought of him loving on Lucas before I had the chance, prompting me to add speed to the equation.

I removed the girls safely from my vehicle and got them to their door in record time. Upon arriving on their doorstep, I was scanned in and given access. With Elle in my hand and the girls at my side, we marched in like a solid unit. That's exactly how it felt, too. The girls were so well-behaved and only moved when I moved although we were in their home.

It was eerily quiet downstairs. Not even Luca was there to greet us. With the girls in tow, we took the right staircase up to the second floor. Suddenly, there was movement and low chatter. We followed the baby's sudden cries into the nursery that had been redesigned for Lucas' arrival.

Elle's time in the beautiful extension of Luca and Ever's room had come and gone. Her decorations were moved into the big girl's room, which had also been expanded. They'd knocked out the wall to combine the room beside it to make space for three growing girls who preferred sleeping together rather than sleeping alone. Elle's nursery was transferred into the new space along with a new crib that would eventually be converted into a toddler's bed.

"Poor thing. TT is here to save you!" I yelled from the hallway before turning the corner of the nursery.

As I rounded the corner, the smile that I'd worn the entire way up the stairs quickly faded. My heart began pumping dramatically, spiking my blood pressure and sending my body into premature shock. Because nothing could've prepared me for the sight before my eyes.

"He'll be fine, nigga. Close the diaper up before he pisses on your black ass," Luca advised.

"What's up, baby?" Laike greeted me, causing me to tear my eyes from the changing table where Lucas was.

"Uh. Hey."

"Fuck wrong with you? You aight?"

"Yes. I'm fine, Laike," I assured him, catching Luca's eyes on me as I turned my body in Laike's direction and then back in Lucas'.

"Then, why are your eyes and shit swollen?"

Keanu's head popped up, neck snapped, and eyes zeroed in on me before I was able to respond. I shifted my weight from one foot to the other, gnawing the inside of my jaw and trying my hardest to be mindful of the next words to leave my mouth because they mattered.

"My best friend just had a baby. A boy, after losing her first child, who happened to be a boy. Forgive me if her redemption has me in my feelings. This birth hit a bit different from the others," I explained.

There was nothing left to be said. Silence coated the space we all occupied. Until his voice penetrated the air.

"Fuck. This little nigga done got my fucking shirt wet." Keanu gasped.

"I told you to finish putting the diaper on." Luca chuckled. "Scoot out of the way and let his auntie handle him. Nigga, you still got some learning to do."

"Exactly why I stayed my black ass over here," Laike added.

"Black where?" Keanu interjected.

"This dick black. If you can't determine that by the color, then I guarantee you can determine it by the size." Grabbing his crotch, my brother thrust in Keanu's direction.

"I'm really happy the girls went to their room." I huffed, almost disgusted with the amount of bickering the three participated in when together.

"Me, too, 'cause this motherfucker has no couth." Luca sighed.

"It's like we didn't come from the same home," I told Luca as I made my way over to the new addition.

"I'm about to go get you a t-shirt so you can get out of that piss," Luca said, patting Keanu's chest.

Though I'd expected him to simply pull back the sliding door that led to his bedroom, he disappeared altogether. I quickly pumped the sanitizer from the cleaning station next to the changing table. I rubbed my hands together as I tried my hardest to ignore the drumming of my heart, the shattering of my nerves, and the wave of emotions.

Stepping next to Keanu, I could feel the heat radiating from his frame. I missed him something awful, but admittedly the pressure of being around him and my brothers simultaneously had dissolved. I assumed it was because we'd separated weeks prior, and I didn't feel as if I was living in secrecy any longer.

"We're getting out of here in a few minutes. I have to go kick shit with my nieces for a bit and then we can roll," Laike shared.

"Bet," Keanu responded.

"Where's Ever?" I asked no one in particular, but I was hoping Laike was the one to answer. I had nothing to say to Keanu. Not today, anyway.

"She was cleaning up and tasked us with keeping an eye on that nigga. He was aight with me until he shitted. Then, Luca made this dude change his diaper. That's taken almost an hour," he explained with a shake of his head.

"Heeeeey, little man," I cooed, staring back at the big, blue-eyed boy on the table.

I listened as Laike's footsteps got further away and a bit harder to hear. Soon, the only thing I could hear was my racing heart and the voices in my head encouraging me to exit as soon as possible. But, with Lucas in my care, it wasn't something that could be done right away. He still needed to be cleaned up, changed, and wiped down.

I started with the organic, damp cloths that Ever kept in a pale just like wipes and wiped down every inch of his tiny body. Lucas didn't like it one bit and squealed the entire time. Once clean, I wrapped him in a small towel and grabbed a onesie while he waited and dried. The tiny diapers made me sigh with obsession before I secured it around his waist. I slid it onto his little limbs as he protested, making the cutest noises.

I appreciated the silence so much, but I could feel Keanu's eyes penetrating me and having a look inside. Attempting to ignore the regurgitation of my feelings for the handsome man that was only a few feet away, I scooped my nephew into my arms with his mother's room as our destination. Though I could've pulled the sliding door back, I wanted to follow Luca's lead. With Ever cleaning herself up, it was possible she wasn't clothed and I didn't want to expose her.

"Lyric," his deep, familiar tenor bellowed in the distance.

The raw, unfiltered emotion that was evoked couldn't be mistaken or missed. Drawn to him like a moth to a flame, my stride halted as I turned on my right heel. The sight of a visibly broken Keanu tore at my heart's strings. Rubbing a hand down his face, he shook his head. I could see the gnawing of his bottom lip as I waited for him to say something... *anything*. Like a sick puppy, I hung onto hope as seconds passed us by.

It wasn't until I released my breath to accept new oxygen in my lungs after a prolonged period that I realized how long I'd been waiting and how much longer I'd be waiting if I stuck around. With prickly eyes and a bruised ego, I turned around and continued toward Ever's bedroom. It wasn't until I made it into the hallway that I rested my back against the wall and released another stream of air. I quickly wiped the tears that fell down my cheeks.